LESSONS IN LOVE AT THE CORNISH COUNTRY HOSPITAL

JO BARTLETT

Boldwood

First published in 2024 in Great Britain by Boldwood Books Ltd.

Cover Design by Alexandra Allden

Cover Illustration: Shutterstock

A CIP catalogue record for this book is available from the British Library.

Paperback ISBN 978-1-80483-960-7

Large Print ISBN 978-1-80483-961-4

Hardback ISBN 978-1-80483-962-1

Ebook ISBN 978-1-80483-959-1

Kindle ISBN 978-1-80483-958-4

Audio CD ISBN 978-1-80483-967-6

MP3 CD ISBN 978-1-80483-966-9

Digital audio download ISBN 978-1-80483-964-5

Boldwood Books Ltd
23 Bowerdean Street
London SW6 3TN
www.boldwoodbooks.com

For my beautiful cousins, Tammy and Maria, two amazing mothers who could give the entire world lessons in love xx

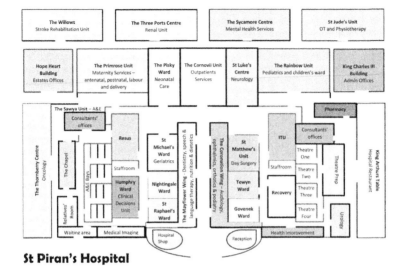

The Willows
Stroke Rehabilitation Unit

The Three Ports Centre
Renal Unit

The Sycamore Centre
Mental Health Services

St Jude's Unit
OT and Physiotherapy

Hope Heart
Building
Estates Offices

The Primrose Unit
Maternity Services –
antenatal, postnatal, labour
and delivery

The Pisky
Ward
Neonatal
Care

The Cornovii Unit
Outpatients
Services

St Luke's
Centre
Neurology

The Rainbow Unit
Pediatrics and children's ward

King Charles III
Building
Admin Offices

The Sawya Unit – A&E

Consultants'
offices

Pharmacy

Resus

Consultants'
offices

The Thornberry Centre
Oncology

The Chapel

Staffroom

St
Michael's
Ward
Geriatrics

The Mayflower Wing - Dentistry, speech &
language therapy, nutrition & dietetics

The Coronation Wing – Audiology,
ophthalmics, orthotics & podiatry

St
Matthew's
Unit
Day Surgery

ITU

Theatre
One

Theatre Prep

King Arthurs Table
Hospital Restaurant

A&E Bays

Staffroom

Theatre
Two

Humphry
Ward
Clinical
Decisions
Unit

Nightingale
Ward

Tewyn
Ward

Recovery

Theatre
Three

Relatives'
Room

St
Raphael's
Ward

Govenek
Ward

Theatre
Four

Urology

Waiting area

Medical Imaging

Hospital
Shop

Reception

Health Improvement

St Piran's Hospital

1

As soon as Danni had got the call to say there'd been a major incident at a building site in Port Tremellien, the adrenaline begun surging through her veins. Her recent promotion to the post of emergency medicine consultant meant she was the most senior doctor on shift. The timing of her new role might not have been perfect, given her personal circumstances, but it was something she'd been working towards for a long time. It also meant the buck stopped with her, and the team needed to be ready to respond to whatever came through the doors.

They'd been told that a dumper truck had demolished the wall of a partially constructed building, where several other contractors had been working. It was the type of emergency that could result in multiple serious casualties, and she'd instructed her team to prepare themselves for that eventuality. They'd faced similar situations before and had been almost overwhelmed by the amount of patients needing their support, but this time the demand on their services had been far less than Danni had anticipated. The driver of the dumper truck had been airlifted to another hospital, and it had been a relief to discover that none of the patients transferred to St Piran's by ambulance appeared to be seriously injured.

Within an hour of the call, the department didn't feel any busier than on a normal day, and the patient Danni was treating in cubicle seven seemed to have escaped relatively unscathed from the accident too. She had been admitted with what appeared to be minor abrasions and was waiting to be taken down for an X-ray as a precaution, but she was clearly struggling to come to terms with what had almost happened.

'I heard the most horrific bang and the wall was already starting to fall by the time I looked up. I was running, but I didn't seem to be moving and I was sure the whole thing was going to come down on top of me.'

'It's okay, Hannah.' Danni reached out as the woman's eyes filled with tears. But this was the reality of emergency medicine. It wasn't all life and death drama, although there was plenty of that. A lot of it involved being there for patients and their loved ones on some of the toughest days of their lives, and as far as Danni was concerned, that was just as important. 'You've been through something really scary, and you can't expect to just brush that off like it was nothing.'

'I just keep thinking about what would have happened if the wall had fallen the other way. It would have killed me for sure, and then Mason would have been left to raise Jessica on his own.'

'Are they your family?'

Hannah nodded. 'My husband and my daughter. Jessie is nine months old, and I've only been back at work for three weeks. I could have left her without a mother.' Her voice caught on the final word and a tear rolled down her face.

'But you didn't.' Danni squeezed her hand, suddenly able to identify so closely with the woman in front of her that she had to swallow hard to stop her own emotions from bubbling up. She'd expected pregnancy to heighten those feelings, but there were moments like this that completely took her by surprise. She could almost feel the terror Hannah had experienced in that moment, and the heartbreak she'd felt at the possibility of never seeing her baby again. The love Danni felt for her unborn son was something she couldn't even have put into words, it felt as if it was in every cell of her body. No wonder her patient was so distraught at the thought of leaving her daughter behind.

'I know you're right.' Hannah closed her eyes for a moment. 'And all I want to do now is to get back to her as soon as possible.'

'You'll be next to go down for X-ray, but I'd like to monitor your blood pressure for a little while longer. It was a bit raised when you got here, which is no surprise, but it's not going down as quickly as I'd like.' Danni gave Hannah what she hoped was a reassuring smile. 'I'm sure it's just everything that's happened today, but like I said earlier, if there are any other symptoms you've been having, even before today, however small they might seem, it's important that you tell me.'

'I know, but I really can't think of anything. Other than the usual stresses of trying to organise childcare and get into work on time. Is this your first?' Hannah gestured towards Danni's obvious bump and smiled as she nodded in response. 'You'll find out about all of that soon enough then! Although I can imagine your job is pretty stressful as it is.'

'I must admit I'm trying not to think too hard about that just yet.'

'I'm sure you'll do a great job, and it's easy to see that you'll be a lovely mum. You've been so kind.' Hannah sighed. 'But as nice as you've been, I just want to get back to Jessie and Mason.'

'I'll see what I can do to chase up your X-ray, and then I'm going to talk to a colleague about whether we need to keep you here if your blood pressure reading stays where it is, or whether we think it's safe to send you home to continue monitoring it.' Hannah's blood pressure had been 140/90 when she'd arrived and had dipped down slightly in the last hour, which meant it had gone from the lower end of a high reading, to pre-hypertension levels. But Danni wanted to see it continuing to fall before she'd feel confident about releasing her. If it didn't reach a normal level, there'd be further tests they needed to run, and Hannah might be sent home with a device to monitor her blood pressure until they were sure it was nothing to be concerned about.

'Thank you, I really can't wait to get out. The light in here is making my eyes feel weird.' In an instant, Hannah's expression changed completely, twisting into the kind of grimace that made it look as though her face was frozen in a scream.

'Hannah, are you okay? What's happening?' Even as Danni asked the question a wave of fear washed over her, as the younger woman started clutching her head.

'It feels like my head is exploding, and I think I'm going to be —' She didn't even manage to finish the sentence before the sickness started. Danni grabbed a disposable kidney bowl and handed it to Hannah.

'It's okay sweetheart, I'm going to get some help.' Yanking back the curtain of the cubicle, Danni's heart started to race as she tried to hold on to the hope that she might be wrong about what was happening.

'I need help in cubicle seven, now.' As soon as she called out, two of the nurses, Aidan and Esther, started running towards her.

'I think it could be an aneurysm.' Danni kept her voice low. 'Hannah needs a scan right now and we need the neurosurgical team down here. If it's burst she'll need nimodipine to try and maintain blood supply to the brain.'

'I'll get the scan sorted.' Aidan was already halfway out of the cubicle.

'I can take care of Hannah if you want to talk to the neurosurgeons?' Esther looked at Danni, but she shook her head.

'No, I'm staying with her. She's got a baby at home.' Danni and Esther had been best friends for more than ten years and Esther knew her well enough not to need to ask any more. Danni tried not to picture herself in a patient's position, to prevent her emotions from clouding her professionalism. But the woman in front of her had a young baby, and it was impossible to stop herself from going there.

'Okay, I'll put in the call and I'll send someone else up to help until I get back.' Esther reached out and squeezed her hand, before Danni moved back towards Hannah, gently pushing her hair away from her face, and giving her a second kidney bowl.

'Jessie.' Hannah managed the single word before another wave of nausea took hold.

'It's going to be okay. I'm going to give you something to help with the pain and some oxygen, until we can get you down for a scan. Then we'll get whatever is causing your pain sorted.' Danni tried never to make promises she couldn't keep, but just this once she refused to let her thoughts go beyond what she needed to do, which included setting up IV access for any medication Hannah might need, and trying to ensure that her brain wasn't being starved of oxygen. Sudden crises were something Danni would never get used to, but as hard as they were, being there for the patients who needed her was what mattered the most. She'd been just ten years old when she'd lost her father, after he'd suffered a massive heart attack at work and there'd been no one around to save him. Over the course of her career she'd learnt to cope with how high the stakes in those kinds of situations were, so that she could do her job, but it never got any easier. And with a patient as young as Hannah, who'd seemed so well just minutes earlier, and who had so much to live for, it was even harder. Especially when

Danni knew only too well the impact that losing a parent could have on a young child. She couldn't let Hannah die, she wouldn't. Jessie needed her mother and Danni refused to consider any other outcome. She couldn't let either of them down.

* * *

The first time Danni had felt her baby move, it had taken her breath away. The tiny life she and Charlie had created suddenly had a power all of its own and she already loved her unborn son with an intensity she couldn't even have tried to explain. But the tears that filled her eyes weren't just tears of joy, there was a sadness she wished she didn't feel too. It seemed horribly ungrateful when she'd been blessed with falling pregnant as easily as she had. But the connection she felt so strongly with a child she hadn't even met yet was a reminder that she'd never experienced anything like that with her own mother, and it hurt more than she wanted it to. It shouldn't matter any more, not now she'd found someone as wonderful as Charlie and they were starting a family of their own, but it did. And as the weeks continued to race towards her delivery date, she just couldn't quite shake off that feeling.

'Is there any room on that sofa for me?' Charlie smiled as he came into the lounge, and Danni shrugged her shoulders.

'I've got a Labrador, a Basset Hound and a bump that people keep telling me already makes me look like I'm full term, and we're all wedged onto a three-seater sofa.' Danni raised her eyebrows. 'How do you fancy your chances?'

'Not very highly.' Charlie grinned and dropped a kiss on her forehead, furrowing his brow as he pulled away. 'You look worn out.'

'It was a tough shift. There was an accident on a building site in Port Tremellien. One of the contractors crashed a dumper truck into a wall, but he was airlifted to another hospital. Some of his colleagues working nearby were brought in to us, with what appeared to be minor injuries, but the surveyor who'd been working on site suddenly developed a thunderclap headache and it turned out she had a brain aneurysm that had burst. They took her into surgery and she's in ITU now, but she's really poorly. I called to see how she was doing and the nurse who answered told me that they'd asked her husband to bring their baby in, just in case it's his last chance. I keep thinking that when she left for work this morning, she must have taken it for granted she'd be seeing her family later. But now she might never get to hold her baby again.'

'Oh sweetheart.' Charlie was clearly prepared to take his chances, and he gave Brenda, their Basset Hound, a gentle shove, encouraging her to move further along the sofa, much to the disgust of their Labrador, Maggie, who got jostled in the process. Wrapping his arms around Danni, he didn't need to say anything else. Their jobs were so different, and yet from the moment they'd met, he'd seemed to understand that sometimes it was impossible for her to separate her work from her home life as easily as other people did. Working as a doctor in A&E was the only job she'd ever really wanted to do, but it came with an emotional cost that just seemed to be rising now that she was pregnant. All of her feelings were much closer to the surface, but never more so than today, with the new mother who might now be separated from her child forever.

'I know I'm being silly, but I had to go to the toilet and cry when they took her up to surgery.'

'You're not being silly, you're being the wonderful, caring person who everyone loves, although no one more than me.' Charlie kissed her gently, and some of the tension she'd been carrying in her spine seemed to ease. Their baby would be so lucky to have a father like him. He was the kindest man she'd ever met, and bedtime stories for their son would be an endless adventure, given that Charlie had written more than ten bestselling children's books. More than that, he made Danni feel safe and loved, in a way she'd never been before, and she knew he'd give that gift to their child too. She really wanted to enjoy this phase of their life together, and all the excitement that came with it, but the anxiety just wouldn't stop building up inside her.

Her brother Joe had spotted it early on, which was the downside of having a consultant psychiatrist for a sibling.

'It's because of Mum and Dad, you know that don't you?' When he'd asked the question, months before, she'd tried to make light of it, joking about psychiatrists always blaming the parents. But he hadn't let it go. Losing their father, the one parent they'd been able to rely on, suddenly, and at such a young age, had made them both aware that stability could be whipped away in a split second, and that life didn't come with a guarantee. Being dispatched to separate boarding schools by their disinterested mother had done nothing to ease those fears, and it meant they hadn't even been able to cling to one another. Joe was right, deep down she knew that. So, even if her job hadn't reminded her on a daily basis how fragile life could be, the anxiety would still have dogged her because of that.

'Have you given any more thought to stopping work a bit earlier, or reducing your hours? I'm worried about you.' Charlie pushed a strand of hair away from her face, as Maggie tried worming her way between them, pushing behind him to get closer to Danni. She'd become more and more protective as the pregnancy had progressed, and she acted like Danni's shadow whenever she got the chance.

'We're so short-staffed at the moment, I just couldn't. Anyway,

I'm fine physically; my midwife says things are going well, even if the baby is a tiny bit on the small side. My blood pressure has also been really good at every check-up and, if work was too much, that wouldn't be the case. I've even managed to give up my border-line addiction to camembert, so I get a gold star for that.' Danni smiled, but then she shook her head. 'I don't think too much time to think would do me any favours anyway.'

'This baby is going to love you, and you're going to be the most wonderful mother he could possibly have asked for. You do know that, don't you?' Charlie held her gaze until she nodded. He understood her fears only too well, never tiring of reassuring her, but the uneasiness was like out-of-control ivy, creeping into all the places that should have been filled with excitement instead. The midwife had said the extra checks were just a precaution, but they fed into Danni's fears that everything she'd ever wanted might still somehow get snatched away.

'Just promise me nothing's going to go wrong.' Even as she asked him to say it, she knew it wasn't fair, but she trusted Charlie more than anyone else on earth and she needed to hear those words from him.

'I promise. We're about to start the most amazing adventure and there's no one else I'd want to share it with.' As he pulled her towards him again, she breathed out at last. Charlie had promised it was going to be okay, and she just had to keep pushing down the fear until the nagging sensation that something awful was about to happen finally went away.

2

Wendy Donahue was about to break a promise. To herself. She'd sworn she wouldn't look at Chloe's Instagram feed again, but seeing what her ex-husband's new girlfriend was up to was a habit she just didn't seem able to break. Like most addicts, she knew what she was doing was bad for her, but the lure was just too strong.

There was a new video and Wendy's fingers twitched as she tried to talk herself out of clicking on it. Chloe would look perfect, like she always did. Even at more than four months into her pregnancy, it was impossible to tell that she was expecting a baby. By that stage in both of her pregnancies, Wendy had been retaining more water than a camel, and had developed melasma – a pattern of brown spots that had covered her cheeks, nose and forehead making her feel horribly unattractive. Chloe was doing that thing pregnant women were supposed to do – but which Wendy never had. She was glowing.

Pressing the screen, the video started to play and Wendy's jaw clenched involuntarily. Chloe was miming a song about best friends, and suddenly both of Wendy's daughters walked into the room too. All three of them had matching hairstyles, and given the length and colour, they must have been wearing wigs. They were such good quality, it would have been impossible to tell that the glossy blonde locks weren't entirely natural. The effect it had was to make the three of them look like sisters. They were lip synching the words to the song, and by the end both girls were leaning in close to Chloe, their heads on her shoulders. All of a sudden, it was like someone had their hands around Wendy's throat and were squeezing as tightly as they could. Whoever said jealousy was an ugly emotion had it spot on.

The words that Chloe had written beneath the post did nothing to ease Wendy's discomfort.

Being best friends with my stepdaughters is a dream come true, but very soon we're going to be The Donahues – party of five – and we'll all have a new best friend to love. #Family #Daughters #BestFriends #Love

Wendy had to fight the urge to scream. She wanted to stand face-to-face with her ex-husband Mike and ask him what the hell he thought he was playing at. For years she'd begged him to consider adding to their family, to have the third child she'd dreamt of, but he'd always shut her down, making the same joke.

'We've got Alice and Zara, so we've already done the A to Z of parenting.' And he'd known exactly what to say to her to stop her harking after the third child that her arms had somehow felt empty without. 'We've got so much to look forward to and, when the girls are out there, following their own dreams, it'll be time for you and me to follow ours. We can do Route 66 like we always said we would, or just decide to spend a month touring Australia and New Zealand. If we have another child we might never be able to afford to put ourselves first, this way I'll finally get the chance to spend quality time with you.'

He'd had the spiel word perfect, and the look on his face had convinced her that he really meant it. For so long she hadn't felt like his priority, and it had made her feel more and more unlovable. She'd been desperate to believe that the only thing standing in the way of him showing her the love she craved was lack of time. She didn't want all the dark thoughts she'd had about not being good enough for him to be the real reason she always felt like she was at the bottom of his list. Except it turned out he'd had plenty of time all along, for other women. A whole string of them, stretching back years, to long before they'd made the decision that they definitely didn't want another child and Wendy had undergone a tubal ligation to make sure it never happened. They'd talked about Mike having a vasectomy, but there'd always been some excuse. He was the major wage earner who ran his own business, so he couldn't risk taking extended time off work if something went wrong. He'd claimed their GP had told him that the chances of complications were far higher for him than they were for her. Even though she'd known it wasn't true, she'd gone along with it, telling herself it didn't matter which of them had the op. All that mattered was their future together, the one he'd painted such a clear picture of.

Only now he *was* getting the third baby she'd always longed for. Maybe after that there'd be a fourth, or even a fifth. None of that was Chloe's fault, Wendy knew that, but it didn't make it any easier to like her. She'd already split up with Mike by the time he met Chloe. The end of their marriage had finally come when he'd been caught with his trousers and pants around his ankles, taking the instruction to love thy neighbour far too literally. The woman's husband, Jeff, had been the one to catch them in the act, in the middle of a barbecue he and his wife were hosting, at the house next door to where Mike and Wendy had raised their girls. After that, it had been like someone had set a bomb off in their lives. Jeff had launched an all-out assault on social media in an attempt to blacken Mike's name, but all it had served to do was pile the humiliation on for Wendy. At first, Mike had begged for forgiveness, but within forty-eight hours he was packing his bags and claiming to be broken-hearted that he'd fallen in love with Julia, their former neighbour. He'd been in tears when he'd talked about how hard he'd fought against his feelings for her, and how he'd never meant to hurt Wendy. His relationship with the new love of his life had lasted less than six months, by which time Wendy had discovered that Julia was just one in a long list of women who Mike hadn't been able to resist 'falling in love with'.

All of which meant that despising Chloe was as pointless as it was unfair, and yet hatred seemed to boil inside Wendy every time she looked at the younger woman's perfect face. The fact that her daughters seemed every bit as captivated by Mike's girlfriend as he was, twisted the knife even deeper.

'She's not even their stepmum, just their father's latest fling.' Wendy said the words out loud, torturing herself by watching the video again. Chloe was beaming with happiness as she performed perfectly choreographed dance moves to the song she was lip synching. When Wendy had confronted Mike after their daughters had found out about his new baby from a friend, instead of from him, he'd tried to wheedle out of taking responsibility. According to Mike, he'd just been waiting for the right moment, but clearly it had never arrived, despite him telling Wendy it would be better coming from him. She wished now that she'd told them herself, as soon as Mike had shared the news with her, she should never have trusted him to keep to his word.

He hadn't handled telling Wendy much better; blurting it out when she'd called him to ask whether he wanted to contribute to driving lessons for their youngest daughter. Hearing him say he was going to be a father again had been like a punch to the gut. He was having a child with Chloe, the girl he'd met when he'd taken Zara to an open evening at the college where she taught, and who was just five years older than Alice. To make matters worse, Zara had later signed up to study art at the same college, and Chloe was now one of her teachers. Wendy had been in bed with gastric flu and a scarily high temperature, on the night Mike claimed to have met 'the love of his life'. That had hurt enough, but it was the affection that the girls had quickly developed for Chloe that had really floored her, and she had no idea how to get over it, or whether she ever would. This wasn't the life she'd wanted, and she'd put up with a less than happy marriage partly in the hope that it might be better in the future, but mainly because she'd wanted to keep her family together at all costs. She didn't want to share her daughters, least of all with a woman who was much closer to their age than she was to Wendy's.

'What are you doing?' Gary's voice behind her made Wendy jump, guilt at being caught looking at Chloe's Instagram account making the heat rise up her neck. She couldn't blame this on a hot flush though, he knew her far too well. 'Are you looking at Chloe's videos again?'

'Only because the latest one has the girls in it.' Wendy's scalp prickled, indignation at Chloe using her daughters as fodder on social media mingling with defensiveness at being caught in the act. 'I've told Mike over and over again that I don't want them all over the internet for any pervert to see.'

'The thing is, Wend, Alice is twenty-one, and Zara is almost eighteen, so I don't think it's up to you any more.' His tone was gentle, and she bit her lip. He was right, as always, and sometimes she found it hard to believe he didn't lose his patience with her. She'd been a neurotic mess when they'd first met at the age of fourteen, and she still was almost forty years later, but for completely different reasons. Getting back in touch with him after so long, and finding out that she still had strong feelings for the first boy she'd ever had a crush on, had been as unexpected as it was wonderful. It had been one of the upsides of having to move back to Port Kara from Port Tremellien.

'I know. I just wish they didn't do all those videos together.' Wendy reached out a hand, pulling Gary down next to her on the sofa. She needed one of his cuddles; they always made things better. 'I know I should be grateful that they're happy spending time at their dad's, but I hate that they have a whole other life with a family I'm not part of. I'm an awful person, aren't I?'

'You're not an awful person, love, and I understand it, I really do. I hated the idea of my kids spending any time with Rachel and Graham, but if I'd tried to stop it, I think it would only have played into Rachel's hands. As it is, Beth and Drew have seen their mum and Graham for who they are. That's why it's us who the kids choose to spend time with when they can, and it's also why Beth and Tom ask for your advice about Albert. You're more of a grandmother to him than Rachel ever will be, and both of his parents can see that. Your girls love you and nothing Chloe does could ever compete with that. Just try to be glad she makes so much effort with them. From what I've seen of Mike, it's lucky they've got Chloe.'

'I know she's good with them, but that makes it worse in a way. They want to go to their dad's to see her, rather than him, especially Zara. It's like Chloe's her idol and, as much as I hate myself for admitting it, I'm jealous. Not of Chloe and Mike, because I couldn't give a damn about him, but of Chloe and *my girls*. I know it's stupid and selfish.' Wendy shook her head, and Gary wrapped his arms around her.

'No it isn't, it's just hard, that's all. But the longer it goes on, the more you'll get used to it. In the meantime, I understand, and I'm here if you want to get it all off your chest.'

'What would I do without you?' She pulled away from him slightly as she spoke, hoping he realised how grateful she was that he'd come back into her life. It wasn't always easy for her to say; it had been so hard for her to trust her feelings, never mind trusting anyone else, after what had happened with Mike. But Gary had broken down those barriers over the past eighteen months. He'd encouraged her to go after the promotion to head of housekeeping at the hospital, and she'd had the privilege of seeing him interact with his patients on quite a few occasions. Gary was a staff nurse, and ten times the man Mike would ever be. Sometimes she felt like tracking down her old neighbour, Julia, and thanking her for being the catalyst that got Mike out of her life, and brought Gary back into it. Only somehow she couldn't put that gratitude into words yet, at least not to Gary. So she had to find other ways to show him just how much he meant to her. 'I didn't even ask you how your day was, but I'll make it up to you. I'm going to cook your favourite tonight.'

'Chicken parmesan?' Gary grinned as she nodded. 'Have I told you before that you're the best thing that's ever happened to me?'

'Far more often than I deserve.' She leant forward, kissing him gently before pulling away again. 'Now tell me about your day.'

'It was busy, as always, but there was a particularly difficult incident. We had a new mum come in, who's now in a critical condition, but it came out of nowhere. Danni was looking after her, and I think it hit her even harder than it normally would, because of the baby.'

'I remember those days; the hormones made me so emotional it scared me sometimes. Poor Danni, and that poor woman. The idea of ever having to leave the girls behind was always my greatest fear.'

'That's why I try to remember to be so grateful for all we've got.' Gary pulled her back towards him. 'And being grateful for having you back in my life is the easiest part of that.'

'I love you.' It had taken her over a year to finally say those words, and that must have been hard for him, but it had meant all the more because of how certain she'd needed to be in order to say them. She really was incredibly grateful for the new life she had, and she didn't want to let anything Mike or Chloe did spoil that. But some things were easier said than done.

* * *

When Gwen had first asked Wendy if she wanted to join Miss Adventures, she'd wrinkled her nose and desperately tried to think of an excuse for why she wouldn't be able to get involved with her friend's latest pet project. Gwen was a retired midwife, who now ran the Friends of St Piran's charity and managed the hospital shop, which was staffed by volunteers. She was also known by everyone as the wisest woman in the Three Ports area, who was never afraid to offer advice, or reveal a tiny bit too much information about her personal life. She had more energy than most people a third of her age, and did everything from performing with her husband as children's magicians, to teaching belly dancing classes with the aim of helping mid-life women reclaim their body confidence. So any club set up by Gwen, aimed at encouraging women to embark on new adventures, was bound to be fun, exciting and quite possibly dangerous. But that wasn't the reason why Wendy had hesitated. It was because Gwen was so hard to live up to. She was almost twenty years older than Wendy, but she was a thousand times more fearless, and she grabbed hold of life like it might run out at any moment. She was the person

Wendy most wanted to be like, but was scared she'd never come close to.

'I can tell by the look on your face that you're running through a hundred reasons why you can't possibly meet up with us once a fortnight, but you do know it's okay to do something for yourself, don't you?' Gwen had fixed her with a look, and she'd known she'd been rumbled. She'd also known that Gwen would find a way to dismiss any protest she might try to make, so in the end she didn't bother. Meeting up once a fortnight for dinner or drinks couldn't do any harm, after all. Just because she went along, she didn't have to join in with any of the adventures that were cooked up during their get-togethers. She had no intention of suddenly signing up for a tandem parachute jump, or paragliding along the Jurassic Coast. It was just some time out to chat to other woman who were over fifty, and who understood one another because they were going through the same thing, or they had done in the past. It didn't mean she was suddenly going to start belly dancing, or that she'd follow Gwen's recent suggestion and sign up to be a life model at the Three Ports College, so that she could see herself in a different light and become more body positive. Even the idea made her want to put on three extra pairs of tummy control knickers, and every item of clothing she owned. She could never be like Gwen, so a bit of vicarious risk taking would just have to do.

'What's it going to be?' Gwen gestured towards the tiki bar behind her, just minutes after she'd arrived for the latest meeting of the Miss Adventures club. 'We've got to make the most of still being able to sit outside during September, and pretending we're in the Caribbean somewhere.'

Gwen's garden really could have doubled for a beach bar. There were festoon lights strung from posts around the seating area, where guests could choose to lounge in swinging chairs, or even a hammock. Wendy had nearly ended up on the floor when she'd sat heavily on a chair, not realising it was going to move and send her hurtling backwards, looking and feeling like a beetle stuck on its back. But what made Gwen's garden feel even more like a beach bar, was the fact that it overlooked the harbour in Port Agnes in one direction, and the end of the main bay in Port Kara in the other. It was a beautiful house that had clearly had decades of love poured into it by Gwen and her husband. The walls of the hallway were lined with photographs of the family she and Barry had built together, and the many adventures they'd shared in their fifty-plus years of marriage. It was a testament to what a long and happy relationship could look like, and it was what Wendy had always dreamt of for herself. Her own parents had modelled something similar, maybe with a few more ups and downs than Gwen and Barry appeared to have had – at least from the outside – and certainly with less adventure. But it had still been Wendy's idea of perfect, and she'd grieved the loss of that imagined future more than the loss of her husband to another woman. The truth was that things had been far from perfect with Mike for years, and she couldn't remember a time he'd ever looked at her the way that Barry looked at Gwen, or her mother and father looked at one another, with pure love in their eyes. The stupid part was that she had that now. Gary had given her that same sort of look almost from the moment they'd reconnected. So, even though grieving for a life with Mike that had never existed was ridiculous, she still couldn't seem to shake it off.

'I'll have one of your Long Island Iced Teas, please Gwen.' Caroline, another member of the Miss Adventures club, smiled. 'I got a little bit addicted to them on our cruise.'

'I'd love to do a world cruise.' Connie somehow managed to lean forward in her swinging chair without tipping out of it. Gwen collected friends easily and, according to Connie, meeting Gwen had got her through a prolonged stay at St Piran's following a serious accident. 'There's so much for Richard and I to catch up on, and that feels like a really good way to cram a lot of places into one trip.'

'It was amazing.' Caroline had the wistful air of someone longing to be back in the place she was talking about. 'We're looking to book another one, but with Esther and Joe getting married we need to wait a while. Although, seeing my daughter as happy as she is now is better than a hundred world cruises.'

'Danni is thrilled about the wedding too.' Connie was still leaning forward in her chair, throwing caution to the wind. 'And with her and Charlie about to make us grandparents, I don't know when we'll fit in a cruise either.'

'So much exciting stuff going on for everyone,' said Frankie. She was Gwen's best friend and worked as a midwife at both the midwifery unit in Port Agnes, and the maternity department at the hospital. 'I've got a little bit more good news to celebrate. My daughter, Nadia, is expecting too!'

'That's amazing.' Gwen swept her friend into a hug. All this baby news was exciting, but there was one upcoming birth Wendy was still dreading, despite the promise she'd made to herself and Gary to focus on their own lives. Mike had let their girls down way too often, but now she was scared he might suddenly become father of the year with this new child. Part of her hoped he would, for the baby's sake, but she didn't want the girls to have to witness that and feel second best. All the times over the years when they'd asked if Daddy was going to make it to sports day, or to their school play, or even if he was going to get home in time to go on a planned weekend camping trip, and he'd let them down. They couldn't have forgotten those things, because Wendy never had, and she didn't want her girls to feel 'less than' in any way. Mike had done that to her, but it would hurt far more if he did that to their daughters. The fact that Chloe was expecting Mike's first son made that seem all the more likely, and Wendy wished she didn't resent his new girlfriend for that as much as she did.

'Looks like the world cruise will be on hold for all of us for a while then, while we take on grandparenting duties!' Connie was Charlie's birth mother, and she'd been reunited with her son a couple of years earlier, after almost four decades apart. She and his father Richard had reunited too, and a new grandbaby was the perfect culmination to a story that had stretched across years of pain and longing for Connie. Her happy ever after with Richard was all the sweeter for all they'd almost lost, and that shone from her face every time she spoke about her family.

'I think that might be true, but I have come up with a more low-key idea we could do for our first group adventure.' Gwen moved behind the bar as she spoke.

'Is that Gwen low-key, or *real* low-key?' Caroline laughed.

'That depends on how the weekend plays out.' Gwen had a typically mischievous look on her face. 'It's a vineyard in the Loire Valley. Apparently, it's got beautiful uninterrupted views for as far as you can see. There's a gorgeous cabin we could rent, with a hot tub on the deck, and fabulous brasseries within walking distance. There's also zip-lining, hot air ballooning and horse riding nearby, for anyone who fancies it.'

'That's all still sounding a bit tame for our Gwen.' Frankie moved closer to the bar. 'I'd expect striptease lessons, or a naked bungee jump at the very least.'

'Oh God, I'll be wearing my boobs as ear muffs if I try that!' Caroline grinned.

'Like I said, we can see where the adventure takes us, but I don't want to put anyone off before we've even got going.' Gwen caught Wendy's eye for just a second. 'Caroline wants a Long

Island Iced Tea, but what about everyone else? A few drinks and I've got a feeling I can persuade you all into a weekend away.'

'I don't need a drink to persuade me.' The words were out of Wendy's mouth almost before she realised she was going to say them, but she didn't want to take them back. She loved being with Gary and spending as much time with him as she could, but she was never going to put her whole life into one person again, the way she had with Mike. She'd spent years making sure she was free to seize upon any time her ex-husband had deemed fit to share with her, letting people down and losing friendships along the way. This was her chance to rebuild that, and she wasn't going to let it go. Gary would never ask her to do that anyway, he was such a different man to Mike. But this was one promise she'd made to herself, which she was absolutely determined to keep.

3

Danni cradled her bump with one hand, and clasped Charlie's hand with the other. This was the fifth scan she'd had, after a decision had been made to give her extra checks following the twenty-week scan, when the baby's measurements had indicated that he was very slightly on the small side. Despite Danni having a huge bump, the baby was measuring in the bottom 25 per cent, so the size was almost certainly down to her carrying a lot of water. The midwife didn't seem too worried about that, or the baby's growth, and had reassured Danni that the measurements were likely to be due to a combination of factors. She'd said it was probably down to Danni having put on so little weight overall, the stress of her job, and most depressing of all, her advanced maternal age. Given how relaxed the midwife had seemed, Danni had been surprised to be offered so many additional scans. She wasn't sure if she was getting so much attention because she worked at the hospital, but they certainly seemed to be pulling out all the stops. Either way, she wasn't going to turn down the extra checks; not when she was carrying a gift she'd feared for so long she'd never be given.

For more than seven years Danni had thought she'd been in love with Esther's ex-fiancé who had strung her along, doing everything he could to convince her that they were star-crossed soulmates, whose difficult childhoods meant they understood one another in a way no one else could. She'd never crossed the line with Lucas, thank God, and in the end the love she had for her best friend had been far more powerful. It was only when she'd met Charlie that she'd understood what love really looked like, and that had heightened her desire to have a family of her own. But she'd been scared she'd left it too late. They were both in their late thirties, and she knew better than most that meant her fertility would have declined.

They'd decided just a year into their relationship to try for a baby, and she'd done her best to manage her hopes, talking to Charlie about the kind of life they could build together if they never had children, all the adventures they could have with Maggie and Brenda. But deep down she didn't know if she would ever really have come to terms with that, or whether Charlie would have either. He was a children's author, after all, adored by thousands of kids who loved his stories. And Danni still had a gap she needed to fill, one that had been there since she'd lost her father. She adored her brother, Joe, and they were really close, but that parent-child bond had been lost when their father had died. She desperately wanted it back, except this time she'd be the parent, and she was going to do everything she could to be the best one she could possibly be.

She'd made a great start by choosing Charlie to be her little boy's father, because she couldn't envisage a better man for the job. He'd been there every step of the way since the positive pregnancy test just a month after they'd decided to start trying. Charlie couldn't do enough for her, and he treated the pregnancy like the miracle they'd felt it was. He'd welcomed the extra scans as much as she had, and he'd never missed a check-up, even when it had meant driving all through the night from a stop on his latest book tour, on the other side of the country, as he had that morning. He'd gone straight to the hospital, and she'd got there earlier than needed, so she could be there to meet him, which was why they still had more than twenty minutes before their appointment. There was only one other patient waiting for a scan ahead of them, so at least there was a good chance of them going in on time. Danni was desperately hoping so, because her bladder was already feeling the strain of all the water she'd drunk in preparation for her appointment.

'I can hear your stomach rumbling from here.' Charlie grinned as the grumbling noise, which had started the moment Danni sat down, reached fever pitch.

'I should have had some breakfast, but I couldn't face it at the same time as all that water. Now it's sloshing around in there like a hot water bottle and I'm so hungry I could eat one of those sandwiches from the hospital restaurant that curl up in the corners.'

'I'll go and get you something now.' Charlie was already halfway out of his seat.

'Don't be silly.' Danni reached out to try and stop him, taking hold of his arm, but he gently shook her off.

'You had low blood sugar at one of your check-ups and you remember what the midwife said?' Charlie raised his eyebrows.

'That I need to make sure I eat regularly, and not skip meals, even if I'm on a busy shift.' Danni pulled a face. 'I'm starting to wonder if it was such a good idea having you at every appointment.'

'I always thought I'd make a great midwife, that's why I listen so attentively.' Charlie laughed.

'Did you really? Funny you've never mentioned that before.' Danni couldn't help laughing, too. 'I think we'd better see how well you cope with the delivery before you decide on a change of career, don't you?'

'Maybe, but one thing I'm confident I can do is rustle up something a bit better than a curly-edged sandwich, and we've still got fifteen minutes until we're due to go in. So as much as I love you, I'm not taking no for an answer this time.'

Just as Danni was about to protest again, her stomach gave another loud rumble and the baby kicked hard. 'Okay, seeing as even our son is complaining about the noise now, I think I'd better let you go.'

'I'll be ten minutes at the most, I promise.' Charlie gave her a quick kiss and headed out of the waiting area.

'You've got a good one there.' The woman sitting diagonally across from Danni gave her a shy smile. She barely looked out of her teens, and she was strikingly pretty with dark hair and bright blue eyes that looked glassy with emotion.

'I know.' Danni returned her smile, but the other woman still looked as though she was on the verge of tears despite her attempts to hide it. 'Are you okay?'

'I'm just being stupid, getting myself all upset over nothing. Sitting here wondering if I'm the only person going to their twenty-week scan on their own.' The woman tried and failed to sniff back the threatened tears.

'Oh sweetheart, I'm sorry, but of course you're not the only one to do this on your own.' Danni got up and moved to her side. 'If you need some company, I can go in with you. I know you don't know me from Adam, but my name's Danni, and I'm a doctor in the emergency department here, if that helps.'

'That's so lovely of you, but I can't ask you to do that. You've got your own appointment to think about. Like I said, I'm just being stupid.' The woman gave a shuddering sigh, seeming to win back control of her emotions as she did so. 'I'm Chloe, by the way.'

'Nice to meet you Chloe and, no pressure, but I'm more than happy to come in if you don't want to do it alone. I know the twenty-week scan is a big one with all the checks. Are you planning to find out the baby's sex?'

'We had a private gender scan at sixteen weeks, so I already know I'm having a boy.'

'Me too!' Danni hadn't missed Chloe's mention of 'we' when she'd referred to her private scan, but she wasn't going to probe further and risk upsetting her again. Anything could have happened in the past four weeks to change the 'we' to a 'me'.

'My partner Mike was at the gender scan and he was so thrilled to finally be getting a boy; he's got two daughters already, you see.' Chloe gave her another shy look. 'They're such lovely girls and I keep telling him he's being old fashioned, but he said he can't help it. He's always wanted a son... I thought when we found that out that he might make the effort to be here for the next scan, but he seems to think there's nothing special about this one now that we know the gender, and he's really busy with work.'

'He probably just wants to take as much time off as he can when the baby arrives.' Danni hoped she was right. 'Are his daughters excited about being big sisters?'

'They really are. Alice is at uni, but Zara comes over whenever she can. She'd have bunked off college to be here with me if I'd told her I was coming on my own, so I kept it to myself. It would hardly be a good look when I teach at the same college, but nothing would have stopped her if she'd known her dad wasn't going to make it.' Chloe gave an audible swallow, suddenly looking even younger than before and it was hard to believe she had a step-daughter at university. There was something about the girls' names that was ringing a bell too; Alice and Zara, she was sure she'd heard them said together before, but the joys of pregnancy-brain seemed to have hit her with a vengeance just lately. Chloe sighed, interrupting Danni's thoughts. 'It's times like this when I miss my mum more than ever. She'd have wanted to be here for me. I was only seven when she died, and sometimes it's hard to even remember her, but somehow, I still know for sure she'd want to be a big part of all of this.'

'Of course she'd have wanted to be here with you; it's hard to imagine a mother who wouldn't.' Danni hadn't been able to stop her voice catching on the last few words and Chloe gave her a level look.

'You can though, can't you?'

'Is it that obvious?' The last thing Danni wanted was to turn the conversation around to her, but maybe it would make Chloe feel better to realise that her life wasn't quite as perfect as it might look from the outside.

'It's probably not obvious to everyone, but it is to me.' Chloe pulled her shoulders back and shook her head. 'When my mum died, my dad remarried quite quickly and my stepmother is... well, let's just say, we've never been close. I always seemed to be in the way, and she had two sons who were clearly the centre of her world, along with my dad. There never seemed to be any room for me, no matter how small a space I tried to take up. I don't know, but I think somewhere along the line I learnt to spot a kindred spirit.'

'You're right in a way, except the woman who has no room in her life for me is my own mother. I lost my dad when I was eight. She couldn't wait to ship me and my brother off to boarding school, and she's never really been interested in either of us since. But we're lucky; my partner, Charlie, was adopted, and he's got two wonderful mothers in his life. It means there are plenty of women around who I can ask for advice, so I'm not really missing out.' Danni was vaguely aware that she was trying almost as hard to convince herself as she was Chloe, but there was no point harking after something she was never going to get.

'Mike still has his mum, but she's in her eighties now and I don't think she approves of me much. I'm only three years older than her granddaughter and she was very close to Mike's first wife, Wendy.' As soon as Chloe said the name, all the pieces of the puzzle suddenly slotted together in Danni's head. She couldn't believe she hadn't put two and two together before. She'd spent time with Wendy socially, and her partner, Gary, was a friend and colleague. Wendy was friend of Connie's too. So, she'd heard about Alice and Zara before – all good. And about Mike – all bad. Danni felt even more sorry for Chloe going into her scan alone as a result, and she wanted to do something to make her feel a tiny bit better if she could.

'Sometimes these kinds of big changes just take a bit of adjustment, but my friend who was a midwife for years always says that babies bring their own love.' Danni rested a hand on her bump as she spoke. 'And I bet, when your little boy arrives, your mother-in-law will see things differently.'

'It might help if she was my mother-in-law.' Chloe frowned. 'I really thought Mike would propose when we found out about the baby. I was sure he was going to when we discovered I was having a boy. He's so desperate to pass on his name, but he still hasn't asked me. So, as far as Veronica is concerned, Wendy remains her daughter-in-law and probably always will do.'

'I know that must hurt, but try to focus on what you have got. You're going to be the absolute centre of your little boy's world, and there isn't a person he is going to want around more than he wants you.'

'I can't wait for that feeling.' Chloe's lip wobbled, tears filling her eyes again. 'It's all I've wanted for as long as I can remember, someone who loves me as much as I love them, and I haven't had it since I lost Mum.'

'You'll have it soon, I promise, and it's obvious how much love your little boy is going to get. He'll be so lucky to have a mum like you. Not every mum is a good one, I know that as well as anyone, but I just know you're going to be great.'

'Thank you.' Chloe suddenly enveloped her in a hug. 'You've got no idea how much what you've just said means to me.'

'Chloe Thomas?' The sonographer called out the name as she came into the waiting room.

'Are you sure you don't want me to come with you?'

'Thank you, but I'll be fine now, because of you. It doesn't matter if it's just me and the baby in there. He's the only thing I really need.' Chloe gave Danni another quick hug as she got up, before following the sonographer into the examination room, just as Charlie arrived back in the waiting area.

'I've found you a pain au chocolat, and some mixed berries.' He smiled and the aroma of pastry and chocolate filled the air, her stomach renewing its rumbling in response.

'You're telling me you managed to get that from the hospital restaurant?'

'I might have had a little jog down the road to somewhere with a bit more choice; I couldn't have you eating a cereal bar and a cheese string from the vending machine.'

'I love you. *So much.*' Leaning forward, she kissed him, still barely able to believe the stroke of good fortune that had brought him into her life. She was so lucky, much luckier than she ever dreamt she'd be, and after her conversation with Chloe she was more determined than ever not to forget it.

* * *

Wendy saw a lot of things in her job that she'd never expected to encounter. Being head of housekeeping wasn't just about doing the things on her job description. She'd found herself comforting strangers sobbing in corridors following a shock diagnosis or the loss of a loved one. She'd helped an injured woman who she'd encountered in the car park, into the emergency department, and reunited a lost child with his terrified mother. That's what came of a job that took her all over the hospital, especially since her promotion meant she now audited the quality of her staff's work across every department. She'd bumped into friends unexpectedly too, who were there for appointments or to visit someone. So maybe it shouldn't have been such a shock to encounter Chloe in the corridor outside the ultrasound department, but it still made Wendy's head shoot back in surprise when the younger woman called out her name.

'Sorry, I didn't mean to startle you.' Chloe smiled and for some reason she couldn't have begun to justify, a wave of annoyance washed over Wendy.

'You didn't.' Her tone was sharp, but she didn't want Mike's girlfriend thinking she had any kind of hold over her, or that her existence bothered Wendy in any way.

'I'm glad I bumped into you anyway.' Chloe's sing-song voice suggested she was completely unaffected by Wendy's response, but why should she care what Mike's fat, frumpy ex-wife thought of her, when she was so perfect in every way? 'I've just been in for a scan, and everything is good with the baby.'

'That's wonderful.' Wendy did her best to sound pleased, and she was genuinely glad that the baby was okay. None of the things that Mike had done were his unborn son's fault, but her face still hurt when she tried to smile. 'I take it that's not why you're glad you bumped into me?'

'No.' Just for a moment Chloe looked crestfallen, and an emotion Wendy couldn't quite put her finger on twisted in her gut, but it felt a lot like guilt. 'I wanted to talk to you about Zara.'

'You wanted to talk to me about *my* daughter?' Wendy bristled as Chloe nodded, and she barely resisted the urge to tell her that she had no right to bring Zara up, she wasn't even her stepmother.

'I'm worried that something might be going on with her eating. She skips meals sometimes, but then I found a load of empty wrappers in her room and some signs in the bathroom that she might have been vomiting.' Chloe's eyes were round with concern, but Wendy was already shaking her head.

'She wouldn't do that. She's not silly; she knows how dangerous that sort of thing is.' Fear had made Wendy lash out, her stomach churning at the very idea Zara could have an eating disorder. Who the hell was Chloe to think she knew Wendy's daughter better than she did? But even as she desperately trying to deny it, her mind started racing through the signs she'd tried so hard to attribute to something else, which were now screaming at her that Chloe could well be right. She still couldn't bear the idea that it was true, and she was nowhere near ready to accept it, so she stood her ground, determined to put Chloe back in her place. 'You're wrong; you don't know her like I do.'

'Of course I don't, but I do know eating disorders.' Chloe sighed, suddenly looking even more fragile. 'I had bulimia and anorexia in my teens, and I can see the signs in Zara.'

'No, no.' The heat flooding Wendy's body was becoming even more intense, as if all the blood was suddenly closer to the surface, and her head was spinning. 'Zara's beautiful and she's loved; why would she feel the need to do something like that?'

'There are so many triggers. For me, having a stepmother who was obsessed with being as thin as possible didn't help. And some accounts on social media actively encourage it.'

'And who's fault is it, if Zara feels pressured by social media!' The heat building up inside of Wendy had boiled over into white hot rage. She could have tried telling herself that all that anger she was directing at Chloe was justified, and that what she'd said proved Chloe was to blame for whatever body issues Zara might have. But something else she'd said had hit Wendy hard too. Having someone in her life who was obsessed with trying to lose weight was something Zara had been exposed to, long before she'd ever met Chloe. Wendy had always wanted to look different, to be thinner, and had tried every fad diet she came across. None of them had worked; in fact, they'd all made things worse, and she was still an apple shape; a dumpling, as Mike had called her ever since she hadn't managed to shift the baby weight after having Zara. It meant that deep down she knew she couldn't blame Chloe for her daughter's issues with her body image, but she couldn't bring herself to say the words out loud. It hurt too much to accept they might be true, and that the reason her little girl might be so desperately unhappy was down to Wendy. It was far easier to deflect the blame.

'This isn't about whose fault it is.' Chloe's eyes were clouded with emotion, but her tone was even. 'I just want Zara to be okay.'

'Me too.' All the air seemed to leave Wendy's body, and the anger went with it, the terror about what her daughter might be going through replacing it and making her shiver with fear. 'How can she think she's not perfect already?'

'I don't know.' Chloe gave another shuddering sigh. 'But I think we need to work together on this. Come up with a way of talking to her about it and getting her the help she needs.'

'Okay.' Wendy nodded, suddenly feeling like she wanted to grab hold of Chloe and not let go until she'd promised Wendy there was a way of making everything okay for Zara. 'What can we do?'

'I think we need to talk to her, gently and calmly, and most of all be ready to listen. It's not an easy process, and if I'm honest I still feel the urge to slip back into old ways, and I still go to a support group sometimes too. It helped me understand what my triggers are, and, for me, it was always worse when I needed some control in my life. Food was something I could do that with, even when I had no control over anything else. It could be very different for Zara, so we have to be ready to hear what she has to say, rather than telling her what we think.'

'You should be the one who talks to her.' As unbearable as Wendy found it that Chloe might be better placed to help Zara than she was, she knew it was true. How she felt about it, and the jealousy that had snaked its way around her heart every time she saw how close her daughters were becoming to Mike's partner, didn't matter. Nothing mattered anymore, except that Zara was okay.

'Are you sure? I don't want to step on anyone's toes.'

'I'm sure.' Wendy let go of a long breath, closing her eyes so she didn't have to look at Chloe when she said what she had to say next. 'I know it must have been hard to tell me and that I haven't made it easy for you to talk to me about the girls.'

'I know how much you love them, but I do too.' Chloe was looking at her when Wendy opened her eyes again and she managed a nod.

'You'll keep me in the loop when you talk to her, won't you?'

'Of course.' Chloe nodded too. 'We're a team now.'

'Uh-huh.' Wendy hated how much she wished that wasn't true, but she managed a weak smile that didn't hurt her face quite as much as the first one had. 'Thank you.' They were just two words that Wendy said over her shoulder, as she headed off down the corridor, but it was probably the most sincere thing she'd ever said to her ex-husband's girlfriend. She just hoped with all her heart that Chloe would know how to help Zara, because she couldn't bear the thought of anything really bad happening to one of her children. And she wasn't sure it was something she could survive.

4

Wendy was trying not to watch every mouthful of food that Zara ate, but it had been hard to relax around her youngest daughter ever since Chloe had forced her to face the possibility of Zara having an eating disorder. She spent far more time in her room than Wendy would have liked, whenever she was at home, but she knew from Alice's teenage years that it was normal behaviour for girls of that age, and it didn't mean she was harbouring some deep, dark secret. But as much as she was desperate to hold on to the hope that Chloe might be wrong, there was no denying that Zara had lost weight. The jeans she'd insisted she'd just had to have, which had cost more than Wendy had ever spent on an item of clothing – including her wedding dress – were hanging off her.

'Why do you keep staring at me?' Zara shot Wendy a look when she caught her mother watching her eating scrambled eggs at a pace a sloth would have found frustratingly slow. The eggs must have been stone cold by now, and both Wendy and Gary had polished off a full English breakfast in the time Zara had been picking at her food.

'It's just nice to have you here for a full day and not have to worry about you rushing off for college, or me heading to work.' Wendy reached forward and brushed a strand of hair away from her daughter's face. 'What do you fancy doing today?'

'Actually I'm going out.' Zara had the good grace to look sheepish. 'I'm sorry Mum, I didn't realise you'd want to do anything. You should have said.'

'I didn't think I had to, seeing as it's my weekend with you.'

'I live here. Dad and Clo are the ones I have weekends with; you get me all the time.' Zara pulled a face and stood up, as if she was already preparing to leave. 'So I didn't think you'd mind, because we can do stuff anytime, and this is a one-off.'

'What's a one-off?' Wendy raised her eyebrows; her daughter was probably about to claim a trip to the shops with her mates was some kind of rare event, but they both knew otherwise.

'Chloe is going to pick some things out for the baby's nursery, and she wants me to go with her.' To Zara's credit, she hadn't lied, but Wendy almost wished she had. At least then it wouldn't have hurt so much.

'Why couldn't she have done it on a weekend you're at your dad's? I can't think why on earth you want to go and look at furniture for a baby's room, anyway. When I tried to get you to come and look at some wardrobes for your own bedroom, you acted like I was violating your human rights.' Wendy wanted to laugh and cry at the same time, at the absurdity of it all.

'It's not just a baby's room, it's my little brother's room. And going shopping with Clo is different.' Zara sighed, and Wendy tried not to resent the way her daughter shortened Chloe's name. It sounded so familiar and affectionate, which was exactly what it was. 'She knows how to make it fun.'

'I see.' Wendy stood up and took her plate to the sink, so her daughter wouldn't see how upset she was. It was all she could do not to snap back that she was sorry she didn't make professional-looking videos of every shopping trip they had, or that she was apparently not fun. She was frightened she'd burst into tears if she said anything much at all. But then Zara wrapped her arms around her mother's waist from behind.

'I'm sorry Mum, I really didn't think you'd mind, and Chloe's only doing it this weekend because there's a sale on at one of the places we're going to. Dad's playing golf or something, and Clo said we could go out for lunch afterwards, and we didn't have any plans, did we?'

'No, we didn't.' Wendy turned around and pulled her daughter towards her. She needed to be more grateful for moments like these. Not every seventeen-year-old would cuddle their mother the way Zara still did, and Chloe had promised to talk to her about her eating. She might have decided that this time alone together would give them the perfect opportunity. Either way, Wendy wasn't going to stand in the way of them spending time together, even if it stung that her daughter clearly preferred spending time with Chloe. This wasn't about Wendy, it was about Zara, and having a good relationship with her father's girlfriend was a huge positive, logically she knew that. Wendy just wished she felt as happy about it as she should.

'You're eating more blackberries than you're picking.' Wendy couldn't help laughing as she looked at Gary, whose purple lips gave him away, before he shrugged and grinned in admission.

'Two for me, one for the pot. That's fair, surely?'

'Just remember that when there's not enough fruit for me to make a crumble.' Wendy shook her head, but she was still smiling. Stealing the fruit was the worst deception she had to worry about with Gary, which was something it was very easy to forgive.

'There must be enough here for a crumble, especially if we're having apple with it.'

'Maybe, but the priority is to have enough fruit for my blackberry jam. I want it to be ready for Christmas. We always have croissants and homemade jam first thing, it's one of our traditions, and I want everything to be perfect this year. It might be the last Christmas Day we get with the girls.' Wendy focused on reaching up for a berry, so she wouldn't have to look at him.

'Why would you think that? Last year was the best Christmas I can remember in a long time. Having all four of our kids together, and seeing how well they get on, especially how good Zara and Alice are with Albert, treating him like he really is their nephew.' Gary turned Wendy to face him. 'All of that could have been so much harder than it has been.'

'The girls adore Albert, and he is their nephew as far as they're concerned. I know they love spending time with Drew, Beth and Tom too. But when their little brother arrives, the draw of being with him at Christmas is going to be even stronger, especially when Beth and Tom take Albert to spend Christmas with his family, or with Rachel.'

'I don't think either Beth or Drew will ever want to spend Christmas with their mum. And even though you're right that Beth and Tom will want to go to his family for Christmas Day some years, Christmas isn't just one day. We can have our family celebration on Boxing Day, or any other day in December, and still make it every bit as special.'

'Do you really think so?' Wendy wanted to believe him. 'It's just that the magic of Christmas is about little children, isn't it? When Mike and Chloe have their son, they'll have all that magic to come again. I missed it so much when the girls outgrew it, and I don't think Christmas was ever the same again for them either. Albert brought it back for all of us last year and I loved every minute of it, but we can't offer that when he's not here. Mike can, though.'

'We can start our own Christmas traditions. Zara will be eighteen soon, so a lie-in, followed by Buck's Fizz and a slap-up breakfast, and then Christmas lunch in the pub later on, might appeal more than you think. I know it does for me.'

'And what if it's just the two of us?' Wendy looked at Gary, knowing she was enough for him, but still needing to hear it.

'That will be perfect too. We can have our family day on another day in December, and base all the celebrations around Albie, but I get the best present of all on Christmas Day. You to myself. We can still have the Buck's Fizz, a big breakfast, and even a walk with Stan, because let's face it, he's not going to let us off the hook.' Stan was Gary's Border Terrier, who'd come as a package deal with his master, but he never left Wendy's side whenever she was around. She and Gary had only been living together full time for three months, but she couldn't imagine life without him, or the little dog, and the house wouldn't have felt like a home without Stan. The girls were besotted with him too, having lobbied for a dog all their lives, but Mike had always been adamant that he didn't want a 'filthy creature' in his house. Wendy just wished she'd stood up to him years before, but it was too late now.

'So there's nothing you'd do differently if it was just the two of us?' Wendy gave him a mischievous smile.

'Nothing except skip lunch in the pub, so that I can spend all afternoon in bed with the love of my life.'

'I thought Stan wasn't allowed on the bed.' She laughed as he pulled her even closer, kissing her in way that left her in no doubt who the love of his life really was.

'Get a room!' The shout made Wendy step back, just in time to see a man race past on his bike laughing uproariously. They were halfway down the steepest hill in the village, and the cyclist had flashed past them so quickly she shouldn't really have been embarrassed, but she was.

'Oh my God.' Wendy's face was flushed with heat, but Gary was smiling.

'Maybe we should take his advice. Have a weekend away, next time Zara is with Mike and Chloe, and we're both off. Beth will look after Stan, or we can get a pet-friendly Airbnb. Make the most of our freedom.'

'That sounds lovely, but only if it's my treat, to thank you for putting up with me.'

'Don't be daft, I thank my lucky—' Gary's response was cut off by the sound of shouting and a high-pitched scream which made Wendy's stomach drop. It sounded like terror, rather than excitement.

'Just brake, Mia, for God's sake BRAKE!' The terror in the man's voice was every bit as obvious, as it carried down the lane. And, as Wendy turned, she saw the little girl on the bicycle careering towards them, her face a picture of fear.

'Daddy!' She screamed the single word. Before Wendy could even respond, Gary leapt into the path of the bike, stopping it hurtling out of control but knocking him backwards. He hit the road with a sickening thud, the little girl and her bike falling on to the ground next to him, just as Mia's father caught up with them and dropped to his haunches beside his daughter.

'Gary!' As she rushed towards him, Wendy's heart thudded in her ears. He'd hit his head and there was a chance he could have been seriously injured, but even before she reached him, he was struggling to his feet.

'I'm fine.' There was a gash on his cheek that was pouring with blood, and an egg-shaped lump had already appeared on his forehead, but in the split second that he'd hit the ground, she'd feared the worst and the relief flooding her body made her skin prickle. She just hoped the little girl was okay too, and that was clearly the only thing on Gary's mind, despite his own injuries.

'Oww, Daddy, it hurts.' Mia was holding one hand in the other, her words punctuated by shuddering sobs.

'I'm know, darling, and I'm so sorry, I should never have let go of the bike so close to the top of the hill. If someone hadn't been here to stop you...' All the colour seemed to drain out of the man's face as he looked at Gary. 'Thank you.'

'It's okay.' He might have made it sound like nothing, but Gary grimaced as he knelt down to look more closely at Mia and there was no doubt he was in pain. 'Do both of your hands hurt, sweetheart, or just one of them?'

'Just this one.' Mia was still crying and her father didn't seem to know what to do with himself.

'I want you to see if you can move your fingers on that hand and make a fist.'

'Oww, howoww.' Mia's face twisted in pain as she tried to follow Gary's instructions.

'Okay, sweetheart. I think you might have broken a bone in your wrist, but we need to get you to the hospital so they can take an X-ray to make sure. Then we can give you some medicine to make you feel better and put a special kind of bandage on it so it doesn't hurt any more.'

'Are you a doctor?' Mia's father finally found his voice again.

'A nurse. I'm Gary. And this is Wendy, who I'm going to ask to do us a big favour and go and get my car, to take us all to the hospital. It'll be much quicker than waiting for an ambulance, and I've got a first-aid kit in there that I can use to stabilise Mia's wrist, and ease some of the pain until we can get her injuries looked at.'

'I'm just so thankful you were here. I can't bear to think...'

Mia's father couldn't finish the sentence. 'I'm Matt, by the way, and this is Mia.'

'I heard you calling out her name, otherwise I might not have seen her in time to stop the bike. You did all you could in the circumstances; it was an accident and they happen to the best of us.' Gary's attempt at a smile turned into another grimace, and the relief that Wendy had felt about his injuries began to ebb away.

'I'm getting the car now.' Wendy didn't even wait for Gary to reply and she broke into a run as she headed back towards their house. She had a horrible feeling that Mia might not be the only one who needed medical attention and she wasn't going to waste a second making sure that Gary got it too. He meant the world to her, and suddenly she was more aware of that than she ever had been before.

5

Danni was still weighing up the decision about starting maternity leave early, when she arrived for work, the morning after she'd discussed it with Charlie. The scan results she'd had earlier in the week were good overall, the baby was definitely growing, but he was still a little on the small side. Neither the midwife nor the sonographer seemed too concerned, even though the baby was still in the bottom 25 per cent. It meant he wasn't actually in the danger zone, but he still needed extra monitoring, and Danni couldn't help wondering whether giving up work might help change that. Except even the thought of going on maternity leave early made her feel guilty, and the truth was she was scared of feeling lonely too.

She was lucky that Charlie would be around a lot, but she was worried about disturbing him when he was working. They'd put a wooden cabin in the garden, which was now his office and, when he was out there, she treated it as if he was in a normal workplace somewhere. She wouldn't dream of just turning up to his office building and asking if he fancied a cuppa and a chat, so she'd made herself a promise that she wouldn't do it once she was on maternity leave. She was so used to being surrounded by people at work, and most of her closest friends worked at St Piran's. As much as she had every intention of making new 'mum friends', it wouldn't be the same as working alongside Esther, Aidan, and the others, and she already knew she was going to miss it.

When it came to family, Joe was the only member she was close to, and she loved him to bits, but even he worked at St Piran's and going on maternity leave felt like she was leaving her support network behind. She'd get the chance to spend more time with both sets of Charlie's parents, which she was looking forward to, but she'd have been lying to herself if she tried to pretend she didn't feel torn. It would be different once the baby was here. But having an extra six weeks of maternity leave before his arrival didn't hold any appeal, except for the fact it might mean he grew a bit more, although the midwife couldn't guarantee it. The department was short-staffed too, and Danni's boss had spent the best part of the week before interviewing to fill the vacant posts, but most of the new recruits would have to serve notice elsewhere first. So not only would she be leaving her friends, she'd be leaving them in the lurch too, which was why she still hadn't decided what to do.

'Gary's been in an accident, and he keeps throwing up.' Wendy suddenly burst through the doors of reception, the jacket she was wearing streaked with blood. 'We've got a seven-year-old girl with us too, with what Gary thinks is a broken wrist. He stepped out in front of her bike to stop her when she lost control, but he hit his head on the road.'

'Are they in your car?'

'Mia's dad is with her in reception, but I didn't know whether I should move Gary again, or if that could make whatever is wrong even worse.' Wendy's eyes widened in fear. 'Did I do the wrong thing bringing him in? It's just he said the ambulance might take hours, but he only started being sick when I was halfway here.'

'You did what you thought was best; try not to worry. It sounds like he might have a concussion, but he's going to need a scan.' Danni put a hand on Wendy's arm briefly, and then turned to see who was around to help. 'Aidan, can you give me a hand please? We'll need a wheelchair.'

The three of them headed outside to where Wendy had abandoned the car by the entrance closest to A&E. Aidan offered to move it for her, once they got Gary out, to avoid having it clamped. Wendy was trembling and she didn't look in any fit state to move it herself, but she shook her head.

'I'll do it. I just need you two to get him sorted, *please*.' Wendy's eyes darted from Danni to Gary and back again, and Danni could understand her distress. Gary had been muttering something about not having time to go shopping, when Aidan had helped him out of the car. It was clear he was confused and he didn't seem aware of the conversation going on around him at all. 'He seemed fine at first, but now he's not making any sense and he's been really sick. I'm so scared of what it might be.'

'Symptoms of concussion or other types of head injury can get gradually worse, but the best thing we can do is get Gary inside as soon as possible and get him checked over. Then we'll know what we're dealing with and how to treat it.'

'Thank you. I'll move the car, and then I'll be in.' Wendy looked as if she was going to kiss the top of Gary's head for a moment, but she stopped within inches of the violent purple bruise that started on his right temple and spread outwards, across his forehead and down towards his cheek bone. There was an obvious lump too and what looked like tiny pieces of loose gravel embedded in his skin.

'We'll take care of him, I promise.' Danni touched Wendy's

arm again, as Aidan pushed his friend towards the doors. Treating one of their own was always something she dreaded, and she couldn't help imaging how she'd feel if she was in Wendy's shoes, and it was Charlie who was dazed, bloodied and confused. She'd seen far too many people lose loved ones during her career, and she'd witnessed the devastation that could cause. She didn't think for a moment that Gary was in that kind of danger, but Wendy's fears wouldn't be alleviated until they knew for certain.

By the time Wendy arrived back in the department, Aidan had already taken Gary down for a scan. If there was ever a fortunate time to have an accident, this was it. It had been one of those once-in-a-blue-moon days, when the waiting times had been short and there was space in cubicles. Danni had put in the call for a scan as soon as they'd got inside, expecting to have to wait at least long enough to be able to monitor all of Gary's vitals. But the opportunity to get him straight in for a CT scan was too good to be missed and, looking at the injury, there was a strong possibility that he'd fractured his skull. There was no sign of any problems with his breathing, or any indication that they should wait, so Danni had agreed for Aidan to take him down for the scan before they did anything else. It left her free to examine Mia and check her over for any other potential injuries, as well as give her some-thing for the pain, before she was sent for an X-ray.

'You're doing really well, Mia.' Danni smiled at the little girl, who looked much calmer now the painkillers had taken effect, and she'd been given a Pirry bear, provided to children having treatment at the hospital by the Friends of St Piran's. Some of the bears, including the one Mia had been given, had slings or bandages, which always helped cheer the kids up.

'He's so cute.' Mia gave her a gap-toothed grin. 'Can he come when they take the pictures of my arm?'

'Of course he can, sweetheart.' Danni smiled again, before

turning towards Mia's father, who'd introduced himself as Matt. 'How are you doing?'

'I can't stop thinking about what could have happened if Gary hadn't stepped out in front of her, and what kind of injury she might have as a result. She could have died.'

Mia's eyes flew open in response to what her father had just said and she suddenly looked really frightened.

'I'm not going to die, am I?'

'Of course you're not sweetheart.' Danni stroked the little girl's hair. 'You're going to be absolutely fine, and you might even get a really cool plaster cast; we do lots of different colours.'

'Can I have blue, please? I love blue, don't I Daddy?' Mia was suddenly beaming, and Danni had to suppress a smile of her own. It was amazing how quickly a child's mood could change, and the mention of a colourful plaster cast had been all it had taken to distract Mia from the idea that she might be dying. 'One day when I'm grown up I'm going to have blue hair like my big cousin, Jasmine.'

'You can have anything you want, darling.' Matt would probably have agreed to it right there and then after the day they'd had. As one of the nurses passed by the cubicle, Danni called out to her.

'Amy, please can you come and tell Mia what colour plaster casts we have? I need to have a quick word with her dad.'

'Of course.' Amy beamed at the little girl. 'Oh my goodness. You've got a Pirry bear; I've always wanted one of those.'

Mia giggled in delight, she and Amy instantly bonding over the stuffed toy, as Danni gestured to Matt to follow her outside.

'What's the problem? Do you think it's more serious than a break? I checked the helmet over for cracks and I couldn't see anything, but if she hit her head—' Matt's words were coming out in a rush and he just didn't seem to be able to stop himself from catastrophising, so Danni spoke as gently and firmly as she could.

'There's nothing seriously wrong with Mia, but I think she gets scared when you talk about what could have happened. I know it must have been terrifying watching her go down that hill, when you couldn't catch her, but she's going to be just fine once the bone has mended. I promise.'

'But what about Gary? If anything happens to him that'll be all my fault too.' Matt whacked a palm against his forehead. 'How can I have been so stupid letting her practice without her stabilisers when we were so close to the top of the hill? If Hailey had been there, she'd never have let me act like such an idiot.'

'Is Hailey Mia's mum?'

'Yes, she's my fiancée, although God knows why she wants to saddle herself with someone like me. She's away on her hen weekend, staying in Dorset, but I don't want to phone her and tell her what happened until I know Mia is definitely going to be okay. I've been scared of something like this happening since the moment I found out Hailey was pregnant, and that I'd turn out to be a bloody useless father just like the one I had. It's taken six years for me to get any kind of confidence around Mia, and I'd finally felt ready for us to try for another baby, thinking I'd got the hang of this parenting business, but I'm just as useless as I've always been.'

'No you're not, it's obvious you're a loving father and that's what kids need more than anything. The only parents who don't doubt whether they're doing a good job are the ones who don't care.' It was a conversation Danni had had with Aidan several times in the past few months, after he'd made the decision to use a surrogate to start a family with his husband, Jase. Aidan had harboured a fear that he'd repeat the mistakes his father had made with him, but she'd told him that nothing could be less likely, and that he and Jase were born to be fathers. She had no

doubt they'd do an amazing job, not least because they knew
better than most what not to do. The weird thing was, it was much
harder to tell herself that her relationship with her own mother
had nothing to do with how good a parent she might be. She
wasn't worried about not loving the baby, because he already
meant the world to her. And, deep down, she knew she had what
it took to be a very different kind of mother to the one her mum
had been. What scared her most was the idea that the baby might
not love her back. She'd have dreams where her son refused to
come to her, and screamed until he was given to Charlie; that
nothing she did could comfort the baby she already loved with
her whole heart. She tried to tell herself it was just the usual pregnancy anxiety, but the fear of rejection still dogged her dreams
and clouded her thoughts in the rare quiet moments of the day.
Knowing that Aidan shared some of the fears because of his own
childhood had helped a little bit, but at least Aidan's dad had
cared enough to have an opinion. Danni's mum Nicola had always
been completely indifferent to anything Danni did and somehow
that felt even worse.

'If anything had happened to Mia, I couldn't carry on. I didn't
know it was possible to love anyone like I love her.' Matt shook his
head. 'I love Hailey too, but I'd die for Mia. The most important
thing in life is for me to protect her. I nearly messed that up in a
way that can't be undone.'

'But you didn't.' Danni held his gaze, wanting to tell Matt she
understood his fears more than he knew. She'd been monitored a
couple of times for low foetal movements, because unless she
could feel her baby moving, the fear that he might somehow be
taken away from her became overwhelming. She'd known both
times that it had probably been down to busy shifts making the
movement feel less noticeable, and that eating something sugary
would probably 'wake him up'. But as soon as she'd got it into her

head that his movements might have slowed down, she hadn't been able to just wait and see. Instead, she'd gone straight to maternity to ask to be monitored. Both times the baby had begun performing what felt like a Cirque du Soleil routine the moment the monitors had been attached, with movements so visible that it looked like he was trying to fight his way out. If the midwives had thought she was wasting their time, they didn't say so. They'd been incredibly kind and reassuring, but Danni still hadn't been able to relax and enjoy the pregnancy the way she so desperately wanted to. In the end she'd accepted it wouldn't be until she held the baby in her arms, and was able to see for herself he was okay, that she'd finally be able to shake off the sensation that something awful was going to happen. Except looking at Matt now, she had a horrible feeling she might never be able to truly shake that sense of dread, and that one of the costs of parenthood was the worry that inevitably came with loving a child as fiercely as Matt loved his daughter.

'Hailey's always telling me I fuss too much, but I'm going to want to wrap Mia up in cotton wool more than ever now.'

'It's scary but you've got to let her take enough risks to be able to enjoy her life.' Danni felt like the biggest fraud in the world spouting off advice, when the thought of getting things wrong with her own child had kept her awake as often as it had during her pregnancy. That was the thing about being a medic: it made her very good at telling other people what they should be doing, even when following that same advice didn't always come easily.

'I know you're right and she's such a great kid, with a real sense of adventure. She makes me laugh every day at the things she comes out with.' Matt smiled for the first time. 'I'm just so grateful to you all, and especially to Gary. I really hope he's going to be okay.'

'I'm going to go and get an update on his scan results now, so hopefully I can give you some reassurance. Although, knowing Gary, he'll want to do that himself. The last thing he'd want is you beating yourself up for the accident. I'll come and find you as soon as I can, but for now there's a little girl who needs her daddy's help to pick out the best colour plaster cast.'

'Thank you.' Matt repeated the words of gratitude before heading back towards his daughter, and Danni rested a hand on her bump to connect with her son in the only way she could for now. The fear might never go away completely, but she had to believe it would ease when she finally met him, and she couldn't wait for that day to come.

* * *

Wendy hadn't left Gary's side since he'd got back from the scan. He was still feeling nauseous, but the terrifying confusion that seemed to have descended on him like a blanket of fog, appeared to be lifting.

'Everything still feels a bit fuzzy. I remember the bike knocking me backwards and hitting the floor, but I don't remember what happened after that very clearly.'

'Don't worry. Danni said it's probably just concussion, but we'll know more once we have the results of the scan.' Wendy hoped she sounded more confident than she felt. Seeing Gary the way she had, unable to string a coherent sentence together, had terrified her.

'Did I hear someone mention my name?' Danni suddenly appeared at the end of Gary's bed.

'I was just telling Gary not to worry and that the scans will tell us more.' Wendy was still trying to keep the wobble out of her voice, but her shoulders relaxed just a tiny bit when Danni smiled.

'You should think about a change of career, and you're absolutely right.' Danni moved closer to the head of Gary's bed. 'I've seen the scans and there is a fracture to your skull, but it's a linear break, which means the bone hasn't moved and there's no need for surgery. Just some painkillers and rest, and you should be back to normal in no time.'

'Don't think I've ever been accused of being normal before!' The return of Gary's sense of humour lifted the final weight off Wendy's shoulders, and she could have kissed Danni. As it was, she kissed Gary instead, but on the shoulder; she wasn't risking going anywhere near the huge purple bruise on the side of his head.

'I'm going to give you a prescription for some slightly stronger painkillers to see you through the first few days, but I want to speak to Zahir about whether we should keep you in for observation overnight.'

'Thank you.' Wendy blew Danni the kiss she'd wanted to give her, and the younger woman smiled.

'My pleasure, but we don't want you pulling any more antics like that, Gary; we need your superhero skills in nursing, and we can't afford to lose any more good staff. But make sure you take it easy and get properly better before you even think about coming back to work.' Danni wagged her finger at him, before turning away and leaving the two of them alone.

'You need to listen to doctor's orders and, if you ever scare me like that again, your injuries will be the least of your worries.' Wendy gave Gary a look that let him know she meant every word. It was still hard to articulate just how much he meant to her; it made her vulnerable in a way she'd been scared to be since discovering Mike had cheated on her. But her feelings for Gary made her vulnerable anyway, so it was futile trying to protect herself, when it was already far too late.

'I think we should get married.' Gary grabbed hold of her hand, and she wasn't sure she'd heard him right. They'd never talked about the prospect of getting married before; she'd assumed he'd never want to go through it again after some of the things he'd said about his first marriage. So she'd never even thought how *she* might feel about it. When she'd married Mike, and had promised until death did they part, the words had meant the world to her, although clearly not to him. As for forsaking all others, she doubted now whether he'd even kept that particular promise until their first anniversary. Gary must still be dazed and confused to blurt out a suggestion like that.

'What are you talking about?'

'There was a time today when nothing made sense, but then I realised you were there next to me, and everything suddenly became clear. I don't want to lose you a second time, and getting married is the only way I can think of to show you that I'm in this for life.'

'I think that might be the concussion talking.' Wendy still wasn't sure whether or not she wanted that to be true. She loved Gary and she wanted to grow old with him, there was no question about that. But she wanted him to choose her every day, because he felt the same way, not just because she was wearing a ring he'd given her. She was almost certain Mike would have left sooner if they hadn't been tied together by both their children and a legally binding agreement, which meant he'd have to hand over half of his assets. She wanted to be Gary's choice, not his obligation, and yet part of her liked the idea of being his wife more than she could admit, even to herself. The last thing she wanted was to make him feel rejected, but she could buy them both a bit of time to think. 'Let's wait until you're fully recovered and see how you feel then.'

'I'm not going to change my mind. I've loved you since I was fourteen and I promised myself I wouldn't let you go a second time.'

'I'm not going anywhere.' Wendy squeezed his hand, hoping he knew just how much he meant to her. She'd never for one second doubted her feelings for him, but she wasn't sure she'd ever fully trust his feelings for her, after what Mike had put her through. It was just one more thing her ex-husband had robbed her of, and she hated the bitterness that had left her with. Mike wasn't worth it, and he'd moved on without a backward glance. She wished she could stop looking back at the life she used to have and focus instead on the promised future that was opening up ahead of her, but sometimes hurt was so deep-rooted it seemed impossible to weed it out altogether.

6

Danni had fallen in love with Castaway Cottage when she was very young, after spending holidays there as a child, back when her father had still been alive and they'd been a 'normal' family. Her mother had always been at least partly absent, despite her physical presence, her mind often elsewhere – where she'd almost certainly wanted to be too. Nicola had never been cut out to be a parent, but Danni's father had done a pretty good job of shielding his children from that while he was alive. Once he was no longer around, Nicola's disinterest had been painfully obvious. Over the years, Danni had often thought about asking her mother why she'd ever decided to have children. It must have been what her father had wanted, and Nicola had simply gone along with it because she wanted to be with him. It had probably never crossed her mind that she might be left to raise her children alone and sending them to boarding school must have been the only solution she could come up with to cope.

Danni's experiences meant that she had thought about what she might do if she was left to raise a child alone, or if Charlie was, and she'd forced him to discuss it before they'd started trying for a baby, even though it was clear he'd rather talk about almost anything else.

'Please, Dan. I don't even want to think about something like that happening.' He'd pulled her close to him and stroked her hair. It would have been so easy just to lie in his arms and forget that bad things sometimes happened, but she'd needed to know they were on the same page before they started on the most important journey they'd ever embark upon.

'I know you don't.' She'd held his gaze, until he'd finally nodded. Understanding why she had to talk about this so badly. It was so important to her to know that any child she had would be loved unconditionally and wholeheartedly, even if something terrible did happen. She knew Charlie would never send a child away. He was going to be an amazing dad, but there were still things they needed to discuss. Danni wouldn't expect Charlie to stay on his own for the rest of his life, if she died, but she had to hear from him that any decisions he made would put their child before his future relationship. She knew what she expected him to say – that their child would always come first, no matter what – but she had to be certain and she needed to hear those things from him. It was only once they'd talked it all through that she was ready to try for the baby they both desperately wanted, and who she was praying would have both parents around for a very long time.

She'd expected it to take at least six months, if they were lucky enough to fall pregnant at all, so conceiving in the first month of trying had taken them both by surprise. They'd already planned a wedding, but she'd have been more than seven months pregnant by the time it came around, and they'd decided in the end to postpone the ceremony until after the baby was born. It had nothing to do with the fact her wedding dress definitely wouldn't have fitted; she couldn't give a damn about that. But they'd both decided they wanted the baby there, and for them all to celebrate becoming a family together. And now she was so close to having the baby she could feel the excitement. Finally, she'd have her little family of three, and Danni couldn't wait.

It was a long time since she'd felt like part of a family, but soon she'd have two. She and Joe had clung to one another in the wake of their father's death, but her heart had been broken all over again when he'd decided to move to Australia. Having him home again had been cause for a celebration, and it was something she tried to do whenever she got the chance. After what had happened to her father, she had a tendency to focus on the what ifs, and worry about things that might never happen, but she was doing her very best to break the habit and focus on all the good things in her life instead. The baby shower Esther had organised would be another wonderful opportunity to do just that. They were holding it in the garden of Castaway Cottage, but providing the venue was the only involvement Danni had had in the day. When Esther had first asked if she could organise a baby shower for her, Danni's instinct had been to say no, because she didn't want to tempt fate. But there were so many people who wanted to celebrate the fact that she and Charlie were starting a family. On the day they'd discovered the baby's sex, her friends from the hospital had thrown an impromptu get-together to mark the news, and they'd all been so excited for her; Esther most of all. So there was no way she could deny her best friend that, or admit even to Charlie just how scared she still was, despite all his reassurances. She hated the fact that she couldn't just enjoy it. Maybe she'd just got used to longing for another life for far too long. And now that she had so much, it felt like she might wake up from the dream at any moment and discover she was back in the boarding school dorm room, crying out for her parents, and knowing they'd never come.

'This is so much fun!' Charlie's biological mother, Connie, put an arm around Danni and hugged her close. She'd joined her on an outdoor day bed, where Danni was catching her breath after trying to chat to as many people as possible. 'I've just added my contribution to the field of flowers, it's such a lovely idea.'

'It really is, isn't it?' Amongst all the party games Esther had organised, she'd also bought a huge canvas where everyone had been asked to paint a flower to create a whole field of them, to welcome the new baby to the world. They could hang it in the nursery as a reminder of all the people who'd cared enough to be there, and who couldn't wait for the baby to arrive. Danni had asked Esther to tell people she didn't want gifts, partly because the idea had given her that feeling of tempting fate again, but mostly because she just wanted to share the day with everyone that was important to her. She should have known that not everyone would follow those instructions, and rejecting gifts people wanted to give would have been churlish and ungrateful. But despite how generous her friends and family had been, she knew the field of flowers was the thing she'd treasure most of all.

'Gilly has painted the most amazing sunflower.' Connie was still smiling, but there was a hint of sadness in her eyes. 'She's the one who gave Charlie his love of drawing. I hope the baby shares that too. Either way he's going to love having grandparents like Gilly and Ray.'

'He's going to love having grandparents like you and Richard too. What child wouldn't want to have a farm to visit whenever he wants to, and be able to ride on the tractor with his granddad?' It was Danni's turn to give Connie's waist as squeeze. 'He's very lucky to have two sets of loving grandparents.'

'I'm sure your mum will fall in love with him too, once's he's here.' The expression in Connie's eyes had changed again, and they'd blurred with tears. 'Try not to let it upset you, darling girl.

You, Charlie, and the baby all have so many people who love you very much.'

'I know and we're really grateful.' Danni blinked back tears of her own. 'I should be used to it by now, but just looking around here at everyone... It's so obvious that someone is missing.'

'She's the one who's missing out and it's her loss. If she doesn't realise what amazing kids she has in you and Joe, then she's an idiot. I'm sorry, but it's true.' Connie took hold of her hand. 'I've wished a thousand times that Richard and I hadn't missed out on seeing Charlie grow up, and knowing that I've got the chance to see his little boy grow up and share in his family life, because of you, has made me happier than you'll ever know. You saved my life after my accident, and you helped me rebuild my relationship with them both. You're an incredible woman, Danni, and I couldn't have asked for a better partner for Charlie, or a mother for my grandchild. I know Gilly feels the same, because we've talked about it.'

'And I couldn't have asked for better mothers-in-law than you and Gilly.' Danni returned the squeeze of her hand. 'Most people worry about having a good relationship with their mother-in-law, and would probably be scared of having that doubled, but I'm so glad I've got you both.'

'Are you two okay?' Charlie suddenly appeared, tilting his head as he looked at them. He didn't miss much, and it was another occasion where she didn't need to say anything for him to know what she was thinking. There'd already been tears earlier in the week, when Esther had suggested a guess the baby photo competition, and she'd realised she didn't have any photographs she could contribute. Not one. After her father's death, she hadn't thought of asking her mother to save them, she'd never dreamt that she'd need to. But then most mothers didn't throw out photographs of their children when they downsized to a new home.

'It's just hormones, you know.' Even as Danni tried to pass it off as nothing, she could tell Charlie wasn't buying it.

'It's a bit more than that.' Connie's voice was gentle, and Charlie moved towards them, crouching at Danni's feet.

'Is this too much? I can tell everyone you're not feeling great, and you can go and hide out until they're all gone. I'll come with you.' Charlie's eyes met hers and she shook her head.

'No, I'm not going to let my mum ruin any more big moments for me.' She'd already told Charlie how much it had hurt when her mother hadn't bothered to show up at her graduation or been a part of any of the other big milestones in her life.

'How about a game of baby Pictionary then? Esther's setting the white boards up and we have to draw baby-themed phrases for our team members to guess.' As Charlie smiled, Danni raised her eyebrows.

'And I suppose you and I are on opposing teams; that's hardly fair when everyone thought the cow I drew when we played at Christmas was a T-Rex.'

'But you're brilliant in countless other ways, so you've got to give me one thing I'm better at. Otherwise, you might not need me for anything.' Charlie pressed his lips against hers for a moment, but she shook her head as he pulled away.

'You're better at so many more things than I am, including always being able to find the positives in any situation, and no one is better at cheering me up than you are.' She grinned. 'So I think I might keep you.'

'Phew!' Charlie pretended to wipe sweat off his brow, and then took hold of Danni's hand again. 'Right, come on, because my team are about to run rings around yours.'

'Oh, you think so, do you?'

'I'm every bit as sure of that as I am of the fact that you're stuck with me until the end.' Charlie kissed her again as she got to her feet, and the hollowed-out feeling she'd had all afternoon was suddenly replaced by a warm glow of contentment. She had a life she loved, filled with people who cared about her, and whom she cared about just as much. But most of all she had Charlie and their baby, and that was more than she could ever have asked for.

* * *

Danni had spent the whole afternoon laughing, mostly at her own attempts to draw the clues Esther gave her. Her depiction of a midnight feed, with what she'd thought was a passable sketch of a mother and baby, had been guessed as a nappy caddy. She just had to hope that their son inherited Charlie's creativity. She'd love it if the baby was like Charlie in as many ways as possible, but she'd never forget how lucky she was to be expecting a healthy baby. Glancing over at Aidan and his husband, Jase, it was even easier to count her blessings. They were sitting with Danni's other friends, including Isla, who'd agreed to be their egg donor. But just weeks after making the offer, Isla had discovered she had chronic myeloid leukaemia. It was a condition that could be managed with medication, in a similar way to diabetes, but if she wanted to do a second round of egg donation, she'd have to stop taking her treatment. Aidan had been vehemently against that idea, and they'd agreed if none of the frozen embryos resulted in a pregnancy, that Aidan and Jase would look for a different donor. After the first round of IVF had failed, Danni hadn't wanted to ask whether they were planning to try again and she'd told Aidan not to feel pressured to come to the baby shower if it was too tough right now. He'd reassured her that he and Jase were fine, and that they'd reminded themselves the odds were stacked against them for it to work first time around. That hadn't stopped her watching her friend at various points in the afternoon, and checking that he and Jase really were managing okay. She'd been relieved to see them both laughing, but she knew as well as anyone that it was possible to put up a front. After all, most of the guests would probably have no idea how terrified Danni had felt for most of her pregnancy, and she wanted to make sure Aidan didn't feel he had to put an act on too.

'We want to go to Australia and New Zealand, early next year, and then on to Japan for when the blossom season is in full swing. We're intending to be away for three months, so we'll see what else we can fit in.' Isla was busy outlining her travel plans to the others, as Danni got to the table. 'Although it depends how long Reuben can be away from the deli before going into meltdown.'

'I think Todd is ready to manage the place now, but I'm not going to pretend I won't be a bit worried.' Isla's boyfriend shrugged, before putting his arm around her shoulders. 'But I wouldn't miss out on the chance to travel with you, not even if it means the business taking a few steps back.'

'Me and your Uncle Jase will be keeping an eye on it for you; it'll give us something to keep us busy.' Aidan gave his nephew a rueful smile. 'And of course we'll make sure Todd is sticking to the recipe for your blondies. Even if we have to taste test them every day!'

'My heroes.' Reuben laughed.

'Come and sit with us and take the weight of that giant beach ball off your feet.' Aidan pulled out a chair for Danni, and grinned.

'Only you could get away with calling me that.' Danni returned his smile, and rested a hand briefly on his shoulder. 'I can't believe the others are having another round of potty-pong. They're such a competitive bunch.' As revolting as the game sounded, it actually involved trying to get ping pong balls into a potty, at further and further distances away, until they eventually got a winner. Both sets of Charlie's parents were playing, along with Gwen and her husband, Barry, and Wendy and Gary, who thankfully seemed to have recovered completely from his head injury. There was a lot of good-natured ribbing and shouting, and she'd had to leave Charlie and Joe umpiring to make sure there were no disputes about who the winner was.

'You know Gwen, she always takes things to the next level.' Esther glanced over in the direction of where a chorus of shouts of 'cheat' had just gone up, quickly followed by more laughter. 'I'm just glad everyone is having a good time.'

'Because of you.' Danni blew her a kiss. 'And I'm going to repay you by helping in any way I can with the wedding. And this so-called beach ball means I can be the designated driver on your hen night. I don't miss drinking at all, but I cannot wait until I can tie my own trainers again!' Danni caught Aidan's eye, heat flushing her face. Here she was, whining on about being a bit uncomfortable, when he'd probably have walked over hot coals to get the baby he and Jase were longing for. Aidan had already told Reuben he wanted to keep busy, no doubt to take his mind off everything for a while. 'I'm sorry, I know this must have been hard for you today and I'm an idiot for complaining about anything to do with being pregnant.'

'Of course you're not.' Aidan exchanged a brief glance with Jase, and then turned back to the group. 'It's handy to hear what the challenges of pregnancy can be from someone in the know anyway, because we're going to need to be ready to step in and help Ellen, our surrogate, with all of that. We weren't going to say anything, as this is your big day, but now that the party is winding down, I've got a feeling you'll want to hear this... Isla already knows, but we got a positive pregnancy test on Wednesday. The IVF has worked this time!'

'That's the best news I've heard in ages.' Danni kissed Aidan on the cheek, and there was a flurry of hugs, congratulations and more kisses exchanged after that. She wasn't the only one struggling to stop herself from crying, and Jase had tears streaming down his face as he turned towards her.

'We can't believe it's actually happening, and there's a lot that could still go wrong, which was why we were originally going to keep it to ourselves for a bit. But what's the point of good news, if we can't share it?'

'I'd never have been able to keep it to myself anyway.' Aidan pulled a face. 'I keep crying every time I see a baby. I don't think I'd be able to keep it to myself if something went wrong either. But like Gwen always says, there's no point in borrowing tomorrow's troubles, and missing out on all there is to be thankful for today.'

'It's going to be okay this time, I just know it is.' Isla got up and walked behind Aidan, putting her arms around him. 'And whatever we decide about more travelling after New Zealand, there's no way we're going to miss being here when you guys become dads.'

'The next few months are going to be so amazing with all of this going on.' Esther smiled as she caught Danni's eye. It was true, and the nagging feeling that had never quite gone away finally seemed to be fading. Aidan was right that good news was for celebrating, and borrowing tomorrow's trouble was a sure-fire way to suck all the joy out of life. She was more determined than ever to only focus on the good things from now on, and push all her worries down as far as they could possibly go. Being surrounding by friends on days like this made it easy, and that was something to celebrate too.

7

There was no such thing as a routine shift in the emergency department, but sometimes things came in patterns, and just lately it seemed to Danni that every other patient being brought in was a child. She'd never been someone who could take a completely businesslike approach to being a doctor, but she could usually bury her feelings deep enough for her to keep the kind of professional distance that was necessary for her to do her job. Except, these days, when it came to children, she was struggling with that much more than she ever had before. When a call came through on the red phone to alert them that ambulances were on the way in with a toddler and his sixty-three-year-old grand-mother, both of whom had been hit by a car, goose pimples had broken out all over her skin. The likelihood of the injuries being minor – particularly for such a small child – was tiny. He was going to be frightened and in pain, and Danni couldn't help hugging her bump tightly as they waited for the first of the two ambulances to turn up.

The adrenaline seemed to flow all the faster once the para-medics arrived, briefing the team on the details of the accident and the pain-killing medication both patients had been given. The little boy's grandmother, Tania, had taken the force of the impact when the car had mounted the pavement, with eye witnesses saying she'd thrown herself between the vehicle and his pushchair. She'd initially been unconscious at the scene, and there'd been an obvious open break in both her left leg and arm. Tania had been sedated and intubated, so that the open fracture could be realigned sufficiently to maintain blood flow to her hand and foot, and she'd been given ketamine to manage the pain.

As a result of the sedation, it was difficult to determine the impact of any head trauma. The paramedics had also described severe bruising and suspected broken ribs on her left-hand side, but thankfully her heart rate and blood pressure had remained stable, so there didn't appear to be any risk of internal bleeding. Danni had only got a brief glimpse of the little boy, who one of the ambulance technicians had said was called Barney, and whose curly blond hair was matted with blood. He was conscious at least, sobbing and calling out, which Danni was hoping would turn out to be a good sign. The sound of him crying for his grandmother made something in her chest constrict. But all she could do was to help the woman he so desperately wanted to be with, while her colleague, Zahir, took charge of treating the little boy.

'We're going to need the trauma surgeons and an anaesthetist down here as soon as possible, but we need a CT first. With so much blunt force trauma on the left-hand side, there's a good chance she could have damaged her spleen.' Danni gave the instruction to Esther, once they were through to resus with the patient and the handover from the paramedics was complete. Aidan, Amy and Isla were already attaching the monitors to ensure that Tania's condition remained stable. She'd been given a GCS of six, due to the fact she hadn't regained consciousness prior to sedation, but there was some response to pain, in both her reflexes and her eyes, which meant there was hope. Although with a score in that range, Danni would have estimated her chances of survival at being less than 50 per cent. And her chances of a full recovery were even lower.

'She's got a heart rate of 130 bpm, and her blood pressure is dropping.' Aidan gave the update on Tania's condition and Danni's heart sank. Both of these changes in her vital signs were indications of internal bleeding.

'Her abdomen is rigid, and it looks like her spleen has ruptured. She needs IV fluids, and we need to prepare for the major haemorrhage protocol.' She'd barely got the words out before Esther headed off, only too aware of how urgent it was to put in the call. They were going to need staff from a range of specialisms available during the CT scan. If Tania's blood pressure dropped again due to further bleeding, specialists would need to administer blood clotting medication, to try and slow down the bleeding until the scan had been completed and she could go into surgery. Amy, Aidan and Isla leapt into action, each of them knowing their roles. And within minutes they'd set up the machine to facilitate the transfusion, despite them not being able to identify where the suspected blood loss was coming from.

'How's her heart rate?' Danni connected the IV to the cannula that the paramedics had put in, hearing Aidan's sharp intake of breath before he responded.

'Still rising. She's at 135 bpm now.'

'Mum!' The doors of resus suddenly flew open as a man, who looked to be in his mid-thirties, charged into the room; the panic in his eyes was obvious before he even spotted his mother lying on the bed. 'Oh my God, is she...'

He stood there with his mouth open, unable to finish the sentence, and Danni stepped in. 'She's sustained some serious injuries, but she's in the right place and the best thing you can do for her now is to go and wait somewhere until we can come and give you an update.'

'I'm not leaving her.'

'I know it's hard.' Danni kept her tone even. 'But you need to let us get on with our jobs. So we can try to make your mother better.'

'*Try*?' The man had seized on the one word that Danni probably shouldn't have used, but her natural instinct was to be as honest as possible. And she jumped as he hammered his fist down on the top of trolley. 'I need you to do more than *try*.'

'We'll do everything possible.' Even in the wake of the man's obvious anger, she wasn't going to make a promise she knew could easily turn into a lie. 'I'm Danni, one of the doctors and if you go and wait in the relatives' room, I promise I'll come and find you as soon as there's more news. But right now, we need to stabilise your mum so that she can go for a scan, and we can work out the best way to treat her. What's your name?'

'Max.' The anger seemed to drain out of him as he spoke, and he suddenly looked so much smaller and far less threatening. 'Mum was looking after my nephew. My sister phoned her when they were on the way home from the park and she heard the accident happen. She was hysterical when she called me. I'm sorry, I know I'm not supposed to be in here, but I just need to know she's going to be all right.'

'It's okay, Max, I'm going to get Isla to take you to the relatives' room now, and I'll come and find you as soon as I can.'

'Please don't let her die, will you? We lost Dad last year and I can't...' For the second time Max was unable to finish his sentence, and Danni's only option was to repeat herself too.

'I promise we'll do everything we can.' As she turned back to Aidan and their eyes met, all she could do was silently pray that everything they could do would be enough to save Max's mother.

* * *

Danni's only focus was to keep Tania safe until she was taken up to surgery. It meant that being forced to spend time with Lucas Newman, one of the trauma surgeons, who also happened to be Esther's ex-fiancé, barely registered on the list of things she was worried about.

'You've done your bit and kept her alive; you can let the experts take over now.' Lucas had given her a tight smile. With any of the other surgeons, she might have assumed they were joking; a bit of inter-departmental rivalry that the different teams would often exchange to take the edge off high-pressure situations. But this wasn't a joke, this was a way of putting Danni in her place, and letting her know exactly what he thought of the job her department did. That type of comment wouldn't have bothered her, even if it hadn't come from a slimeball like Lucas, because she knew how vital her team's work was, and just how good they were at it. They'd kept Tania as stable as possible, until the scan had revealed that the bleeding was coming from a ruptured spleen. After the handover with Lucas, Tania had been rushed up to theatre for a splenectomy, and to pin unstable fractures in both her leg and arm. She was going to survive, and would make as full a recovery as possible, because of what the team in A&E had done. Lucas might want to puff up his chest and say it was all down to him, but Danni would make sure her staff knew how much she valued them, and how proud she was of what they did on a day-to-day basis. Although it was Tania's son who needed to hear from her first.

'I'm sorry not to have got here sooner.' Danni addressed Max as soon as she entered the relatives' room, and he looked up at her, his face deathly pale.

'She's gone, hasn't she?'

'No, she's doing as well as can be expected and we've managed to stabilise her condition.' Danni gave him a smile she hoped was comforting. 'She's up in surgery now, where they'll be removing her spleen and ensuring the fractures are realigned.'

'Can she have a normal life span without a spleen?' The fear in Max's eyes was still apparent and she hoped that was something she could help alleviate.

'Thankfully the liver can work a bit harder to make up for the removal of the spleen and take over most of its functions. There's a slightly increased risk of infections becoming more serious when you're living without a spleen, but I can assure you that the risk in adults is very small.'

'So she's going to be okay?' Max's tone was a blend of hope and trepidation, and she knew what she said next would be what tipped the balance.

'It's going to be a long road to recovery, but there's every reason to be really hopeful. There was no sign of a significant head injury, and even though there'll be a long period of rehabilitation, she should regain full use of her arm and leg.'

'Thank God.' Max leapt to his feet and threw his arms around Danni, spinning her in a circle, before he suddenly seemed to realise what he was doing, setting her down and letting her go. 'Sorry, that's probably the last thing you needed in your condition.'

'It's fine.' She smiled, soaking in the moment. There were far too many times when she had to pass on the worst possible news, so days like that were priceless. 'Has someone been to talk to you about Barney?'

'My sister and brother-in-law are with him. He's got a greenstick fracture to his lower right leg and suspected concussion, but because of Mum he's going to be okay, and because of you, she is too.'

'I just did my job, but it sounds like what your mum did for Barney was what really saved a life today. You must be so proud of her.'

'She's always been an amazing mum, and she loves being a nana.' Max smiled. 'So it doesn't surprise me in the slightest that she'd put her life on the line for Barney. Although I suppose anyone would do that in the same circumstances; it's instinctive, isn't it?'

'I'm sure most people would.' Danni's attempt to return his smile made her cheeks ache. Nicola couldn't even make time to meet up with Danni when she'd suggested travelling down to Bristol to meet her mother for lunch. She'd wanted to share the pictures from the twenty-week scan, and she'd even found a place close to her mother where they could go for a 4D scan together, now that she was past the twenty-four-week stage. She'd hoped if her mother saw the baby that she might somehow develop a bond with her grandson. It was stupid really, when she barely had a bond with the children she'd given birth to, but somehow Danni still couldn't quite bear to let go of that hope. Tania had put her life on the line without a moment's hesitation, and Barney had a grandmother who loved him more than life itself. Danni and Charlie's baby would have that kind of love from his parents, but she couldn't help feeling sad for him that he'd never have that from his maternal grandmother. Buried far deeper than that was the pain that Danni carried from never having that kind of love from her own mother. It still mattered, even after all this time, and she had a horrible feeling she'd never stop grieving for the one thing she was never going to have.

8

Wendy snuck a glance at her reflection in the mirror. She'd never imagined she'd be wearing lingerie like this again. A red and black bra and matching lacy knickers made her feel risqué, but even she had to admit they were an improvement from the greying underwear she'd favoured in the latter years of her marriage, when Mike had seemed to stop noticing her at all. She knew she should have worn nice underwear to feel good for herself, but back then she'd forgotten what that was like. Lately, she felt better about herself than she had in years, and it made her want to wear nice things, even if she was the only one who'd see them.

What made putting on her newest purchase feel all the more racy was that it was 3 p.m. on a Saturday, and she was fully intending to wake Gary up from his post-night-shift slumber with an offer she knew he'd appreciate. Gwen's pep talks and the advice of the others in the Miss Adventures group, was starting to help shift her confidence in the right direction, at least a little bit. Gary had told her countless times that she was beautiful, but it hadn't made a lot of difference to how she felt about herself. It was the advice of her female friends that was doing more to change that. They understood how she felt, in a way she didn't think Gary ever could, and she was doing her best to follow their lead. Taking care of the body she had now – rather than the one she'd always wanted, but was almost certainly never going to get – had become more of a priority since she'd joined the group. What she found harder to admit, even to herself, was that the conversation she'd had with Chloe had influenced her thinking too.

Wendy wanted Alice and Zara to see her loving herself just as she was. She might not be able to go that far yet, but faking it was something she'd grown adept at. The idea that she might have had something to do with Zara's disordered eating broke her heart. Part of her had wanted to tell Chloe where to shove her comments, and to suggest that Zara's problems probably had more to do with her father getting her art tutor pregnant, than any fad diet Wendy might have been on. But she had to admit Chloe was right; she'd been a role model for self-hatred and shaming her own body for as long as she could remember. Gwen had given her advice about how to love her body and Wendy had nearly choked at the thought of some of the suggestions; she'd rather clean the hospital toilets with her own toothbrush than let strangers see her naked. So this was a compromise and buying good quality, ever-so-slightly naughty underwear, for the eyes of a man who for some reason thought she was sexy, even when she was wearing jogging bottoms and an old T-shirt, turned out to be something she could do.

The blackout curtains were still drawn, and she didn't want to turn the light on and be caught in its harsh glow – she was a long way from being that confident yet. Instead she left the torch of her mobile phone on, setting it down on the bedside table, giving just enough light to softly illuminate the room. Zara was at her dad's and Alice was at university so there was no fear of getting caught out, or of making either of her daughters wish they could rinse their eyeballs out with bleach, just so they could unsee the horror of being confronted by their mother's sex life.

'Gary. Wake up.' She shook his shoulder gently, letting her hair fall forward to brush against his skin as she leant over him, the scent of her perfume filling the space between them.

'You smell gorgeous.' The first compliment was out of Gary's mouth before he had even opened his eyes. But when he did, he gasped. 'Oh my God, Wend, what are you trying to do to me? You look amazing.'

His body was already responding as she drew back, allowing him to see the full effect of the gravity-defying miracle of such an expensive bra. Even she had to acknowledge that her boobs hadn't looked this good since before she'd had the girls, and for a moment she felt not just beautiful, but powerful too.

'I was going to bring you breakfast in bed, but seeing as it's already three o'clock, I thought you might prefer some afternoon delight.' Even as she said the words, Wendy's toes curled under her. Gwen had talked about how she'd reinvigorated her love life following a crisis of confidence in her fifties, and it was Gwen who'd mentioned the phrase. It had sounded far more alluring in Wendy's head, when she'd rehearsed the line, than it did out loud, and part of her was already dying inside. But when she looked at Gary, his eyes were shining.

'If I'm still dreaming, please don't wake me up. I'd pinch myself, because I can't believe how lucky I am to have you in my life, but I don't want to risk it.'

'You're not dreaming and you're about to get a whole lot luckier.' The glass of wine she'd had for bravado while she was getting ready was the only reason she could even say the words, and she was determined to ignore the heat that rose up her neck every time she tried to say something sexy.

'I love you.' He reached for her hand, and she was about to respond, when the shrill ringtone of her mobile phone suddenly filled the room, jangling her senses and making her feel oddly exposed in what should have been the most intimate of moments, even before she glanced at the caller ID.

'I'm so sorry, but I think I should get this. Alice doesn't usually call unless there's something—'

Gary cut her off, his tone gentle. 'It's fine. I understand. It'll give me time to have a quick shower; just promise me you'll still be wearing that when I come out?'

'I promise.' Counting her blessings to have found such an incredibly kind man, Wendy pressed the button to accept the call.

'Hello sweetheart, everything okay?'

'Why do you always think something's wrong whenever I call you instead of you calling me?' Alice laughed, not giving Wendy a chance to reply. 'I know, I know, it's what mother's do, and I'll understand when I am one. Don't worry, everything's fine, I just wanted to let you know I'm on my way home for a couple of days.'

'Oh brilliant! What time will you be here?' Wendy had missed her older daughter so much since she'd started university in Exeter, and an unexpected extra visit home made her heart soar. The promise she'd made Gary was already forgotten as she reached for a robe, hoping that her daughter wasn't already too close and that she'd at least be given enough warning to get changed.

'Probably Monday lunch time.'

'But I thought you said you were on the way home now?' Wendy's spine went rigid as she waited for her daughter to answer, knowing what she was going to say.

'I'm going to Dad's first. I want to spend some time with Zara, and we're going to see the new Marvel movie with Chloe. Then tomorrow she's taking me to bottomless brunch in Port Tremellien, so I'll need to sleep that off I reckon. Clo obviously can't drink at the moment, so I'll have to have enough mimosas for the two of us! As soon as I get up on Monday, I'll head over to your place.'

It took all Wendy had not to respond to the fact that her daughter had described the home where her bedroom was as *your place*, but she couldn't keep the disappointment out of her voice. 'I'm working on Monday.'

'I know, but we can have dinner together and watch a film on Netflix or something, before I head off on Tuesday morning. If Gary's not working, can you ask him if he'll make that Beijing chicken he does. I haven't been able to stop thinking about it since I had it last.'

'I'll ask him.' Jealousy was prickling Wendy's scalp and she had to clench her jaw to stop herself from asking why Alice had never wanted to do anything like go out for bottomless brunch with her mother; or why she'd rather do something like that with a woman who was currently tee-total. She knew the answer already. That would be embarrassing, or 'tragic' as the girls would probably term it. Whereas doing it with Chloe was more like going out with a friend. She was beautiful and cool, and someone both the girls seemed to want to be like, instead of a sad, middle-aged cringe-fest like their mother.

'Are you okay Mum? You sound upset?'

'No, I'm fine.' Letting Alice know just how hurt she was would probably make the idea of spending time with an over-emotional, menopausal woman even less appealing. So, she passed her sadness off as something else. 'I've just got a bit of headache that's all.'

'Okay then, I'll see you on Monday evening. Love you.'

'Love you too.' As the call disconnected, Wendy's whole body seemed to go into a slump that even the miracle bra didn't stand a chance of reversing. She was never going to be able to compete with Chloe, and she was scared that she was always going to come off second best to a woman who she didn't want to be a part of her children's lives, let alone her own. Suddenly she felt the opposite of beautiful and powerful, she was back to being plain old Wendy, rejected by her ex-husband and their daughters, and no amount of positive thinking or expensive underwear could ever make up for that.

When Joe had proposed to Esther, he'd asked Danni if it had upset her. He'd told her he was worried that she might not approve, given the warning she'd issued not to rush her best friend into anything she might not be ready for, after her broken engagement to St Piran's most hated man. But Danni hadn't been upset; she'd been delighted that two of the people she loved most in the world were getting married, and that her best friend – who'd she's always seen as a sister – would soon be one for real. And it was obvious that Esther hadn't felt pushed into anything. Her relationship with Joe might have progressed quickly, but they'd been friends for years and they'd already had such a solid foundation to build upon. When Esther had asked if Danni minded that she and Joe would be getting married first, now that Danni and Charlie had decided to wait until after the baby, she hadn't needed to think about her response to that either. It didn't matter one bit which of them was first, all that mattered was that they'd both found genuine happiness in the wake of Lucas's attempts to come between them, and they were closer than ever. So her tears on the evening of Esther and Joe's pre-wedding party, in lieu of the usual stag and hen do neither of them wanted, had nothing to do with her being anything less than thrilled about their imminent wedding.

'Right, I'm finally ready. Sorry.' Charlie dropped a kiss on the top of her head, as he came over to where she'd been waiting for him on the sofa. He'd been to London for a couple of nights to meet with his agent and a TV production company who had optioned one of his books for a Christmas special. The train he'd been due to catch home had been cancelled, and he'd arrived back almost an hour later than planned, which meant he'd had to rush in and get showered, while Danni waited for him in what passed for her best party attire these days. At five feet, ten inches tall, she'd never been much of a one for high heels, but pregnancy made comfort even more of a priority and she was wearing white pumps and an empire-line dress that made the most of her newfound bust, but gave the baby plenty of room to perform the kind of somersaults he seemed to be practising a lot just lately.

She'd gone through her handbag while she was waiting for Charlie, taking out the empty packets from her current obsession with ginger biscuits, and making sure she had enough Rennie to re-tile a bathroom floor for the inevitable attack of indigestion she'd get as soon as they'd eaten. That was when she'd found the envelope that Charlie's mother had given her. Gilly had handed one to Danni, and one to Connie at the baby shower, telling them she'd had copies made of the best photographs from the first couple of years of Charlie's life. Connie had seized on them, taking them out straight away and exclaiming in delight at the sight of the chubby-fisted little boy she'd felt she had no choice but to put forward for adoption. Danni had put the photographs away and tried not to look too closely at the ones Connie had waved around. She hadn't taken her copies out of her bag since, but not because she'd forgotten them.

On the day of the baby shower, she hadn't wanted to end up

crying again over the fact there wouldn't be any photographs of her for their baby to look at when he got old enough to want to see what his parents were like as young children. Her mother hadn't thought it worth keeping any of them when she'd sold the house after her father's death. Danni had been too young to realise the impact of that back then, and now it was too late to do anything about it, but she hated the fact that Connie's reaction had made her feel envious of Charlie. Even now, when she'd convinced herself that looking at the photographs wouldn't be anything other than a wonderful glimpse of what their own son might look like, the tears had still slid out of her eyes. Brenda and Maggie had picked up on it straight away, with the Labrador resting her head on Danni's knee and staring up at her with big soulful eyes. Brenda had emitted a melancholy howl, before lying heavily across Danni's feet, in what she knew was an attempt to comfort her. She'd given herself a good talking to then, determined not to let Charlie see how ridiculous she was being, crying over the loss of something she'd never had. Danni had thought she was doing brilliantly; the tears had been wiped away by the time he'd come down from his shower, but Charlie knew her far too well.

'Are you okay, Dan? You don't look like your normal self.' Joining her on the sofa, much to Brenda and Maggie's disgust, he waited until Danni met his gaze.

'I'm just being stupid.'

'You've never in your life been that.' Stroking his fingers across the back of her hand, he waited.

'Okay, over-emotional then.' Danni sighed as her vision blurred with the tears she was determined not to shed again. 'I'm making a drama out of nothing.'

'I hate the thought of anything upsetting you, so will you just tell me what's wrong, please?' Charlie's tone was gentle.

'It's self-centred and ridiculous, but it makes me sad that I don't have a single photograph of me as a young child. I've got a few copies of primary school photographs that my great aunt's son, on my dad's side, sent me after she died, but no one I've spoken to on either side of my family has one of me as a baby. My great aunt tried to pass off one of her grandson, Seb, as me but he had white-blond hair and loads of freckles and there's no way I can have gone from that to this.' Danni had a cloud of curly dark hair that it had taken her most of her life to learn to tame, and her skin was olive toned. Joe was curly too, but his hair was a reddish brown. Neither of them were the child in the photograph their great aunt had tried to give them. 'It's like no one cared enough to take one, and they certainly didn't care enough to hold on to a copy if any were taken. I know it shouldn't still matter to me now, but for some reason it does.'

'Of course it matters and you've got every reason to be upset.' Charlie pulled her closer to him. 'I can't do anything about the photographs from back then, but I can promise you that we're going to make thousands of amazing memories with our little boy, and I'm going to document all of them. You'll be in every photograph I take, and I never want you to feel for a single moment like you don't matter enough to me. You're the person I love most.'

'I don't deserve you.' She touched his face, as a smile played around his lips.

'I'm afraid you're stuck with me anyway.' He kissed her then and all the emptiness inside, that always appeared when she thought too much about her mother, was filled up again by Charlie, in a way only he could. They had a future with a family of their own, and the past didn't have to haunt her any more unless she let it. So she didn't want to waste another moment looking back.

9

Danni hadn't expected to dance as much as she had at the party, but the decision to hire a nineties band had been a stroke of genius, even if she did say so herself. When Esther had announced that she and Joe didn't want traditional stag and hen dos, but a far more casual get-together, Danni had been determined to organise it, to take the load off Esther's shoulders. Charlie had offered to help too and Connie and Richard had insisted that the party be held in their barn on Trengothern Farm, which had been strung with thousands of fairy lights, instantly transforming it into a magical place. The idea of hiring a nineties-themed band had come from discussions with Esther and Joe, about the music the four of them had always loved. That era had been the soundtrack to Esther's childhood, and to the teenage years for the other three, all of whom were at least five years older than the bride-to-be. Danni and Esther had barely been off the dancefloor all evening, but it was the Spice Girls medley that that pushed Danni over the edge in the end. Even Amy and Isla, who were both still in their twenties looked done in. Unsurprisingly to everyone who knew her, it was left to Gwen to maintain a St

Piran's presence on the dancefloor, while all of the others sat a few songs out and tried to recover.

'I'll tell you what I want, what I really, really want... somewhere comfortable to sit down.' Danni put her hands against the small of her back, arching it to stretch against the weight of the baby.

'Me too and I haven't even got an excuse.' Esther grinned. 'Gwen seems determined not to sit down until the band has a break and forces her to.'

'It shouldn't be long now; they'll stop when the food arrives and he said he'll put some background music on then.' Danni had considered continuing the nineties theme with the food, but when she'd googled party foods of the decade, the indigestion that had been ever present since the early part of her pregnancy went into overdrive, just from looking at the suggestions. Instead, she'd copied what Connie and Richard had done for one of their previous parties at the farm, and booked a couple of food trucks to give everyone more of a choice.

'Will the background music be from the nineties, too?' Isla raised her eyebrows as she asked the question. Danni couldn't help wondering if her friend found the decision to play the music of her youth all night as baffling as she had when her dad had insisted on playing his favourite records from the sixties at every get-together her parents had hosted when she was a child.

'He might change it up and play some modern stuff. I love Lijah Byrne's new song.' Esther had a dreamy look on her face. 'I think it's perfect for our first dance, but I don't know if Joe is quite so keen.'

'He's brilliant, isn't he? I think I read somewhere that he grew up around here.' As Danni turned to the others, she didn't miss the look that Amy and Isla exchanged.

'Can I tell them?' Isla directed the question at Amy, who pulled a face for a moment before nodding.

'I don't suppose it matters. It's hardly a secret, is it?'

'No, but it is a claim to fame most of us will never even get close to.' Isla leant forward conspiratorially. 'Guess who Lijah Byrne's first love was?'

Even before Danni could open her mouth, Amy interjected. 'I didn't say I was his first love, I said I was his first girlfriend.'

'Really!' Esther's eyes shot open in surprise. 'So does that mean some of his songs are about you?'

'I highly doubt it.' Amy shrugged. 'He's probably forgotten I even existed. After all, he has thousands of people throwing themselves at him now. When I knew him, he was cute in a geeky way, obsessed with music and always making up melodies. I never dreamt he'd make it big, and I don't think he did either.'

'Is he as lovely as he seems to be on TV? None of the fame appears to have gone to his head.' Danni found it fascinating that Amy had never mentioned knowing Lijah, given that he was one of the most famous musicians around, but the younger woman just shrugged again.

'He was always really genuine and down-to-earth when I knew him, but he didn't have any cause not to be, given that his career back then consisted of busking and delivering the *Three Ports News* on his weekly paper round.' Amy laughed. 'He was a nice guy, though, and I like to think fame wouldn't have changed him that much, but I haven't spoken to him in years.'

'I keep telling her she should get in touch.' Isla gave Amy a pointed look. 'What's the worst that could happen?'

'A restraining order?' Amy laughed again and stood up, signalling the end of the conversation. 'I'm going to get a drink; what does everyone else want?'

By the time Amy had got back with the drinks, the

conversation had moved on, and she seemed relieved at the change of topic. Maybe Danni wasn't the only one who'd decided to focus on looking forward, in order to move on from the past.

* * *

'Here you go.' Esther's dad set down two Belgian waffles piled high with cream, strawberries and chocolate sauce in front of Danni and his daughter.

'You shouldn't be waiting on us, Patrick, you should be letting us look after you.' Danni's admonishment was gentle and the truth was it was lovely to see him looking so well. It had been a tough twelve months for him and Esther's mother, Caroline, but he was now in remission from the prostate cancer which he'd tried to keep secret, and which had pushed their marriage to the edge as a result.

'You two ran around after me and Caroline non-stop during the treatment. The least we can do is repay the favour now that I'm almost back to my old self.'

'Yes, and our girls are the ones who need looking after now.' Caroline's eyes met Danni's for a moment. It was a term she'd used to describe the two of them almost from the start of their friendship. Esther's parents and grandparents had welcomed her into their family, as if she really was part of it, and she loved them for it. 'You're both so busy with work, Esther's got so much on with planning the wedding, and you need to be taken care of even more, with the baby so close to arriving. I just can't wait until he's here!'

'Charlie and I were talking about it, and we wondered if you and Patrick would be willing to be the baby's godparents, alongside Esther and Joe?'

'Willing to? We'd be honoured, wouldn't we, Patrick?' Caroline was beaming.

'We really would.' Patrick wiped his eyes with the back of his hand. Like Danni, his emotions were much closer to the surface these days.

'The only trouble is, we're not sure what that will look like yet and whether we'll do the whole church thing, so in the meantime I wondered if you'd mind filling in for the vacant Nana and Grandpa position on my side. Charlie's got two sets of parents, but the first thing my mother said when I told her I was pregnant was not to expect her to babysit. The second was that she wanted the baby to call her Nikki. Although I don't suppose he'll call her anything much, given how infrequently he's likely to see her.' Danni tried to smile, but it came out a bit wonky, and Caroline wrapped her arms around her.

'You've got no idea how much we'd love that, and we really do see you as our second daughter. We always wanted another child, not least so that Esther would grow up with a built-in best friend, but it didn't work out that way. At least we thought it hadn't, but then you came into our lives and it was as if it was always meant to be. Esther finally had the best friend we'd always wanted for her, and you filled the vacant position in our family, like you were made to be there.'

'This baby is going to feel so lucky to have you; I know I do.' Danni rested her head against Caroline's shoulder for a moment and Esther reached out and squeezed her hand. She could have been jealous of the relationship Danni had built with her parents, but she'd always said how happy it made her. Danni might not have been born into their family, or have been fortunate enough to have a mother like Caroline, but her life was filled with people who *chose* to love her and she knew how lucky that made her.

10

Wendy was scrolling on her phone, but every so often she glanced furtively around her to make sure no one was looking. She was doing something she'd promised herself she'd stop doing, and looking at things that made her feel so guilty her face had gone hot. But staying away from diet advice, and off the sites that claimed they had the answer to her finally getting a so-called bikini body, was much harder than she'd imagined. Especially now Gary had proposed. She'd wondered if it was a knee-jerk reaction to his accident, and his obvious confusion in the wake of his head injury. But he'd mentioned it again three times, and had assured her that there was nothing he wanted more, and when she'd finally realised her meant it, there'd been no hesitation in her answer.

When she'd said yes, he'd swept her into his arms, before stopping and looking at her. She hated the place her mind had gone to in that moment, immediately thinking he must be comparing her to his first wife. Deep down, she knew that was her own insecurities talking, but it didn't stop her imagining how she'd look in the wedding photos, compared to the pictures of his first wife's recent wedding. It was how Wendy had found herself scrolling through photos on Gary's ex-wife's Facebook page, trying to imagine a scenario in which she might look half as good as Rachel in her Net-A-Porter dress that a quick Google search revealed had cost more than Wendy's car. But even if she had been able to spend almost eight thousand pounds on a dress, she still wouldn't have looked anything like Rachel, never mind Chloe. She was probably thirty pounds heavier than both of them, and six inches shorter than Chloe.

She'd started to look at wedding dresses for the more mature bride instead. Most of the suggestions of tea-length, 1950s-style dresses, or well-fitted suits were a world away from the fantasy she had of what she wanted to look like. Whatever she wore, she'd come off second best again, and the thought of doing that on what was supposed to be the happiest day of their lives together made her weaken her resolve. All she wanted was one photograph of their wedding she'd be happy to have up on the wall. And the advertisement that had just popped up seemed to promise it all.

> Think you've tried every diet going? Then this one's for you. In three months you could lose more than forty pounds! It's changed my life, let it change yours too! It really works!!!

Wendy clicked on the link at the bottom of the post, which took her to a website filled with before and after photos of women who'd looked like she did now, but who just months later were posing by a poolside in swimsuits that Wendy wouldn't have got over one thigh. She clicked on a video. One of the women talked about how different this diet was and how it had changed her relationship with food forever. According to the successful slimmer sharing her story in the video, all she needed to do to maintain her weight loss after the initial three months was to make sure she had three of the company's ketone drinks a day, and then she just ate normally. Even as a little voice inside Wendy's head whispered to her that she'd been here before and ought to know better, a louder voice was growing in excitement. Maybe this really was the one. After all, these other dieters had all failed before and this diet had turned things around for them. What did she have to lose, other than the weight she'd tried a hundred times to shift before? Okay, so it was an expensive programme, and the initial twelve weeks consisted of a diet made up of what looked like astronauts' food. She'd start straight away on drinkable ketones to suppress her appetite, and continue with those once she was at her goal weight.

Just one more diet couldn't hurt, as long as she kept it quiet and made sure Zara didn't know what she was doing. It was the worst kind of hypocrisy, she couldn't deny that. It was already eating her up inside that she wasn't the one helping Zara, even though she knew it was in her daughter's best interests. Chloe had been through the same experience, and she was someone Zara could relate to. The chances were that Chloe would also be far more successful at treading the fine line between encouraging Zara to open up, yet not coming off like she knew what was best for her. Everything Wendy had read suggested that trying to give advice or act like the answers were easy, was the worst possible thing someone could do. The trouble was, as a mother, she always wanted to fix her girls' problems, so being as hands-off with Zara as she was had been incredibly difficult.

What she hadn't admitted to anyone, even herself, was that a lot of the symptoms of eating disorders had resonated with her. At the very least she had disordered eating from years of yo-yo dieting, and telling herself that the next diet might be the one that worked. It was crazy how easily she could slip back into such toxic habits, but instead of facing up to it, she was still trying to make excuses for why just one more time couldn't hurt.

It wasn't until she finally looked up that she realised that Gary had been watching her. Dropping her phone on to the coffee table, she got to her feet.

'What's the matter?' Smoothing her dress, she took on a defensive tone.

'Am I forcing you into getting married? You keep asking me if I'm sure, but I'm starting to wonder if it's you who isn't certain, and I don't want to put any pressure on you.' Gary held her gaze, his warm brown eyes filled with nothing but love, and she shook her head. Despite the insecurities she was struggling to shake, she was more certain of her answer than she'd been of anything in a long time.

'No, I want to marry you, but we don't need to rush do we?'

'Are you sure, because if you want to stay living together instead, I can cope with that, as long as it's forever.'

'No, I'm sure. I know it's old fashioned, but I want to say *my husband*. I feel fourteen again whenever I say my boyfriend.' Wendy grinned, and Gary caught her around the waist.

'You make me feel like I did back then all the time. I never thought I could be this happy again.' He kissed her, working the magic of making her forget everything else for a little while, the way he always did. All the comparisons with women far more beautiful than she would ever be ceased to exist too, and she promised herself that this time she really wouldn't be sucked back into another diet. Gary loved her the way she was and she'd already spent far too long fighting against her own body, trying to be something she'd never be. She was going to stay strong and keep working on her self-confidence instead. It was time to break the cycle and lead by example; it was the least she could do for the poor body she'd already put through so much, and even more importantly, for Zara.

She wouldn't be signing up for wonder weight loss in twelve weeks, or remortgaging the house to buy a dress that might make her look like she'd lost thirty pounds. Instead, she wanted to start planning the wedding, and any money she might have wasted on those other things could go towards celebrating with the people they loved the most.

* * *

The rush to work the next day, and getting Zara off to college, meant Wendy felt as if she was running to catch up all morning. It wasn't until lunchtime that she had a moment to start looking at the wedding venue websites she wanted to talk to Gary about. She was so engrossed in her phone as she walked along the corridor, that she almost missed Chloe altogether. She was certain she would have done, if it hadn't been for the shuddering sigh Chloe had taken, a sob catching in her throat.

'Are you okay?' Wendy's eyes drifted to the small baby bump that Chloe was cradling with one hand.

'I'm scared.' They were just two words, but they conveyed so much, and the expression on Chloe's face said even more. She wasn't just scared, she was terrified, and her eyes were swollen from crying. She might not want to open up to her partner's ex-wife, any more than she already had, but either way, Wendy couldn't leave her standing in the corridor.

'It's going to be okay. Whatever you're scared of, there are people who can help.' Wendy had no idea what lay at the root of the other woman's fears, but she needed to say something to help her, the way she would have done if it had been one of her own girls standing in front of her. 'Do you want to come and sit down for a little while? I don't think you should drive anywhere until you're feeling a bit better. We can go to my office, or get a drink in the restaurant.'

'A hot drink would be good; I can't seem to stop shivering.' As Chloe spoke, Wendy couldn't help noticing the shakiness of her voice, or the goose pimples that had broken out all over her arms. It was a warm day, almost stifling in some parts of the hospital, so the reason Chloe couldn't get warm had nothing to do with the temperature.

'Come on then, let's go and get you a drink and then you can tell me if there's someone you want me to call.' Wendy turned towards Chloe, who seemed frozen to the spot, until she gently took hold of her elbow, guiding her down the corridor towards King Arthur's Table, a name the hospital restaurant could never hope to live up to.

By the time Wendy had brought a hot chocolate over to Chloe, her eyes already looked less raw from crying than they had a few minutes earlier, but she was still wearing that same dazed expression she'd had in the corridor, as if she was searching for someone in the distance, who hadn't yet come into view.

'Here you go.' Wendy set the cup down on the table in front of her, suddenly feeling awkward. Whenever they'd spoken before, the subject of their conversations had always been the girls. It was the only reason Wendy could have imagined them ever needing to talk, and now, in the wake of Chloe's obvious distress, she had no idea what to say. She had to say something, though. 'So... is there someone I can call for you?'

It was such a stupid question. Gary had recounted stories about the difficult calls he'd sometimes had to make to patients' relatives in his job, but Chloe had a mobile phone. It wasn't like she'd been taken into A&E, and her phone had been left behind at the scene of an accident, or she was too poorly to be able to make the call herself. But Chloe's reaction had taken Wendy by surprise and she didn't just shake her head to decline the unnecessary offer; a fresh crop of tears filled her eyes, the first one plopping down on to the table in front of her almost instantly.

'Oh, I'm sorry, sweetheart.' The term of endearment had come out of nowhere, but in that moment it felt entirely natural, as Wendy reached out for the other woman's hand. 'I'm useless at this, it's why I'm in housekeeping and not medicine. Oh, and because being a nurse sometimes involves having to touch people's feet, I can't stand feet.'

Wendy was babbling, desperately trying to find the right thing to say and failing horribly, but Chloe's expression had suddenly changed, and she laughed through her tears. 'I keep thinking how amazing the midwives caring for me are. The things they have to look at all day long...'

Chloe's expression flipped back again, and something inside Wendy's stomach flipped over too. This had to be about the baby.

'Is that where you've been, to see the midwife?'

'I need extra checks. I've been telling everyone my scans have been clear, but they found something wrong.' The fear in Chloe's eyes was so naked now, it made Wendy catch her breath. Guilt washed over her too, for the thoughts that had crossed her mind when she'd first heard Mike and Chloe were expecting a child. But the baby had just been a concept then, an unwelcome idea, not the reality presented by Chloe's growing bump, or the flickering heartbeat Wendy had seen on one of the scan videos Chloe had posted on her Instagram account. She didn't want to wish that baby away, despite the twinge of envy she felt every time the girls talked about their little brother with excitement in their voices.

But it still felt as though those unwelcome thoughts, which had kept Wendy awake in the beginning, were somehow responsible for what Chloe was going through now. She had to force herself to ask the obvious question, worried that Chloe would see right through her concern to the bitterness that had coloured her reaction when she'd first heard Mike was having another child.

'Is it the baby?'

'No, he's okay. But they've found something on one of my ovaries.' Chloe glanced up, suddenly looking barely more than a child herself.

'Is it...' This time Wendy couldn't bring herself to say the word, but the goose pimples she hadn't been able to believe Chloe was experiencing had broken out on her skin too.

'They're almost certain it's a benign cyst, but my mum died from ovarian cancer and I can't help worrying that they've got it wrong.'

'That must be so scary.' Wendy's chest ached as she looked at the young woman in front of her, who desperately needed the mother she'd lost far too soon. 'Are there any checks they can run to put your mind at rest?'

'They're monitoring it to check if it grows, and if it does they want to remove it while I'm still pregnant. They're saying the risk of anything happening to the baby is really low, but I can't lose bean. He's the only family I've got.'

'No, he isn't. You've got the girls and Mike.' It was weird how quickly things could change. Half an hour ago, Wendy's throat would probably have constricted at the thought of someone else laying claim to her daughters, but it was true. Chloe had done nothing but welcome Alice and Zara with open arms, and show them the kind of love that Wendy knew deep down she should be eternally grateful for, even when it was hard to share them. 'What does Mike say about the operation?'

'He doesn't know. He was too busy to come to the twenty-week scan, which he knew was the most important. He had a meeting he couldn't miss apparently. It was probably on the golf course; that's if I'm lucky.' Chloe caught Wendy's eye and an unspoken understanding passed between them. 'So, I haven't told him about the cyst, because he didn't even care enough to ask. He just assumed everything was okay, because that's the way life always turns out for him. As long as it doesn't affect Mike and what he wants to do, nothing else matters. I'm scared about the cyst, and about losing bean, but I'm also terrified that I'm having a baby with a man who's exactly like my father. I thought I'd finally found someone who cared about me.'

'I sure Mike cares about you…' Wendy trailed off for a second time. It was hard to justify the behaviour of a man whose actions were indefensible, especially when she knew Mike far too well to be able to assume he had the best of intentions towards Chloe and the baby.

'When I told him how much I wanted him to come to the twenty-week scan, he just told me there was no need to worry, because in his exact words: "*I make great babies. Wendy carried two beautiful ones with no problems, so you'll be fine too.*"' Chloe bit her lip, putting her hands over her bump. 'Sometimes I think he wishes this had never happened. I think it's only the fact that this one is a boy that's giving him any cause for excitement. It feels like he's been there, done that, and it's all old news to him. I just want someone to be excited about this baby.'

Chloe's words took Wendy back to a place she didn't want to visit. No one had ever been able to get to her the way Mike could. Sometimes his selfishness had made it feel as though her blood was actually boiling. Now it was surging through her veins in the same white-hot way. He was doing it all over again, putting himself, first, last and everywhere in his list of priorities. She could still remember how alone that had left her feeling, particularly during a difficult pregnancy with Zara, and she could see that same aching loneliness reflected in Chloe's face. He'd got away with acting like this for years, and he was clearly arrogant enough not to see any reason to change. Hate was a strong word, but in that moment it was how she felt towards her ex-husband. And, much to her surprise, she wanted to somehow try and make things better for Chloe.

'I'm sure there are loads of people in your life who are excited.' Wendy had an almost overwhelming urge to reach out and take Chloe's hand, but she kept her arms clamped to her sides instead, even as Chloe shook her head.

'When my mum died, my dad found someone else almost straight away and she definitely wished he didn't come as a package deal. It didn't matter that she had two sons from her first marriage, I was the one in the way and she made sure I felt it. Worse than that was my father never did anything to try and make up for it. That's why I need the girls to know how much I want them around, and it's why I encourage Mike to have some one-on-one time with them too...' It was Chloe's turn to trail off.

'Not that he does, right? And he probably doesn't appreciate all that you do either.' Wendy took a deep breath. 'But I do, and I want you to know that.'

The realisation of just how much Chloe did for the girls had crept up on Wendy recently, even though she'd desperately wanted to deny it. If Chloe was an important part of their lives, surely that somehow diminished Wendy's role. Except now she could see that Chloe hadn't been trying to compete with her, she'd been attempting to fill the gaps left by Mike, because she understood exactly how his indifference would make them feel.

'They make it easy. They're such great girls.' Chloe closed her eyes for a second, before opening them again and looking straight at Wendy. 'It just makes me so sad that when you asked if there was someone I could call, there's no one I could think of who cares about me and the baby the way I need someone to right now.'

'Alice and Zara do.' Wendy nodded to emphasise her words. Chloe had shared a painful secret with her, and it was time to do the same. 'They love you, so much that I have to admit I sometimes find it hard, but it's you they want to rush over to their dad's place to see, not him. And they are so excited about the baby. He's already really loved, and not just by you.'

'Oh my God, thank you.' Chloe's eyes filled with tears again, but the tortured look on her face was gone. 'You've got no idea how much that means to me to hear, Wendy. The girls are so lucky to have you and I know this sounds really strange in the circumstances, but I wish I'd had a mum like you around.'

Maybe it was a weird thing for her ex's girlfriend to say, but the truth was that Wendy was easily old enough to be her mother, and something about the young woman had brought the maternal instinct out in her too. That didn't mean they were suddenly going to become best friends, or confidantes, but the bitterness she'd felt about another woman muscling in on her life, and her children, had all but evaporated. Chloe's life wasn't perfect – far from it. And like almost everyone else, her online presence was a façade, aimed at presenting her life in a certain way, which meant it would have been absolute madness for Wendy to envy it, when she had already so much to be thankful for.

11

One moment Danni was standing talking to Zahir about a patient, and the next moment the floor seemed to be rising up to meet her. Putting out a hand in an attempt to steady herself, she took a clinical trolley with her when she went down, causing a horrendous crash in the process that seemed to alert the whole department to what had happened.

'Oh my God, Danni!' Esther was at her side within seconds, appearing out of nowhere like Super Girl on a mission to save the day. 'Are you okay? What happened?'

'I don't know, I just went really lightheaded, and it felt like my legs were going to give out from underneath me.' Danni looked at the chaos around her. 'And apparently they did.'

'Don't you dare even try to get up yet.' Esther put a hand on Danni's shoulder to make sure she couldn't disobey her command.

'I'm fine. I think I just need a snack or something. My blood sugar has been low at some of my checks.'

'Maybe, but it could be your blood pressure, or low iron, or...

like you say, just that you haven't eaten recently enough. But, whatever it is, I want to get you checked over properly, so you're not moving until I've got a wheelchair, and then we're going up to the maternity unit so that they can assess you.'

'You can be a proper sergeant major sometimes, do you know that?' Danni couldn't even pretend to be upset with her friend. Knowing that someone cared as much as Esther did was a gift that she would never take for granted.

'I'm only looking out for you, because you don't look out for yourself the way you should. Now promise not to move, while I get you a wheelchair.'

'I'll keep a close eye on her.' Aidan dropped a wink as he looked at Danni, but she knew he'd keep his word. The friends she'd made in her job were like family to her. Working in emergency medicine had a way of bonding people together for life, and she couldn't have chosen a better group of people to be bonded to.

'I'll be two minutes.' Esther dashed off and Aidan was as good as his word about not letting her stand up. Although he did allow her to sit up, so he could take her blood pressure, asking in his lilting Irish accent whether she and Charlie had found it difficult to pick out a name for the baby, almost certainly in an attempt to distract her from worrying.

'I want to wait until he arrives. I feel like we'll just know when we see him.' She smiled at the look on his face. 'Clearly you think that's a mad idea?'

'We're probably the mad ones, spending most of our spare time talking about a baby we don't even know we're going to get yet.' Aidan pulled a face. 'I'm Mr Upbeat most of the time, and getting a positive pregnancy test was obviously huge, but there's still such a long way to go. Every time the phone rings, or I get a message and see it's from Ellen, I have to hold my breath until I'm certain it's not bad news. I wish I was one of those people who could just assume the best until proven otherwise, but every so often I get this creeping fear.'

'Me too.' It was a relief to Danni to be able to admit it to someone and to know they understood. She and Aidan had shared some of their fears before, and she didn't have to pretend around him that she always felt positive. 'I don't know why I can't be more like Charlie; he looks on the bright side of everything. But we know where it comes from, don't we? And sadly, we also know that not all childhoods are happy ones.'

'You're not wrong, but we can learn from the mistakes our parents made and be all the better at it for our own kids.' Aidan pulled another face. 'Do I sound convincing, because I'm trying to convince myself!'

'You'll be a great dad, I know you will and I'm not so worried about that bit. I just wish I could see that the baby's all right. I keep saying to Charlie that there should be a zip or something I can open, so I can have a little peek inside and make sure he's okay.' Danni laughed again. 'But Charlie reckons I'd look all the time and it would be like when someone opens the oven door too often to check on a cake. The baby wouldn't get cooked properly.'

'We're both in for our share of soggy bottoms either way, and I can't wait.' Aidan squeezed her shoulder. 'The good news is your blood pressure looks fine.'

'Does that mean I can get up?'

'No!' Esther arrived back just in time to lay down the law, and she and Aidan helped Danni into the wheelchair as Esther delivered her next order. 'I've got my lunch break now, so I'm taking you up to maternity and I'll treat us both to a portion of chips from the hospital restaurant. It might not be the healthiest option in the world, but it'll give you a quick energy boost if the midwives say you're okay to drive yourself home, and it'll help me get to the end of the shift.'

There was no point Danni saying that she had no intention of going home, unless the midwives insisted. If she was given the all-clear, she'd be heading back to A&E to finish her shift. They were already short-staffed as it was. But starting that argument with Esther was something she wasn't going to do until she had to.

* * *

The maternity department was unusually quiet when they arrived and Danni was immediately checked over, before being hooked up to a foetal monitor, all of which gave reassuring results. Her blood was taken, and she was asked to provide a urine sample, and within minutes, Heike, the midwife looking after her, had come up with a possible reason for why Danni had fainted.

'There's a trace of some blood in your urine, which indicates an infection, probably caused by the baby getting bigger and putting more pressure on your bladder.' She gave Danni a reassuring smile. 'It's fairly common in pregnancy, but you're going to need some antibiotics to make sure it doesn't get worse. There's a chance the fainting was caused by something else, like anaemia, but we'll know more once we get the results of the blood test.'

'But she needs to rest either way, doesn't she?' Esther's tone was insistent and it had taken all Danni's powers of persuasion to stop her calling Charlie back from Bristol, where he'd gone to consult on set with the TV company who were making one of his books into a Christmas special.

'Rest would be a good idea at this stage, but I know that's difficult in your job.' Heike was still smiling, but Esther frowned.

'Perhaps it's time you put yourself first and started your maternity leave now.'

'Anyone would think you wanted to get rid of me.' Danni grinned, but there was still no softening in Esther's expression.

'I just want to make sure you and the baby are okay.'

'I know.' Danni sighed. 'But sitting at home overthinking all the things that could go wrong between now and the baby arriving sounds like hell to me. Not to mention how guilty it will make me feel. I'd rather be at the hospital with all of my friends looking out for me, and covering for me if I need a slightly longer break. I just forgot to eat this morning, that's all, and that, along with a bit of a UTI, must have done it. But I promise I won't skip any more meals, and that I'll tell you or Aidan if I feel even a little bit dizzy again.'

Esther narrowed her eyes for a moment, and then turned to Heike. 'What do you think? Is it safe for Danni and the baby if she continues working?'

'There's no problem with your blood pressure, so as long as you take breaks whenever you need them, and make sure you eat regularly, you should be okay with lighter duties. I'm guessing that's what was suggested during the risk assessment?'

'Yes, I've been taken off the list for the in-hospital cardiac response team, and I'm not doing any pre-hospital shifts with the paramedics now either. But I can still deal with all the minor issues; burns, broken toes, lacerations, that kind of thing. I can even do some of that sitting down if I need to.'

'Nothing I say is going to change your mind, is it?' Esther sighed as Danni shook her head. 'Just know I'm going to be watching you like a hawk and, if anything like this happens again, I'm getting you straight home, even if I have to carry you over my shoulder.'

'I'd like to see you try.' Danni had a good eight or nine inches on her friend, but she still wouldn't have bet against Esther if it came down to it, and she was clearly backing herself too.

'You know I could if I had to.'

'You probably could, but you won't need to. Once I've had those chips, I'll be ready to tackle anything that comes through the doors.'

'As long as it's a minor injury.' Esther gave her another pointed look.

'Yes, Mum.' Danni laughed again and a warm feeling settled in her chest. She might not have a real mum who loved her the way mums were supposed to, but she had a best friend who cared about her in a way many people never experienced, and that was a blessing which needed to be counted.

Being on lighter duties meant that Danni saw a quicker succession of patients than she might normally have done. There were some who definitely should have gone to their GP instead of turning up in A&E, including Sam, a rugby player who'd been brought to tears when she'd examined his foot, shortly before diagnosing him with an ingrowing toenail. Then there were the others whose injuries made it clear from the moment they arrived that A&E was the right place for them. Clifford was one of those people. His face was obviously swollen, and he was wincing in pain before Danni even had the chance to ask him what was wrong.

'Just put me down, doc, can you? I've had enough. I can't sleep for the pain, but if I could close my eyes and not wake up, and all the pain would be gone, that would be all right by me.' Clifford sat down with a thud, grimacing and clutching the side of his jaw. His records showed he was eighty-two, and she'd heard this sort of remark from patients before, when a catalogue of illnesses had become too much for them to bear. But Clifford's records didn't reveal any serious health complaints, so if they could get to the bottom of what was causing the pain, there was every chance his desire to find a permanent way out of his current agony would pass too.

'I'm really sorry you're in so much pain, Clifford, but hopefully we can sort that out. I just need to ask you a bit more about what's been going on, if that's okay. It's dental pain, is that right?'

'It's more than pain. I've snapped a tooth and I think it's infected.' Clifford grimaced again.

'That sounds horrible. Have you seen a dentist?' Danni braced herself for the response she was almost certain was coming. Over the past few years, she'd seen more and more patients arriving for emergency care with problems that should have been dealt with by a dentist, but there just weren't enough of them, especially in more rural areas. She'd been told about people who'd had their name down on waiting lists for years to get an NHS dentist, because every practice in their area was closed to new patients. For those people who couldn't afford to go private, it ended up leaving a gap for emergency medicine to fill, or worse still for the patients themselves to try and fill. She'd had one patient, in London, who'd attempted to fill his own tooth cavities with a compound he'd bought online, and who'd ended up poisoning himself. So, Clifford's answer to her question came as no surprise.

'I haven't got one. I stopped going after my wife, Blanche, died. She used to make all the appointments, but I didn't realise it was more than two years since I'd been, until I rang them up and they told me they'd taken me off their list.'

'I'm so sorry to hear that you lost your wife.' It had always touched Danni's heart when a patient talked about their loss, but that was something else that hit her even harder these days. The thought of something happening to Charlie woke her up in the night too. The idea of Danni's life without him in it was unthinkable. And, despite her forcing them to talk through what would happen if one of them died, what still scared her most of all was the idea of their child being robbed of having Charlie around. She knew only too well what that was like. There was no time to dwell on the irrational fears that she couldn't shake just lately, Clifford needed the full focus of her attention. 'How are you coping with everything else at home? The admission notes said you damaged your tooth in a fall? Did you sustain any other injuries?'

'No, I tripped on the corner of the rug and hit the side of my face on the edge of a coffee table. It's just as well I didn't knock myself out or I'd still be lying there. There'd be no bugger to come by and find me.' Clifford attempted to laugh, but it came out as more of a strangled sob, and Danni couldn't tell whether it was because of the physical pain he was in, or the emotional kind.

'So you're living alone, and you don't have any regular visitors?' Another little piece of Danni's heart felt like it was breaking for the man in front of her and, when she looked at him again, his eyes had gone glassy.

'It's my own fault. When I split up with my children's mother, I should have fought harder to see them. Instead, I took the easy route, met Blanche and made her my whole world. I told myself that Tracey and Darren were better off without me. Maybe they were, but either way I'm reaping what I've sewn. There's no one who'll check if I'm knocked out on the floor, or even to care if I'm dead or alive.'

Danni didn't trust herself to speak for a moment; the emotion that was rising up in her throat felt as though it might overwhelm her. Her mother had chosen a new life with her partner, Paul, instead of spending time with her children. But maybe there'd been a reason for her doing so, even if it was only in Nicola's head. For the first time Danni questioned whether her mother had thought the same thing; that her children were now better off without her. Whatever the history with Clifford and his kids, she'd have to have a heart made of stone not to feel sad for someone who believed no one left in the world cared about him. She might not be able to change how he felt, but she wanted Clifford to know there were people who would care enough to check on him.

'I'm going to have a look in your mouth now, because I suspect from the swelling on your face that there's an infection. If there is I'll prescribe you some different painkillers and a course of antibiotics, which should help alleviate some of the symptoms and allow you to get some rest. I'll also refer you to one of the dental surgeons to discuss options for extraction or further treatment.' Danni took a breath. 'I think it would be a good idea to run some blood tests, just to make sure there's nothing else going on that might have contributed to your fall. I know you said you tripped, but it's better to err on the side of caution. I'd also like to make a welfare referral for you, so you can get some support with things like finding a new dentist, and looking at whether there might be any hazards in your house that could cause another accident. They can discuss whether you might like to be part of a befriending service too, where volunteers come in for a chat on a regular basis, so you have someone keeping a bit of an eye on you, and caring that you're doing okay. How would you feel about that?'

For a moment Clifford didn't say anything, and if she'd had to guess how he was going to respond, she wasn't sure she could have done. She'd experienced every kind of reaction to that kind of offer in the past, from outright refusal to even discuss it, to being told where she could stick her referral and to stop being an interfering busybody, by a ninety-three-year-old lady who said she had no intention of letting other interfering busybodies over her threshold, since she was perfectly capable of looking after herself. But Clifford's eyes had gone glassy again.

'I'd like that.' It was a simple statement, but there was a chance it could change Clifford's life. Physical pain was almost always easier to treat than the emotional kind, but when Danni went home from work at the end of every shift, she wanted to know she'd done all she could to alleviate both.

12

The smell that greeted Danni as she opened the door to Castaway Cottage on Friday evening made her stomach rumble. Charlie was making his famous Thai green curry and the scent of spices in the air reached her just seconds before Maggie and Brenda came hurtling down the hallway, overjoyed to see their mistress and hailing her arrival with loud howls of delight.

'Oh hello, girls, yes, yes, I love you too.' Leaning down slightly, she patted the dogs, who weaved their way around her in tighter and tighter circles, as if they were trying to deter her from suddenly attempting to leave again.

'Is any of that love reserved for me?' Charlie's voice was deep and warm, and the most welcome sound she could possibly have heard.

'Any love not already used up on these two is always reserved for you.' Danni couldn't help smiling when she looked at him. Sometimes she still struggled to believe she'd found Charlie in a twist of fate, in such a great, big, world where their paths might so easily never have crossed. It was incredible that after coming so close to losing everything for someone like Lucas, she got to wake up every day with the best man she'd ever met instead. 'I've really missed you, but I didn't think you'd be home this early.'

'I missed you both too much to stay on any longer.' Charlie gently rested one hand on her bump and put the other arm behind her back, which was the closest he could get to hugging her and the baby for now. 'I finished reviewing the scenes they wanted me to look at, then had a quick detour to Hanham on the way home to pick something up.'

'Hanham?' Danni shook her head, trying to dislodge the sensation of it being stuffed with cotton wool. There were only two people she knew who lived in Hanham, and she couldn't even begin to imagine why Charlie would need to go to the village, let alone why he might actually want to visit them. 'That's where Mum and Paul have their barge moored at the moment.'

'I know. Come on, I've got something to show you in the other room.'

'But why on earth were you in Hanham?' She had no idea why Charlie was acting so mysteriously, but all he did was shrug.

'You'll understand when I show you.' He put his hand in the small of her back, applying gentle but insistent pressure to get her to move along the hallway.

'If it's my mother's body, I want you to know that I love you enough to help you hide it. I even understand why half an hour in her company would be plenty of time to drive you to murder. But after the shift I've had, I'm not digging the hole.' She might be laughing, but she couldn't push down the nagging unease that was building up inside her. If her mother was sitting waiting for them on the sofa, it was going to ruin Danni's evening. All she wanted was to have dinner, and curl up with Charlie and the dogs. She couldn't face her mother without prior warning; it was something she needed to mentally prepare for at least a week in advance. Once upon a time she'd have dreamt of her mother turning up as a surprise, but her reaction to the news she was going to be a grandmother had driven an even bigger wedge between them than there had already been.

She'd been tempted to tell her mother that she was the last person she'd want to babysit her son, but instead she'd just nodded, adding their latest encounter to the catalogue of painful memories between them. If death could come from a thousand small cuts, so could the death of a relationship and it felt like that day was getting closer and closer. As much as she wished her mother's reaction to the baby news could have been a turning point in their relationship, she had to accept that the less contact they had, the better Danni felt about herself. It was why the idea of her mother sitting waiting in their living room, was almost as unwelcome as it was unlikely.

'What's in the box'? Her eyes were drawn to it as soon as she went into the room. It was a battered-looking cardboard box, with the name and logo of her father's favourite brand of wine stamped on the side of it. She could suddenly picture him so clearly, with a glass of red in his hand, the way he always seemed to relax after work, telling her the latest story he'd made up about two explorers called Danni and Joe, who went on a seemingly endless series of adventures. She'd always loved those stories, far more than anything she'd ever read, and for far longer than most kids her age would have done. She'd been ten when he died, and bedtime stories had long since been forgone by her peers. But Danni would happily still listen to them now if she could, and she wished he'd recorded some of the stories, so that she could hear his voice again. But none of them could have known he wouldn't be around to retell them to his grandchildren, let alone not even living long enough to see his daughter go to secondary school.

'Something I hope you'll like. Sit down and take a look, although you might need these.' Charlie pushed a packet of tissues closer to the box as he spoke. 'I'm going to pour you a nice cold drink, and I'll be ready if you need me for anything else, but I think you might need this moment alone.'

'Okay.' Danni's hand shook slightly as she followed Charlie's instructions, sitting down and reaching for the lid of the box, when he disappeared towards the kitchen. As soon as she saw the words written on the top, in loopy handwriting, she wanted to call after Charlie again and ask him to tell her what she was about to see. But he'd said he thought she needed to do this alone and she trusted him completely. It meant she was ready to face whatever was coming, even if the sight of the words: '*J&D – the early years*' were making her heart race so fast she could feel it.

Undoing the flaps on the top of the box, which were tucked into each other as a makeshift seal, she caught her breath as she peered in. There, right at the top, was a yellowing heart-shaped photo frame, which must once have been white, containing a picture of her father, with two children on his lap. One a toddler, dressed in navy blue shorts and a T-shirt covered in pictures of tractors, and the other, a little girl, in a forget-me-not blue dress, with a cloud of curly black hair that the ribbons attempting to contain it had no chance of keeping under control.

'It's me.' Danni said the words aloud, unable to keep the wonder out of her voice. It was like discovering the Holy Grail, or seeing a unicorn suddenly gallop past the window. Something she'd thought didn't exist any more, that had been lost forever, was staring her in the face. Putting the photo to one side, she began sorting through the rest of the contents of the box. There were more photographs, about thirty in total, some of them in frames, and others loose. They were all of her and Joe, either with or without Danni's paternal grandparents. There was only one with her mother in, and from what Nicola had said, there'd been no love lost between her and her in-laws. It was a group photograph, from what must have been Danni's first Christmas. They were all sat at a table laden with food, a Christmas tree in the background. Everyone was smiling, except Nicola, who looked as though she'd rather be almost anywhere else in the world. It wasn't a picture of motherly love by any stretch of the imagination, but she was cradling Danni in her arms, while Joe sat next to them on their father's lap, and it was obvious they were a family. Or at least that they had been once upon a time. If Charlie had given Danni a winning lottery ticket it wouldn't have meant as much, and she'd probably have been less surprised. By the time he came back into the living room, there were tears streaming down her face and she was screwing up her eyes and opening them again, half in an attempt to blink the tears away, and half to check that she wasn't imagining things, and the photographs would suddenly disappear again. Maggie had her head on Danni's knee, the way she always did when she sensed someone was upset. And Brenda had hauled herself on to the sofa, edging as close to Danni as she could possibly get without actually being on her lap.

'Are you okay, sweetheart?' Charlie sat down on her other side, putting an arm around her shoulder, and she nodded a couple of times, unable to speak at first. It took several attempts to try and get hold of herself, before she finally managed to respond.

'This is amazing, but I can't believe it. I don't understand, how did you...?' She couldn't even finish the question. Instead, she picked up one of the loose photographs, gently smoothing out one corner that had been folded over somewhere along the line.

'I rang your mum the day after the baby shower. I always knew that not having any photographs of you and Joe when you were young got to you. So, I asked her if there was any chance there were some she'd forgotten about.'

'She always said she had to chuck out anything that wasn't

essential when she sold the house and moved on to the barge.' Danni had challenged her mother more than once about it, reminding her that most people would consider photographs of their children the one thing they'd save in a fire, never mind hold on to when they downsized. But Nicola had claimed that sorting through all the stuff was still too painful, even eight years after losing her husband. Danni had been in her last year of boarding school at the time her mum had moved in with Paul, and hadn't thought that much as a teenager about wanting photographs that documented her own history and, by the time she did, a few years later, it was too late. Whatever photographs had once existed, they'd all been thrown out. Along with the rest of the precious mementos that marked the most important events in her family's life, everything from her parents' wedding photographs to the last holiday they'd all had together, in Port Kara, before her father's sudden death.

'She did and it doesn't sound like her own mother was much more sentimental than she was.' Charlie was clearly trying to do his best not to sound judgemental, but he couldn't quite stop the slight curl of his lip. 'And if there had been any photos at her parents' house after they died, I'm guessing they'd have gone the same way as the others, if your mother had had a hand in clearing the house.'

'The only photographs I ever got were passed on by my great aunt's son, after she died, when I was still at uni. But they were just a handful of school photographs, nothing like this.' Joe and Danni had been at boarding school when their maternal grand-parents died, and their other grandmother was a widow who'd passed away about a month after they'd lost their father, so that had been a dead end too. Danni narrowed her eyes as she looked at Charlie again. 'Which leaves me still completely clueless about where you found them.'

'It was a bit of a mission. The truth is, I finished up the last of the work in Bristol late on Wednesday evening, and went to see your mum first thing Thursday morning, but there's a reason I still didn't make it back until this afternoon. It's also why I said I might not be home until tomorrow, because I wasn't sure how long it was going to take.'

'You're going to have to tell, because right now the only solution I can come up with is that you went and rummaged in every landfill site in the South West trying to unearth these things.'

'Not quite, but it might have been my next step if Paul hadn't said something. I was asking your mum if there were any friends she could think of from back when you were young who might have a photograph of you as a baby, and she said no. But then he mentioned Audrey. It turns out she was your paternal grandmother's best friend, and with your dad gone it was Audrey who had helped your great aunt clear out your nan's house when she died. As you can imagine, Nicola had told them at the time that she didn't want anything from the house. But about five years ago, Audrey's daughter reached out to your mum on Facebook, to tell her that Audrey had passed away too and that there were a couple of boxes of your grandmother's things in her loft, mostly old photographs. Apparently, Audrey and your great-aunt had split the things they didn't want to throw away between them, in case Nicola changed her mind one day. Audrey's daughter asked your mum if she wanted them now that her mother's house was being sold, and...' Charlie's mouth turned down at the corners, and she reached out for his hand.

'It's okay, I think I can guess what her response was.' Danni's heart was thudding in her ears now. He'd said 'a couple of boxes'; that might mean there was more.

'It was a long shot that Audrey's daughter would still have the boxes, but I had to try. Paul managed to find the old message on your mum's Facebook account, and he messaged her back explaining. I must admit I hugged him when she replied to say they were now in her loft, because she hadn't been able to bear to throw them out. She said I was welcome to collect them, but she lives on the Llyn Peninsula, or she could post them on. I couldn't bear to think we might get this close and then risk them getting lost. I still didn't know for sure whether there'd be any of you and Joe.'

'That's in North Wales, isn't it? You drove all the way up there?' Danni would have sworn that she couldn't love Charlie any more than she had that morning, but she could feel it growing and making sure that all those empty spaces that had left her hollowed out for so long were now full up.

'I made it to Karen's house by late evening yesterday. She and her wife, Rosie, welcomed me in like an old friend. We went through all the boxes she had, and she told me as much as she knew. She loved your nan, and she was always sad that your mother had cut off contact, and that she hadn't been able to keep in touch with you and Joe as a result. She'd love to meet you. She's got loads of stories about your grandparents, and your dad. Apparently, they went to school together. She and Rosie insisted on making me dinner and putting me up for the night, and I know you're going to love them. I hope it's okay, but I've invited them down to see us when the baby arrives, and told them there'll be an invite to the wedding too. Karen is desperate to see you. She said she thought about reaching out to you and Joe on Facebook, but she assumed that your mother hadn't wanted the photographs because they were just duplicates of what she already had, and that after all this time you'd probably have no idea who she was.'

'Did she say if anyone calls her Kay?' Another flood of emotion was washing over Danni, and it enveloped her like a warm embrace when he nodded.

'Yes, that's what her wife called her. Why, do you remember her?'

'Auntie Kay.' The smile on Danni's face was making her cheeks ache. 'Oh my God, I almost thought I'd imagined her. She was around loads when we were little. She always had a cupboard full of treats when we visited with Nan, and she gave the best cuddles. But we never saw her again after Dad's funeral and I thought she wasn't interested in us once he was gone, but it must have been because Mum cut off contact. I can't believe you've seen her, or that she kept the photographs for all those years. And most of all I can't believe how amazing you are for turning into my very own Poirot and tracking these down. I didn't think there was a better gift you could ever have got me, but putting me back in touch with Auntie Kay... She knows so much about mine and Joe's early life, and about Dad too. Mum never wants to talk about any of that, even if she remembers it. I don't think I can ever repay you for giving me that link to my childhood back.'

'I'd do anything for you, and it was nothing really.' Charlie's gaze met hers and she could see how tired he was. He'd probably been on the road for the best part of the last two days. He'd also gone to visit her mother, a challenging woman he barely knew, and had difficult conversations, all in an attempt to find something he didn't even know existed. It was the best thing anyone had ever done for her, and she would never forget it.

'I love you so much.' Danni threw her arms around his neck. 'And it finally makes sense why I keep worrying about something bad happening. It's because it's impossible to believe I got so lucky, and I'm scared something is going to happen to take away the family I always wanted. But that's stupid, because all you do is keep making it better, and I've got to stop wasting all my time worrying. I'm sorry I've been such a nightmare.'

'You've never been anything like a nightmare. The fact that

you care so much and want everything to be okay is one of the things I love about you, but it's just one on a very long list. I do want you to take it a bit easier, though.' Charlie pulled away slightly and gave her a level look. 'I got a tip-off that you had a bit of a funny turn today.'

'Essie promised me she wasn't going to say anything.'

'She didn't, Aidan did. Then Isla, then Amy.' Charlie laughed. 'You've got no idea how many people care about you. I know that's something it's not always easy for you to believe, but it's true.'

'It's getting easier to believe, especially since I met you.' She leant forward again to kiss Charlie, thanking whatever twist of fortune it was that had brought them together, for at least the hundredth time.

* * *

Watching Alice and Zara running through the sprinkler in the garden, chasing after Gary's grandson, Albert, was like having them both back as little children again. Their laughter was filling the air as they hoisted Albert between them, swinging him backwards and forwards through the water and making him giggle like it was the best day of his life. Albert might not even be three yet, but he already understood that the simple pleasures in life were the best ones, and the whole day had been a good reminder for Wendy of that too. The weather was glorious for October and it was the type of day when she felt incredibly lucky they lived on the Cornish Atlantic coast. The smell of salt was in the air, lingering with the aroma of the barbecue Gary had taken charge of. They'd been joined by Drew, Beth and Tom and by Gary's parents, Janice and Bob, and Wendy's parents, Barbara and Roy. Her sister, Louise, had brought her family along too, and it had been one of those perfect family days, when the cobalt-blue sky had never faded, and she'd laughed so much her stomach muscles ached.

'You're so lucky, you know that don't you?' Louise had taken her to one side earlier in the afternoon, while Wendy had been opening another bottle of wine. 'My kids are all related to one another by blood, and they don't get on half as well as your two and Gary's kids. You've all fitted together like it was always meant to be.'

'It honestly feels like it was.' The warm glow Wendy experienced in that moment hadn't just been down to the wine and the sunshine.

Louise had put an arm around her waist and given it a squeeze. 'You really deserve this, Wend. Mick the Prick put you through hell but look at you now.' Louise had insisted on changing the shortened version of Mike's name to Mick, so that it rhymed with prick, after the extent of his infidelities had come to light. And she used his new nickname at every opportunity she got.

'Thanks sis, I'm finally starting to believe this all had to happen for me to get what I really needed, and I'm happier than I can remember being for years.' It had been on the tip of Wendy's tongue to add *most of the time*, but she didn't want to spoil a perfect day talking about something she knew she had to get past. Being envious of her daughters' bond with Chloe was ridiculous, and no doubt Louise would remind her she should be grateful for that too. It had been easier since she'd realised Chloe's life was nowhere near as perfect as she painted it online. She'd even texted Wendy to beg her not to say anything to anyone about the cyst on her ovary, and that the things she'd said about Mike were just her hormones talking and making her over-emotional. If anything, it made Wendy feel sorry for Chloe. She couldn't tell the person she was supposed to be closest to about what was worrying her, and she'd blurted it out to his ex-wife instead. But it still hurt Wendy to see Zara's face light up when she got a call from Chloe and the speed with which she always fired off a response. Sometimes Wendy had to wait the best part of a day to get an answer to the simplest of questions. Deep down she knew it was normal for her girls to take her for granted, and she could see the attraction of wanting to spend time with Chloe. Begrudgingly, Wendy could even admit to sort of liking her, and it was impossible not to admit that Chloe had a good heart, and that she'd had a hard time. But that still didn't stop her wishing that a step-mother figure didn't have to feature in her girls' lives at all. She knew that was crazy too, because the break-up with Mike which had led to that, was the same thing that had brought Gary back into her life. And like she'd said to Louise, she wouldn't change that for the world. None of it was logical, but then feelings often weren't.

'Thank you so much for a wonderful day, Wendy.' Beth came over with a still-dripping-wet Albert, who was wrapped in a towel and nuzzled in her arms. 'Albie's had the best time, but we need to get him home for a bath before bed. We can't wait to do it again and I've told Dad you're all invited over to ours on the next weekend he's got off.'

'That will be really lovely, and I meant what I said about a sleepover for Albie next time.'

'You'd love to have a sleepover at Nanny and Granddad's, wouldn't you?' Beth looked down at her little boy, who gave a squeal of delight and nodded vigorously. 'He's almost as excited as me and Tom!'

There was a flurry of goodbyes after that, and when everyone went home, leaving only Wendy, Gary and the girls, she felt strangely bereft. It wasn't just because her parents and her sister's family had gone, she missed the presence of Gary's family too.

She genuinely liked all of them, and she'd quickly grown to love his children and grandson, in a way that felt entirely natural. Louise was right, she really was lucky. Wendy was just reaching for a bottle of rosé that needed finishing off, so that she and Gary could toast the perfect day, when Alice suddenly appeared.

'That was so much fun, thanks Mum.' Wendy's eldest daughter planted a kiss on her cheek.

'It was great, wasn't it? Where's Zara?' A tiny frisson of anxiety fluttered in Wendy's chest. It really had been a wonderful day, but she'd found herself watching her younger daughter to make sure she was eating, and she'd followed her upstairs after the barbecue, listening outside the door to make sure she couldn't hear Zara making herself sick. She'd suspected that's what was happening, when she'd overheard tell-tale sounds a couple of times before, but both times Zara had insisted she'd just been coughing. After what Chloe had said, Wendy doubted that was true, but a big part of her still desperately wanted to believe it. How could her beautiful daughter hate her own body so much that she wanted to punish it in that way? It didn't bear thinking about.

'She's just gone to get changed.'

'I don't blame her after how wet you both got with Albie. I think PJs all round sound like a good idea.' Looking at Alice, Wendy suddenly realised she'd changed too, into a pretty floral skater-style dress. 'You look nice, but are you sure you wouldn't be more comfortable in your pyjamas, too? We can sit and watch a movie; there's loads of leftovers and I could make some popcorn.'

'Dad called about twenty minutes ago.' Alice dropped her gaze and moved from foot to foot. 'I know we're not due over there until next weekend, but he and Chloe want to take us both out for dinner; they've got big news apparently.'

'Bigger news than when they found out they were having a

baby? Shame they didn't tell you that themselves.' Even as she'd tried to bite back the barb, it slipped out, and she didn't miss the look that crossed her daughter's face. 'Sorry ignore me, go, have fun.'

'Thanks, Mum.' Alice gave her a brief hug and she tried to relax her muscles, so that her daughter wouldn't realise how rigid her spine had gone. 'I think we're going to stay at Dad and Chloe's tonight, so I'll drop Zara back in the morning and then probably head straight back to uni.'

'Sounds great.' She kept her voice falsely bright, painting on a smile in the hope Alice wouldn't realise quite how much she resented Mike and Chloe for eating into the time she had with her daughters. Instead, ten minutes later she waved them both off and wished them a good time again, before heading back to retrieve the bottle of rosé, and pouring all of the wine she'd intended to share with Gary into her own glass.

'Hey gorgeous, what's up?' Five minutes after she'd gone back into the garden, he came out. She was sitting in a garden chair, staring into the middle distance, and he put a hand under her chin, gently tilting her face upwards so that she had to look at him.

'The girls have gone to Mike's.' She couldn't keep the bitterness out of her voice this time and the truth was she didn't even try. 'He's got something big to tell them apparently. He's probably proposed to Chloe, and the girls will be all excited like it's the best news ever.'

'It will be good news though, won't it? They're already expecting a baby.' When Wendy didn't answer him, taking another huge slug of wine instead, Gary sighed. 'This really bothers you, doesn't it, the idea of Mike marrying someone else?'

'It's not that, it's...' She couldn't finish the sentence without revealing how petty she was, or how ridiculous she was being.

Half an hour before, she'd been basking in the light of her brilliantly blended family, but she didn't want that for the girls when it came to her ex's new family. Maybe it was because she wanted to punish Mike for being the one to rip their family apart, but she knew she should want that same closeness on his side, for the girls' sake, and she couldn't let Gary see how selfish she was being. Not again. They'd been through all of this before, and she knew everything he'd said about it in the past was right. Yet, despite that, some part of her still couldn't seem to accept the situation and just be happy.

'What is it then, Wendy? Because that's what it looks like from here. At least Mike and Chloe want the girls to know they're getting married. You haven't even mentioned us getting married to them.' Gary looked so hurt it made her heart ache, and she tried to reach out to him, but he shook his head. 'And the way you're reacting to the idea that Mike and Chloe might want to get married, makes me think you wish you were still with him.'

'I don't, not like that. It's just the girls... I never wanted things to get this messy. I wanted the kind of family Mum and Dad had.'

'So is that what today was for you? *Messy*?' Gary's voice cracked on the last word as he stood up and took a step away from her. 'There was me thinking it was pretty damn perfect, and all you could see was a big mess.'

'I didn't mean that. None of this is coming out the way I want it to and I know I'm being stupid.' Guilt swept over Wendy. She was acting like a spoilt cow and ruining the day for Gary, a man who'd never done anything except show her love and kindness. In his position, she wasn't sure she could ever have forgiven what she'd just said; it made their life sound like something she could barely tolerate. It wasn't true; she wished she could rewind time and make it all come out the way she'd intended, but it was too late. Gary was upset, and he had every right to be.

'No, I think I've probably been the stupid one, letting myself believe you wanted all of this as much as I do, and that I could make you as happy as you make me.'

'I do and you have, Gary *please*.'

He shook his head again, already walking away from her. 'I don't think you know what you want and, until you do, I should probably give you some space.'

'Where are you going to go?' Panic was surging up inside Wendy now. If Gary walked out there was always a chance he might not come back, and she didn't even want to try to imagine her life without him. But for some reason she couldn't bring herself to tell him that, despite a big part of her wanting to beg him not to leave.

'Don't worry, I'll take the camper van.'

'You can't, you've been drinking.'

'I've only had the non-alcoholic beer. I had a headache and I took some strong painkillers. I didn't want to say anything in case it put a dampener on things, but I'll be okay to drive. I've got it all set up for when the girls want to take it to that festival, so it's ready to go. I was going to tell them tomorrow.' There was such sadness in his tone and another wave of emotion surged up inside of her, for this man who'd spent all his spare time in the last week getting an old camper they'd bought ready, so her daughters could take it on its first outing and have fun at a music festival. Gary really was the kindest man she'd ever met, but when she tried calling out to him again, he just raised a hand and carried on walking. Alone in the garden, which had rung with laughter just an hour before, she was suddenly terrified that she'd left it too late, and that she might just have blown the best thing that had ever happened to her.

13
_____

'I'm thinking of trying paragliding; apparently there's no freedom like it. You'd be up for that wouldn't you, Wendy?' It took a moment for her to realise that Gwen was waiting for an answer, and she didn't even remember what the question had been. She'd got up after a night of reaching out into the empty space in the bed where Gary should have been, which had made anything but fitful sleep impossible.

Making a pot of tea, she'd headed out of the side door of the house, planning to knock on the camper van door and apologise for how she'd acted the day before. Gary was bound to be back by now, the frustration he'd clearly felt the day before at least partly out of his system; except the camper wasn't there. He hadn't cooled off and come home, and the instant she realised that, the dread had come back. What if he never came back, and she really had blown it? Rushing back inside, she'd tried to call him, but it had gone straight to voicemail. Her WhatsApp messages went unread, and there were no replies to her texts either. She'd thought about calling Drew or Beth, or even Gary's parents, but what was she supposed to say? That she had no idea where he was, and that she'd been such a jealous cow she'd somehow convinced Gary she was still in love with Mike.

It had taken all of about ten minutes after he'd left for her to put herself in his shoes. If he'd thrown a hissy fit because his ex was getting engaged, she'd have assumed that meant he still had feelings for Rachel. So it was no wonder he'd assumed the same about her. In the dark of the night, she'd forced herself to face up to that question and whether there was any truth to it. She'd really thought about it, and she was absolutely certain there wasn't.

The idea of being with Mike was so alien, as if their time together was a life someone else had lived, or something she'd watched in a film. She couldn't imagine being his wife, and the thought of touching him, or worse still of him touching her, was horrifying. But, somehow, a part of her was still grieving for the picture she'd envisioned, of a perfect family unit that had never been split apart by divorce. She had no idea how to reconcile that, without somehow leaving Gary feeling like what they had was 'less than' as a result. All she knew was that she had to try, because she couldn't lose him. Their conversation from the night before had been playing on repeat, ever since she'd discovered the camper still wasn't back, so it was no wonder she'd barely heard what Gwen was saying. She'd only come to the Miss Adventures get-together in an attempt to stop obsessing over how she'd left things with Gary, and the easiest thing to do was to murmur incoherently and nod along. She didn't even realise what she was agreeing to, until Caroline's mouth dropped open.

'You're going to go paragliding with Gwen?' Caroline looked at Wendy, shaking her head. 'Please tell me you're not up for this too, Connie, and that I'm the only sane one here.'

'Oh no! I can hold Wendy's coat, and you can hold Gwen's. I'll also take as many pictures as you want, but you won't get me up there.'

'I didn't mean—' Wendy's protest was cut off as Caroline turned to Frankie.

'What about you, are you on team crazy or team sane?'

'It depends how you look at it.' Frankie grinned. 'Because I have signed up to do a tandem parachute jump. A few of us from the Port Agnes midwifery unit are doing it to raise money for the MS therapy centre. They've done so much to help Ella since her diagnosis, and they do some really great work. I'm scared out of my mind at the prospect of jumping, but I just think about how scared she must have been when she got her diagnosis, and any fear I have doesn't even compare to that.'

'That's such a great attitude.' Wendy looked at her friend. Frankie was probably a decade older than she was, and from what she'd shared since they'd joined the group, it was obvious she'd been through a lot. Her own marriage had broken down, her son had tried to force her to choose between him and her new partner, and her daughter had been trapped in an abusive marriage thousands of miles away, until she'd finally escaped back to Cornwall. There must have been an imagined future that Frankie had grieved for when her marriage had broken down, but if she was still struggling with that, she never let it show. She wasn't the only one who'd been through a tough time. Connie had been separated from Charlie for almost four decades, after his adoption, but she'd said the last thing she wanted to do was to waste the years she would now get with him, wishing that the past could be different. And Wendy had a sneaking feeling she could learn from all of the others in the Miss Adventures club. Maybe doing something she'd never have dreamt of doing in her old life would be the start of shaking it off altogether, and letting go of what she'd expected her life to look like. Mike would have laughed at the idea of her paragliding, and told her she could never do it. Gary, on the other hand, seemed to believe she was capable of anything. So, if she hadn't completely messed up, she already knew she'd have his support.

'How do we sign up for this paragliding, then?' She wanted to put her name on the dotted line of an agreement she couldn't get out of, before she chickened out. And there was something else she could do that would make her even less likely to back out. 'Maybe we could join forces with the midwives, and get some sponsorship for the paragliding to raise more funds for the MS centre.'

'That's a brilliant idea.' Gwen picked up her mobile phone. 'This is the site I've found. We can either do a tandem jump taster session, or a full day with training where we get to fly solo along the Atlantic coast. If we're talking sponsorship, we could always do it with a twist.'

'If you're about to suggest naked paragliding, I'm retracting my offer of coming to take photos!' Connie laughed. 'I love you both, but there are some things that can't be unseen, and there's a reason not all of us would have made good midwives.'

'I was thinking about fancy dress, or seeing if we can get some local businesses to sponsor us, if we wear a shirt with their logo on, but maybe Connie is on to something.' There was a mischievous glint in Gwen's eye, which suggested she was joking, but you could never be sure. That would be one adventure too far for Wendy, and she needed to shut it down.

'Fancy dress it is then? Shall we choose a date and get it booked in now? I'm guessing we might have to wait until the spring, as the weather is bound to break soon. But I want to pay up front; that way I won't be tempted to back out.' Wendy's feet were already tingling at the thought, the same way they did whenever she was in a tall building. This was definitely feeling the fear and doing it anyway.

'How about the last Sunday in April? That gives us six months, which should be plenty of time to drum up sponsorship.' Gwen raised her eyebrows as she waited for a response, and it was Wendy's last chance to duck out. Instead she found herself nodding vigorously, and handing over her credit card for Gwen to secure the booking. It was time to embrace the new life she'd found herself in, and taking to the sky above the Atlantic coast might just make her appear cooler than Chloe in her daughters' eyes. At least this once.

* * *

There was no urgency for Wendy to return the serving dish her sister had brought with her to the barbecue, laden with her famous macaroni cheese. But when Gary still hadn't got back with the camper by the time she returned from her get-together with the Miss Adventures girls, she needed someone to talk to. It had been all very well in the heat of the moment agreeing to go paragliding with Gwen, and it felt like she was taking a huge leap out of her comfort zone, but doing that wouldn't suddenly solve her problems. A future that might not include Gary felt very bleak, and no amount of adventure would make up for that. She had to do something to fix the rift she'd caused between them and, if she confided in her sister, Louise would offer up some advice. She always did, whether it was asked for or not.

'You didn't need to rush over with that. We're meeting up at Mum's on Saturday, aren't we? It could definitely have waited until then.' Louise was already eyeing her up suspiciously when she opened the door to find Wendy standing there clutching the large Pyrex dish.

'You really know how to make a girl feel welcome.'

'Don't be daft, you're always welcome.' Louise stepped aside for her sister to come in. 'But why do I get the feeling that the reason you're here has nothing to do with returning a dish?'

'I don't know, why *do* you get that feeling?' Wendy's eyes met her sister's for a moment, and Louise shrugged.

'Because you look like you've been awake half the night worrying about something; your eyes are red rimmed and your cheeks are all blotchy.'

'Maybe I should just book into your place and have myself put down.' Louise worked as a veterinary nurse at a practice on the coast road that led towards Port Tremellien, but she should have been a mind reader.

'Or you could just tell me what's bothering you, and what you think you might have done to mess things up with Gary.'

Wendy shouldn't have been surprised; her sister had always been able to see right through her. As soon as Louise ushered her into the kitchen and turned on the coffee machine, it all started flooding out. By the time Louise put a coffee in front of her, Wendy had recounted the whole sorry tale and her sister was giving her another appraising look.

'So you think you're grieving for this amazing life you were going to have with Mike, one that was going to be just like Mum and Dad's?'

'Well maybe not amazing, but at least it would have been neat. A family with a husband and wife, a couple of kids, and no cobbled-together extension that I didn't ask for, tacked on to the side of it.' It was the only way Wendy could explain it. She'd described her version of the picket-fence lifestyle she'd envisioned, with 2.4 children, but Louise was already wrinkling her nose.

'There was a slight flaw in that plan though, wasn't there?

Mike was already erecting extensions, or at least erecting something, all over the place, when you were supposed to be this *neat little family*. What Mum and Dad have is built on nearly sixty years of togetherness, and continuing to choose to be together because they make each other happy. You and Mike didn't do that. And, yes, he might have been the one who cheated, but I want you to look me in the eye and tell me honestly that he made you as happy as Gary does. And that you wanted to spend time with him, the same way you do with Gary.'

'I wanted us to spend time as family and—'

Louise held up her hand, cutting her sister off. 'No! I'm not talking about what you wanted for the *girls*, I'm talking about what you wanted for *you*. I don't think it was Mike; I'm not sure it ever was. He made you feel bad about yourself and criticised you all the time, doing whatever he wanted while you picked up the slack. I'll never understand why you put up with it for so long and, even when you first got together, you never lit up around him like you do with Gary. I mean sometimes it makes me want to throw up.' Louise laughed. 'But it also makes me incredibly happy to see you like that. I used to laugh when we were teenagers and you told me he was the only boy you were ever going to love and that all you wanted to do was marry him one day. I thought you were wrong, but you weren't. He's still the only man you've ever really loved, isn't he? And you still want to marry him, don't you?'

'Yes.'

'So what the hell are you playing at?'

'I've got no idea. I just want Gary to come home, even though I still feel bad for the girls that things with their dad have come to this. I should have known Mike wasn't up to the job of fatherhood.' It was a relief to admit it, even to herself, but she still couldn't shake the nagging guilt that she'd built her daughter's lives around a relationship that her heart had never been in, in quite the same way as it was in this one. She would never regret having a relationship with Mike, because without him she wouldn't have the girls, but as irrational as it was, she still wished she'd given them a different father. Things would have been so much better if Gary had been their father, but she'd saddled her children with a dad who only really cared about himself. And she couldn't help wondering if part of the fault for that lay with her. Maybe if she had loved Mike with the same intensity she loved Gary, he might have been able to focus on someone other than himself, and that was why she felt guilty, but Louise had seen right through her once again.

'Quite frankly it's a miracle in a world full of chance meetings that you found Gary at all, and what you feel for him is something an awful lot of people don't get to experience in their lives. So don't you even for a minute feel guilty because the one man you've ever truly loved turned out not to be your children's father. The girls are happy, they love Gary, and they clearly love Chloe too. The new people who've been brought into their lives as a result of the divorce are just a bonus as far as they're concerned. So you can stop beating yourself up about it and start enjoying it.'

'I want to, more than anything, but I seem to be intent on spoiling what we've got, by being jealous of Chloe.'

'Because she's with Mike?' Louise sounded as if it was the most ridiculous thing she'd ever heard. 'You should feel sorry for her.'

'I do, but I hate the fact the girls love her so much and, before you say, I know that's stupid and that I should be grateful she's so kind to them. Even I can see she's a lovely person, but I just can't seem to get used to the idea of sharing them. Chloe has really helped with some issues with Zara, and I thought I'd turned a corner as a result and started to adjust. But the girls seem to want to spend all their time with her and it really hurts. I wish it didn't, but it does. That's why I've been harking after the neat little family that never even existed. It's got nothing to do with wanting Mike back.' It was true, she knew that without a shadow of a doubt now, because the news from the girls that Mike and Chloe were engaged hadn't bothered her a bit, in the wake of Gary leaving. All she wanted was for him to come home.

'And you think that's something worth sabotaging your relationship with Gary for?' Before Wendy even had the chance to answer, Louise shook her head. 'First off, all kids of the girls' age want to pull away from their parents in one way or another. There's nothing remotely unusual about that. Secondly, you said yourself that the family you're grieving for never even existed, so let it go and be thankful that the girls are surrounded by people who care for them, despite the fact there are no biological ties. No one can have too many people who love them, and it's not a competition. Just because they love Chloe, it doesn't mean they love you less. Any more than them thinking Gary is amazing affects their feelings for you. Did the love you had for Alice diminish because of how much you loved Zara once she was born?'

Louise finally hesitated long enough for Wendy to answer. 'Of course not.'

'Well this is exactly the same.'

'How did you get to be the sensible one out of the two of us?' Wendy smiled, but it didn't reach her eyes. She'd been such an idiot, and she was terrified of just how much her stupidity might have cost her.

'I always have been. You just need to listen to me more.' Louise put an arm around her sister's waist. 'You can still put this right.'

'What if it's too late, and Gary doesn't want to come back?' Even saying the words out loud was like a kick in the stomach.

'Just bloody well tell him you've never loved anyone the way you love him, because it's obvious he feels the same way about you. Or even better, find a way to show him. Strip naked and invite him to come and ravage you, whatever it takes.' Louise was starting to sound like Gwen's apprentice, but Wendy had a better idea, one she hoped might just work. She was going to have to go to her parents' house first and hope to God that their tendency for hoarding hadn't diminished over the years, because she needed all the help she could get to make things up to Gary, after the way she'd been behaving.

* * *

The text Wendy had sent Gary had been simple:

> I'm so sorry for yesterday, if you get this message, please meet me by our cave, at Ocean Cove, at four o'clock xx

She'd looked at her watch approximately every ten seconds since she'd arrived at about half past three. She didn't want there to be any chance of him arriving before her, but if he was more than fifteen minutes late they'd run out of time for her to say what she needed to say. The tide came in quickly at Ocean Cove, and far too many people had been cut off by the water over the years, and had needed to be rescued. But it wasn't just the threat of the incoming tide that was making her obsessively check her watch, it was the fear that he might not turn up at all.

It was about five minutes past four when she looked up and saw him walking along the beach towards the mouth of the cave where she was waiting, sitting on a rock. It had been their hideout when they'd dated the first time around. Ocean Cove was in Port Agnes, far enough away from their homes in the neighbouring village, but still easy enough to get to whenever they wanted to escape. It was somewhere they could go to kiss, and talk, and kiss some more, where no one would rap their knuckles against the door, or worse still, fling it open to check whether the two of them were up to no good. She understood now why their parents had done it, but back then she'd just wanted time on her own with him.

They'd gone on lots of dates in the two years they'd been together as teenagers, simple things like the cinema, or to the travelling funfair that pitched up on the old common grazing ground in Port Tremellien twice a year. But the cave had still been the place she'd most loved being with Gary. They'd set out a little picnic blanket, pretending they were in their own apartment somewhere and talking about how they'd do it for real one day, when they were both grown up and earning good money. Except Wendy's father had been made redundant and had taken a job in Birmingham, which had been the start of all those plans for the future unravelling. The whole family had followed him a year later, and it had broken Wendy's heart. She'd begged to be allowed to stay, and she and Gary had hatched every plot they could come up with to make it work. But they were barely sixteen and they didn't have enough money for a deposit on a shoebox, never mind a flat.

They'd written at first, in the days before mobile phones and emails, never mind social media. But when she hadn't got a reply to two letters in a row, and her friends at the new college she went to had spelled out what that meant, she'd given herself a good talking to and had vowed never to write to Gary again. What she hadn't known then was that he'd been in hospital with a burst appendix. By the time he'd recovered and written back to her, she'd decided it was too late. Her friends had told her not to be the sort of girl who waited around until someone found the time for her. So when the letters with his distinctive handwriting began to arrive, she'd thrown them straight in the bin, without even reading them. She'd known if she looked at them the temptation to reply would be too much, and she didn't want to let her new friends down. Eventually he'd given up too, and even when Wendy and her family returned to the Three Ports area a few years later, they didn't speak. She heard from mutual friends that he was engaged to Rachel, and not long afterwards she'd met Mike.

It was only when Gary had reached out on Facebook, more than three decades after the last letter they'd exchanged, that it became obvious how easy it would have been to avoid so much heartbreak. All she'd needed to do back then was be honest, to ignore what her friends had said about needing to be 'cool'. It was so ironic when she thought about how little notice she'd taken of that advice once she'd met Mike, and all the things she'd put up with from him. She should never have been persuaded into ignoring Gary's letters. She should have reached out to him, to tell him how she really felt, and that she wanted him in her life no matter what, even if she had to take the risk of getting hurt. But she wasn't about to make the same mistake twice; it was time to be completely honest. Except it was Gary who spoke first in the end.

'I'm sorry I've been a pig-headed idiot all day and not answered your texts. I just needed a bit of time to think, but I should have let you know instead of giving you the silent treatment.'

'I deserved it.'

'No, you didn't.' He reached for her hand as he drew level with her. 'We're not fourteen any more, but I acted like a spoilt kid yesterday. It just gets under my skin when I realise Mike still has the power to hurt you. He was never good enough for you, and I wish you could see that.'

'I do; there's only one person who's ever been good enough for me.' She took a deep breath. 'I just have to hope I'm good enough for him.'

'And who exactly is this lucky man?' He was smiling now, and she finally felt her shoulders relax a bit.

'He's standing in front of me.' She moved to the side slightly, so he could see into the entrance to the cave. 'I thought you might like to join me for a picnic for old times' sake.'

'Oh my God, is that what I think it is?' Gary laughed as he spotted the spread she'd laid out on the picnic blanket behind her. There was a plate of French Fancies, a big bowl of cheesy Wotsits, some cocktail sausages, and a bottle of Tizer. All of which the two of them had thought were the height of sophistication back when they were fourteen. As she nodded, he spun her around and kissed her, before pulling away again, still laughing. 'This is brilliant! Why didn't I think of this?'

'Because it was my turn to try and show you how special you are to me; you do that for me every day. And if a French Fancy washed down by some Tizer can't seduce you, I don't know what will.'

'All you have to do is look at me. Exactly like you did back then.' When he kissed her again, for a moment it really was like the hands of time had been wound back all those years, only it was better now. He'd been a good kisser even then, but he'd definitely perfected his technique over the years, and she appreciated everything about him more this time, because she'd already lost him once.

'Come on, we haven't got long before the tide turns, and you risk having to watch your French Fancies float away. There's something else I need to show you too. Something I found at my mum and dad's place.' She grabbed him by the hand, pulling him into the entrance of the cave. It was more of hollow really, just deep enough to fit the spread-out picnic blanket and to partially obscure them from view.

'If it's an artic roll, I think I must have died and gone to heaven.' He laughed again and she joined in, even though nerves were beginning to flutter in her chest. It had been a running joke back then, whenever her parents had invited Gary round to tea, that they needed to stockpile the artic rolls, because it had been his favourite dessert and no amount of it was too much. She just hoped he wouldn't be too disappointed when it didn't turn out to be that.

By the time they were sitting side by side on the blanket, her heartbeat was thudding in her ears. She was about to give Gary something she'd found in a drawer, under the divan bed in her childhood room. The scrap book had survived a lot: the four years they'd spent in the Midlands, while the family home had been rented out, and even half a day in a bin in Birmingham, where she'd thrown it when she'd made the vow never to write to Gary again. But something had made her retrieve it, and when it hadn't been ruined, it had seemed like a sign. She'd told herself she was keeping it so that the grown-up version of her could one day look back at the memories it contained, and smile at the innocence of the young girl who'd written it. By then she'd be incredibly successful, of course, and even more sophisticated than a French Fancy. She'd probably be married to Simon Le Bon, or George Michael, and they'd laugh together at her childhood romance with a boy named Gary, who she could hardly remember. Except he'd never faded from her memory, and deep down she must have known her decision to keep the scrapbook was because she couldn't bear to part with it. Either way, she was just glad that she hadn't. Pulling it out of the large canvas bag she'd hidden it in, she let go of another long breath.

'I want you to have a look at this. It's where I kept every photo, every cinema ticket stub, the cards you sent me, and the letters I got from you when I was first in Birmingham. All the pages are headed up.' Her hand was shaking as she handed it to him.

'Oh Wend, this is amazing.' A smile lit up Gary's whole face as he turned over the first couple of pages, laughing at a photograph on the page labelled up 'Beach Days'. 'Although I'm lucky you ever agreed to go out with me, when I had hair like that.'

'You were the best-looking boy in Port Kara; you still are.' She rested her head on his shoulder, smiling as she watched him reliving old memories every time he turned a page. When he got to the first of the letters he'd sent her in Birmingham, which was stuck onto one of the pages, he started to read it, but she reached out and touched his arm.

'You can read them all later, but we'll run out of time if you read them now. I want you to skip past the letters to the next part.' Gary looked at her quizzically for a moment, before doing as she asked, stopping when he came to a flyer for the restaurant where they'd had their second 'first date', stuck onto a page labelled *Second Time Around*. It turned out old habits died hard; she'd rifled through the memory box she'd been keeping ever since their reunion, finding things to add to the scrapbook once she'd retrieved it from her parents' house, but it was the first empty page she really wanted him to see.

'Just flick a few more pages further on.' She was holding her breath as she watched him do as she asked, and she didn't breathe out even when he turned to the page where she'd written the last label: Our Wedding.

'Does this mean—' She kissed him before he could finish the sentence, following her sister's advice and showing him in the best way she could think of how much he meant to her, because she knew she'd start crying if she tried to speak. When she pulled away, she finally found her voice.

'It means I want to marry you, even more than I did when I started that scrapbook. I love you, I always have and I always will. So, if it's not too late, I want to say an unreserved yes to the question you asked me when you had your accident, and to thank you for coming back into my life and making me happier than I've ever been.'

'I can't imagine anything better than being your husband, but what's happened since yesterday? You seem like a different person.'

'I decided to go paragliding dressed as a flying squirrel.' She couldn't help laughing at the look that crossed his face. She'd explain it to him later, but all he needed to know for now was that she loved him in a way that she'd never loved anyone else, and there wasn't a single thing that could happen that would ever change that. She'd never felt so certain, so secure, or so loved in return. It might not be the neat little image she'd had in her mind of how things would turn out, but she wouldn't change it for the world. And she'd rather let the tide come in to carry her away, than ever risk losing Gary again.

14

One of Danni's responsibilities as a consultant in the emergency room was to mentor new team members and the appointment of Eve Bellingham had been a welcome relief. Having a new doctor on the team was much needed, especially with Danni being restricted to lighter duties, and the impending start of her maternity leave. Eve was only thirty, but had specialised in emergency medicine since completing her training, which meant she was already a senior doctor and Danni couldn't imagine needing to provide much in the way of mentoring, other than around the specifics of how St Piran's operated its emergency department. She'd met Eve when she came in to be interviewed, and Danni had been asked to give her a tour around the department. Eve had been easy to talk to and someone Danni had felt would fit in with the team, so it had been welcome news to hear she was joining them.

Eve's first day on the team passed quickly. It was a typically busy day in A&E, without much time to stop and chat, but Danni had checked in on her whenever she could, and it was almost as if she'd always been there. She worked quickly and without fuss, not missing a beat when a four-year-old who'd come in with a high temperature and listlessness, suddenly projectile vomited all over her. She'd changed into clean scrubs and got straight back into it, diagnosing the little girl with a nasty case of norovirus and making sure that protocols were followed to minimise the risk of the infection spreading within the department.

'She's going to be a real asset to the team.' That's what Danni's verdict had been, when Dr Moorhouse, the department clinical lead, had asked for an update on Eve's progress. Admittedly there hadn't been any major incidents or life and death admissions during her first shift, but Danni had no reason to believe that Eve wouldn't be able to handle those with every bit as much ease as she had the day-to-day stuff.

Eve's second shift started off slowly. It was unusually quiet but, like Danni, she was experienced enough to know you never commented on that, unless you wanted a sudden deluge of patients. The waiting room was less than half full, which was a relief to Danni as there'd been times lately when it was standing-room only. The rural position of the hospital and the size of the population it served, meant they hadn't yet had an occasion when they'd had patients waiting on trolleys in the corridor, but she'd seen plenty of that when she'd worked in London and she often got messages from her former colleagues talking about how it had become even more difficult. So, the chance to finally catch up with Eve to find out a little bit more about her, and begin to develop a working relationship they could build on, was one that Danni didn't want to miss.

'Which hospital did you say you were at before?' She set down the cardboard cups she'd brought back from a quick coffee run to the Friends of St Piran's shop. Eve had offered to go when Danni had asked if anyone wanted a drink, but there was only so much taking it easy she could do.

'Jimmy's. I stayed on after my training.' Eve's face had taken on a slightly wistful look. Jimmy's was an affectionate nickname for Leeds General Infirmary, an internationally renowned teaching hospital, which was a world away from somewhere like St Piran's. It made Danni's next question an obvious one.

'What made you want to come down here?'

'The quiet life.' The way Eve said it, with an upward inflection at the end, made it sound more like a question than an answer. As if she was testing whether anyone would believe her. But Danni had harboured her own secret reasons for leaving behind a job in a busy London hospital and taking refuge on the Cornish Atlantic coast, none of which had anything to do with wanting a quiet life. At this stage of her career, if Eve was ambitious, there probably couldn't have been a better place for her to work than Jimmy's, so there had to be more to it than wanting a life by the sea. Danni wasn't going to push her for an explanation, though; it was none of her business if Eve didn't want to share the real reason. And the truth was, she was just grateful to have her new colleague on board. Jimmy's loss was almost certainly St Piran's gain.

'I don't think our jobs are ever going to give us the quiet life.' Danni smiled. 'But it's certainly a beautiful place to live. I love being able to take the dogs out on a walk along the cliffs after work, or going in for a swim whenever the mood takes me. I was at King's College Hospital before I came here, and I thought I'd miss the city life, but I wouldn't trade this for the world.'

'So you'd never want to go back?' Eve's eyebrows shot up, half-disappearing behind her fringe. Clearly she wasn't so certain that she wanted to stay.

'I thought I might want to at first and I even contemplated it in my first year here. I think it's because of the reasons I came in the first place. I was in a bit of a toxic relationship with a colleague, that wasn't really even a relationship in the proper sense, but it was still messing with my head and stopping me from getting on with my life.' Danni shrugged; it was funny how easy it was to talk about all those wasted years trailing around after Lucas and hoping that her best friend would fall out of love with him, so that they could be together in the way she'd been convinced they were meant to be for so long. But it had all been an illusion. She'd never really loved Lucas, and he'd certainly never loved her, he'd just been an incredibly skilled manipulator. She thanked God every day that it was her love for Esther, which had always been far stronger than the illusion of loving Lucas, that had stopped her crossing a line she would have regretted forever. She wasn't embarrassed to talk about what had happened, even with a new colleague. Everyone in St Piran's seemed to know the story anyway, so it was best that Eve heard it from her. It might also make her more wary if her path crossed with Lucas's, because a beautiful young woman who was homesick for her old life, and who might be a bit vulnerable as a result, would be just the sort of person he'd hone in on. 'Then he decided to follow me to Cornwall and I thought about heading back to London, but I love living here, and the friends I've made since I started at the hospital are great. There's a sense of community here too that I never found in London. This is my home and it's where I met Charlie, so it feels like our place too. And it's definitely where we want to raise our son.'

'I can see the appeal of all of that, but I'd never have left Leeds if it hadn't been for...' Eve hesitated for a moment, her breath seeming to catch in her throat before she continued. 'My fiancé was brought up around here, and he needed to move back to be closer to his parents. So of course I came with him.'

'But your heart is still in Leeds?' As Danni asked the question, she didn't need to wait for a response, it was written all over Eve's face even before she nodded. 'You can always go back.

No decision about your career is forever unless you want it to be.'

'I hope so.' Eve seemed to shake herself, then she smiled. 'But the decision about how long I stick around might well hang on just how good or bad this coffee turns out to be.'

'It's lucky Danni got them from the hospital shop and not the vending machine then, or you'd probably be handing in your notice by the time you'd finished it.' Aidan marched towards them, clearly having caught the tail end of their conversation. 'The good news is, if you know where to go, you can get just as good a vanilla latte in Port Kara as you can anywhere else. And I really need a decent coffee right now.'

'Tough night?' Danni looked at Aidan, who had dark circles under his eyes and a lot more stubble on display than he usually did, which suggested either a change of image, or that he'd started his day in a bit of a hurry.

'We had a call from Ellen last night. She'd had a bit of spotting.' Aidan shook his head. 'Jase went into full panic mode and to be honest I wasn't much better. So the pair of us got in the car and drove an hour and a half to meet her at Derriford Hospital in Plymouth. She didn't want to go into the Early Pregnancy Unit without us, because she couldn't face it alone if she'd lost the baby. By the time they called us in, I'd convinced myself it was over. I think it was the only way I could cope, facing the worst head on before I even got the news.'

'Oh Aidan, you shouldn't even be here.' Tears were pricking Danni's eyes, and she couldn't believe he'd come in to work, but he was shaking his head again.

'It's okay, they saw a heartbeat. Can you believe it? A tiny flickering little sign that our baby wants to stay around to meet us. Neither of us could sleep when we got in, we were so excited.' Aidan smiled and his whole face was transformed, the joy of discovering that the baby was hanging in there so obvious that even a relative stranger like Eve seemed touched by the moment.

'Oh congratulations, that's amazing.' Her voice sounded thick with emotion, but Danni was struggling to get any words out at all. Instead, she hugged him hard for at least twenty seconds, before she let him go and was finally able to respond.

'Why didn't you tell me? And why didn't you take the day off?'

'Because that would have ended up with you taking on even more work, and I'm not having that.' Aidan wagged a finger at her and grinned. 'You know there's not an agency nurse on the planet who can match up to me.'

'That's true, in more ways than I can count.' Danni laughed at the look of mock outrage on her friend's face, seconds before the red phone started to ring, notifying them that a trauma call was on the way. 'Looks like it's just as well I've got the A team on today.'

'I'm on it already, boss.' Aidan gave her a mock salute, and moved to answer the call. There was a serious emergency on the way and, until it was dealt with, that was where the focus of everyone involved needed to be.

* * *

The trauma call was for a thirty-year-old male called Freddie Summers who'd fallen over twenty feet whilst working on the roof of a building. He'd been unconscious at the scene and incoherent following the accident. The paramedics had stabilised him, he'd been intubated and sent in for a scan almost as soon as he'd arrived at the hospital. Shortly after the call about Freddie, there'd been another trauma alert, this time about a road traffic accident involving several casualties, and the plan for Danni to stick to light duties had to be put on hold. Eve had proven every bit as adept at coping with the drama of a more serious situation as Danni had hoped she'd be, but they'd barely had a chance to talk for almost two hours. Freddie was still in the department with his family at his bedside, awaiting a space in theatre and ITU, where he'd need to go as soon as a bed became available. The scan had shown a severe head injury, which looked as if it could be life changing for both Freddie and his loved ones, and Danni just hoped the neurosurgeon would be able to do something that would make a significant difference, although sadly not even the most skilled surgeon could perform miracles.

She was on her way back through the department, and finally able to catch her breath, when she spotted Eve coming out of one of the cubicles. She was just about to call out to her new colleague, who was about twenty feet ahead of her, to check how she was doing, when Freddie's heavily pregnant wife, Lauren, who they'd met when he was admitted, suddenly appeared in the corridor in front of Eve.

'He's not going to get better, is he?' There were tears streaming down the young woman's face, her mascara creating rivers of black as she stood in front of Eve, desperate for an answer that could give her some hope. But Eve seemed to have frozen to the spot.

'Do you even care!' Lauren began hammering her hands on Eve's chest, but she still didn't react, even as Danni caught up with them.

'That's not going to help anyone.' Catching hold of one of Lauren's arms, Danni had to weave her head to one side to avoid being struck by the woman's other fist as it flew upwards. But then all the fight seemed to go out of her.

'No one's doing anything. He's just lying there getting worse and worse, and you're letting him.' She was sobbing so hard it was difficult to make out what she was saying, but Danni folded her into her arms, the two of them standing awkwardly bump to bump, as Eve remained rooted to the spot.

'He's being kept stable, and he'll be taken into surgery as soon as there's a theatre available. It will be within the next hour.' It was a promise Danni could make, because she'd been there when Freddie's options were discussed, and the team had considered whether transferring him to another hospital might get him into surgery sooner. In the end, the decision had been taken for him to stay at St Piran's, because the air ambulance had been on another job when the emergency services had been called, and there were no beds available in the nearest specialist units. There was only a very small neuro-surgical team who operated out of St Piran's, but they'd been able to call enough members of the team in. That didn't make the waiting any less hellish for his family.

Isla and Aidan had rushed towards Danni, clearly worried that something was going to kick off. But she silently mouthed over Lauren's shoulder that it was okay, and they backed off, watching from a distance, ready to step in if she needed them.

'I can't do this on my own, I can't have this baby by myself. I need Fred, we're a team and if he's, if he's...' It was a sentence Lauren couldn't finish and Danni wished with all her heart that she could reassure the other woman that she'd get her husband back, exactly the way he had been that morning, but there was a very good chance that their lives had changed forever.

'The surgeons deal with these kinds of head injuries all the time and there are rehabilitation services which can make a huge difference too. Right now, the important thing is that he's stable and ready for his operation. But you need to take care of yourself and the baby too. It won't help Freddie if he's got to worry about the two of you.'

'I can't leave him. His mum and dad are with him, but I still can't go.' Lauren looked completely exhausted as she stepped

back from Danni. It was as if she was being pulled in two direc-
tions and Danni didn't know what to advise. She had no idea how
she'd have reacted in the same circumstances.

'They're ready to take Freddie up to surgery.' It was Zahir who
broke the silence in the end, as he came into view.

'Oh, thank God.' It was a good job Danni was close enough to
reach out and steady Lauren, otherwise she suspected the other
woman might have ended up in a heap on the floor. The tears
didn't stop flowing, even as she turned to look at Danni, and then
towards Eve, who still hadn't said a word, but there was a tiny
spark of hope in her eyes. 'I'm sorry, I can't believe I lashed out
like that, but I was so scared.'

'Don't worry, I just hope he's okay.' Eve's chin wobbled as she
finally spoke, the intake of air afterwards shuddery as she
breathed in.

'I need to see him before he goes. Just in case.' Lauren was
already pulling away, desperate to say a goodbye to her husband,
which none of them knew whether he'd be able to hear. The
hardest thing about Danni's job was that sometimes the outcome
for her patients was completely out of her control. She'd done all
she could for Freddie and his family. The rest was in other
people's hands now, and the forces of fate. But what she could do
was talk to Eve, and try to get to the bottom of what had caused
her new colleague to completely freeze. Danni just hoped it wasn't
something that would affect what had seemed such a promising
future at St Piran's for Eve.

* * *

'I'm sorry, I don't know what happened. I just had no idea what to
say to her.' Eve hadn't even given Danni a chance to ask the ques-

tion when they got into Dr Moorhouse's office, where she'd suggested they go for a chat.

'We all have moments that affect us in unexpected ways, but you must have had to deal with family members going through this kind of thing before.'

'More times than I want to count.' Running a hand through her dark, glossy hair, Eve seemed so put together and in control, yet she'd been like a rabbit in the headlights when Lauren had approached her. It didn't make any sense, unless it had reminded her of something far more personal. Danni had been there herself, and she was going to take a chance that her hunch was right.

'My dad died of cardiac arrest when I was ten years old. It was what made me want to become a doctor, but it still hits me hard every time I find myself in a situation like my dad faced that day. The first couple of times I froze, and for a while I wasn't sure it was something I could get over. But with the support of my colleagues, I found a way. If the situation with Freddie and Lauren is like that for you, I want you to know you can talk to me.'

'My f...' Eve hesitated for a moment, then swallowed hard and met Danni's eyes. 'My friend sustained a serious head injury in an accident, and I was with him at the hospital. Like Lauren, I was waiting for someone to tell me he was going to be okay, but they never did, and he never was. Nothing anyone said to me that day helped, and I desperately wanted to find something to say to her today that would – even a little bit – but I couldn't seem to open my mouth.'

'I want to say it gets easier and it does, but not all by itself.' Danni reached out and gently squeezed her arm. 'I don't think I'd ever have got past it if I didn't get some help to process what it feels like to be back in a moment when you felt so helpless. Have you spoken to anyone about this before?'

'No. It's just that the circumstances today were so similar in a lot of ways. Freddie was the same age as my friend, and I was there by the bedside with his parents, who were distraught too. I didn't realise it could still hit me so hard, and I'm scared I'll let everyone down and won't be able to do my job.'

'Of course you can do your job, and with the right support this will make you even better at it. There's nothing the families of our patients need more than to be shown some empathy; you can do that in a way that people who haven't experienced something similar just can't do. I do think it would help you to speak to someone about it though. Maybe one of the hospital counsellors would be a good starting point?'

'I think it would.' Eve nodded. 'Thank you so much for understanding and not just tearing a strip off me for being useless.'

'You've been great today, and I can already tell you're going to fit in perfectly. Do you do hugs?' Danni smiled, as Eve nodded. Hugging her new colleague, she hoped she was right, because there was no doubting Eve had a lot to offer. She wouldn't be around soon, because of her maternity leave, but the team at St Piran's had a way of pulling together unlike any other she'd ever worked with, and she couldn't be leaving Eve's future at the hospital in better hands.

15

Wendy had been laying the groundwork to get a puppy for the past few weeks. It seemed like the perfect antidote to her increasingly empty nest, and she knew now which breed she wanted. From what she'd read, it would also be a good fit with Gary's Border Terrier, Stan. The breed was supposed to be incredibly affectionate and very loyal to their favourite people. It was exactly what she needed, a little dog to depend on her, who she wouldn't have to share with another household. Gary had questioned whether now was the right time for a second dog, considering their plans to get married, and the hope that they might be able to have an exotic honeymoon somewhere, but she could tell she was starting to win him round, and he'd begun to send her videos of dachshund puppies falling over their own feet and doing other impossibly cute things. She was just watching another video Gary had sent her, when her phone started to ring. It was Zara.

'Oh Mum, thank God!' Her voice was high and reedy, and even without seeing her face Wendy could tell she was close to tears.

'Are you okay? What's wrong?' Fear prickled her skin, and she was already in flight or fight mode with the need to get to her youngest child.

'Yes, no... It's not me, it's Chloe.' Wendy's immediate reaction was to sigh with relief; all the scary scenarios that had flitted through her mind in less than ten seconds had disappeared, but then she heard the panic that was still in Zara's voice.

'Mum? Mum? Are you there?'

'Yes, darling, but if something is wrong with Chloe, why haven't you called Dad?'

'He's not answering. He's away on a golf trip with Uncle Tony and you know what it's like when they're playing, he won't even look at his phone until he comes off the course. Mum, please, I know it's weird me phoning you about Clo, but I think she's really poorly and she won't let me call an ambulance. She keeps crying because of the pain.'

'Where does it hurt?' Wendy felt as if her blood had gone cold, and she had a horrible feeling she knew what Zara was going to say before she said it.

'Near the bottom of her bump and she's been sick a few times too. I don't know what to do, and she just keeps saying she wants Dad. I can't do this on my own, Mum. I just can't. *Please.*' Zara was pleading now, but she didn't need to, Wendy had already snatched up her keys and she felt close to tears herself.

'Okay sweetheart, I'm coming straight over now, but I want you to call the ambulance. Never mind what Chloe says, she needs medical help.'

'Thank you, please be as quick as you can. I'm really scared.'

'I know you are, sweetheart, but it'll be okay. I'll be there in ten minutes, I promise.' Ending the call, Wendy dashed towards the front door. From what Chloe had said there was every chance this had something to do with either the pregnancy itself, or the cyst on her ovary, and Wendy had no idea how dangerous that might be to either Chloe or her unborn baby. All she knew was that she desperately wanted them both to be okay.

* * *

Zara was standing in the open doorway when Wendy pulled up outside Mike and Chloe's house. Her face was almost as pale as the white shirt she was wearing, and her eyes were red rimmed and puffy.

'I'm scared she's dying; she can't even stand up now and when I phoned for an ambulance they said it was probably a miscarriage, but they might take two hours to get here. They've got a backlog of jobs.' Zara threw herself into her mother's arms as Wendy reached her. 'Don't let her die, Mum, you've got to do something.'

'If she's as bad as you say, I'll take her to the hospital myself.' Wendy gently extricated herself from her daughter's embrace. 'But try not to worry. There are a lot of reasons she might be having pain and it doesn't necessarily mean she's losing the baby.'

'I think that's why Chloe doesn't want to go to the hospital. If she gets there and they tell her she's lost him, I don't think she'll cope.' Zara shivered and Wendy nodded. Her daughter shouldn't have had to witness this, and if Mike had answered his bloody phone neither of them would be here, but all they could do was their best to help Chloe until they could track him down.

'I'll speak to her and make her understand she needs to do this.' Wendy took her daughter's hand, and followed her down the hallway and into the sitting room where Chloe was curled up on the sofa, with her knees drawn up to her chest, still crying and in obvious pain. Something inside of Wendy stirred, and it was almost as if it was one of her own daughters lying there.

'Oh sweetheart, what's going on?' Crouching by the sofa, Wendy pushed Chloe's hair away from her forehead.

'The pain is so bad, it's feels like something is crushing my insides on the right-hand side of my groin. It started off as a dull ache, but it's got worse and worse.' She looked at Wendy, her eyes filled with fear. 'I'm losing him, aren't I?'

'I really hope not, but we need to get you to hospital, so they can take a look at you both.'

'I can't bear to hear them tell me he's gone.' Chloe buried her face in the cushion and when Wendy put a hand on her shoulder, it felt rigid with tension.

'It might not be that, it could be the cyst, and the sooner you get seen the better it'll be for you and the baby. The ambulance will probably take a while, but I can drive you in.' She kept her voice level and did the best she could to sound hopeful, but this amount of abdominal pain in a pregnant woman was terrifying to witness, and she could only begin to imagine how scary it was to experience.

Chloe turned to look at Wendy again. 'Only if you promise you'll stay with me until Mike arrives.'

'I promise.' It was an easy commitment to make in the end, and she told herself it was because she'd do the same for anyone in that kind of distress, even a total stranger. But the truth was she felt something more for Chloe than just passing sympathy. She wouldn't have been able to define what that was if her life depended on it, but it was there all the same.

* * *

Chloe had been sick at least three times on the fifteen-minute journey to the hospital, and Wendy had questioned whether they should have waited for the ambulance, but once they were on the road she wasn't going to stop driving. When she'd run upstairs to try and find Chloe some bits to take into the hospital, she'd asked Zara to phone the ambulance again for an update, and they'd said at least another hour. They couldn't just sit around and wait. Wendy parked as close as she could to the entrance to A&E, without blocking access for the ambulances, but she couldn't have cared less if she got fined a month's wages for parking there. All that mattered was getting Chloe the help she needed. Wendy had debated whether to take her straight to the maternity department, but she had no idea if it was a pregnancy-related issue or not, and her money was still on the ovarian cyst. Either way, she figured that the emergency department were best placed to deal with it, and she didn't want to delay Chloe getting seen by someone who could help her for a second longer than she had to.

Thankfully, the first people Wendy had spotted when she'd burst through the doors of the emergency department had been Amy and Isla, who'd rushed out with a trolley to bring Chloe inside. Taking Zara to the relatives' room, Wendy had said she wanted to get them both a drink, while they waited to hear when they could see Chloe, but the truth was she wanted to see if she could reach Mike. Whatever the reason for his fiancée's pain, he needed to be here, and Wendy was ready to tell him that in no uncertain terms. When she tried her ex-husband's number, she wasn't surprised that it went straight to voicemail, but she had something else she could try.

'Alright, Wend. I didn't expect to see your number flash up on my phone.' Tony Poston had been Mike's best friend since they were at primary school together, and they'd been as thick as thieves in the five decades since, which was why Alice and Zara had always called him Uncle Tony.

'Me neither, but I'm trying to get hold of Mike. *Urgently*.' She was in no mood for small talk, and Tony and his wife Vanessa had made it perfectly clear whose team they were on over the years, but especially since the divorce.

'I can't help you there.'

'Really?' She tried and failed to keep the irritation out of her voice. 'Only I was told he was playing golf with you.'

Tony laughed. 'Christ! This is even more of a blast from the past. I thought the days of me bullshitting you to cover for Mike were long gone, but apparently not. I've got no idea where he is, but he's not with me. Just don't tell Chloe.'

Tony laughed again, and if Wendy had been face to face with him, she'd have landed a punch right on his nose. She was so angry, but the rage she felt had nothing to do with all the times Mike's best friend had lied to her; it was entirely reserved for what the pair of them were putting his fiancée through. 'Well maybe you'd better try and find out where he is, because I'm with Chloe in the hospital. She's in agony and she might be losing the baby. So, tell that selfish bastard you're always so willing to defend to get his arse to St Piran's now, or I swear to God I won't be responsible for my actions.'

'You're joking.' Tony sounded shocked, but Wendy still felt like punching him.

'Even a moron like you must know I'm not joking about something like that.' Wendy cut off the call before Tony could answer. The adrenaline that was pumping through her was making it feel as though her veins were closer to the surface than they had been before. She had no idea how she'd react if Mike suddenly turned up, but she wasn't entirely sure she wouldn't be capable of murder.

* * *

Despite the warmth of the room, Wendy was still shivering as she grasped the hot chocolate between her hands. Stealing a glance across the room, she noticed Zara shiver too. Neither of them could relax and every time there was the sound of footsteps in the corridor outside, Wendy held her breath, but no one had come in yet. And then came the knock on the door.

'How are you doing?' Esther gave a half-smile as she walked into the room and it was all Wendy could do not to cry, but she gave a small shrug instead, and glanced towards her daughter.

'We're just worried about Chloe.'

'She's been sent for a scan and she's on an IV because we're concerned about dehydration and we also wanted to be able to give her stronger painkillers, but Chloe asked if you can go in there to be with her before they give her the results of the scan. I can stay with Zara if you want?'

'No!' Zara's response seemed to echo in the room, and Wendy looked at her daughter. She had more right to be with Chloe than Wendy did, and if the news was bad, she was probably better placed to comfort her soon-to-be stepmother than Wendy was.

'If Chloe's okay with us both being there, I am too. I've tried to get hold of my ex-husband, because he's the one who should really be here, but I haven't had any luck.'

'I think she's going to need a friendly face.' The downturn of Esther's mouth would have said it all, even if Wendy hadn't picked up on the implication of her words. Whatever the news was, it wasn't going to be good.

* * *

Chloe had been moved into a private room after her scan. She was hooked up to an IV as Esther had said, but there was no foetal heart monitor and the last shred of hope that Wendy had been holding on to drifted away. Chloe was ashen and she flinched when they came into the room, like a dog that expected to be beaten.

'Thank you for being here. I couldn't look at the screen while they were scanning me and I told them I didn't want to know what they'd seen until I had you with me, but I'm sure they'd have said if everything was okay.' She whispered the words to Wendy, her eyes filling with tears as she spoke. Chloe shouldn't have needed to be grateful to her partner's ex-wife for being there in her hour of need, but Mike had left her with no choice. Wendy knew that might not make him the worst person in the world, but it made him the worst person in hers. She'd tried so hard not to hate him after the way their marriage had ended, for the girls' sake if nothing else, but there was no denying how she felt about him now. She'd wasted so much time thinking that Mike leaving had destroyed their chances of having a perfect family life, and wishing that things could be different. When the truth was he'd been hellbent on destroying their chances of being a happy family right from the start. He was too selfish to put anyone but himself first; he'd let them down over and over, and yet she'd still spent years convincing herself that holding their family together was better for the girls than the alternative. What a fool she'd been, but she couldn't bear that Mike was making a fool of Chloe too, and hatred wasn't a strong enough word for him any more. She couldn't focus on that right now, though; the energy those feelings took up was needed elsewhere.

'It's okay, sweetheart.' Wendy had stopped seeing Chloe her rival in any way, and all she cared about now was that somehow she'd survive this. But looking at the fragile young woman, who'd already told her she had no one to rely on, she was terrified this might be the final straw. When Ravinder Parvid, one of the consultant obstetricians, came into the room and introduced herself, less than two minutes after Wendy and Zara had got there, her expression made Wendy's heart feel as though it had hit the floor. Ravinder took a deep breath and then said the words none of them wanted to hear.

'I'm so sorry.' The wail that filled the air came from Chloe, but the pain in Wendy's chest almost made it feel as though it had come from her. She held the younger woman's hand, as Ravinder outlined the terrible results of the scan. The cyst on Chloe's left ovary had suddenly increased dramatically in size, twisting it and cutting off the blood supply. They couldn't be sure whether it had been a direct cause, but the blood supply to the placenta had been compromised and her baby had died. All of the young woman's worst fears had come true and her anguish was unbearable. It was almost ten minutes before Ravinder could outline to Chloe what was going to happen next. It took that long for her to be able to stop sobbing, and Wendy held her the whole time, the front of her top soaked through with Chloe's tears by the time she was able to cope with being told what would happen next.

'Ovarian torsion requires emergency surgery and we're preparing theatre for you now. We're hoping we might be able to save your left ovary, but there's a chance we may have to remove it if the blood supply has been cut off for too long.'

'What about the baby? Will you take him out too?' Chloe was gripping Wendy's hand so tightly it hurt, but she was glad of the physical pain, it was almost a relief.

'We wouldn't if you weren't already going under a general anaesthetic, but I think it would be best in this instance.' Ravinder patted Chloe's shoulder, and Wendy let go of the breath she hadn't even known she was holding. The thought of Chloe having to give birth to her son after losing him was unbearable. Nothing could make this situation any better, but there were definitely things that could make it worse.

'Will I be able to see him?' The desperation in Chloe's voice was breaking Wendy's heart again and, when she stole a glance at Zara, her daughter was frantically wiping tears out of her eyes.

'You will, but I think it would be best if we wait until afterwards for me to advise you whether I think it would be a good idea. I really am so sorry.' Ravinder sounded like she meant every word, and as Chloe started crying again, it was echoed by Zara's inability to stifle her own tears. This was agony for all of them, even Wendy. They had no idea where Mike was and she dreaded to think what he was doing. Now wasn't the time to wonder whether Chloe would ever be able to forgive him, but one thing Wendy knew for certain was that she never would.

16

Wendy hadn't known if she should stay at the hospital until Chloe came out of her operation, but there was still no sign of Mike, and Zara had begged her mother to wait with her. Alice was on her way too, having got a call from her younger sister. They both wanted to be there for their father's fiancée, and yet the man himself was probably with another woman, either not knowing or not caring what Chloe had gone through. If someone had told Wendy when they'd first split up that she'd later discover Mike was still being unfaithful, despite having a beautiful and much younger partner, she'd have imagined that giving her some kind of satisfaction. After all, it meant that the cheating had nothing to do with her, or that she'd let herself go and only had herself to blame for him straying, as she'd feared at the time. Yet she felt nothing but anger and sadness that Mike was still up to his old tricks.

The young woman lying in bed recovering from major surgery was already broken by the loss of her son, and no one with an ounce of compassion could have taken any satisfaction from Mike's absence. But the sadness she was feeling wasn't just sympathy, or even empathy for another woman caught up in the same web of lies she'd been caught in for so long. The pain was deeper than Wendy would ever have believed possible, and she'd needed to hide from Zara in the toilets so that she could sob until her chest ached. And the truth was she wasn't just waiting for Chloe to come around from the operation for Zara's sake, she was doing it because she couldn't bear to leave her in the hospital and just walk away.

'Mum, Chloe wants you to come in.' Alice had arrived ten minutes earlier, and had exchanged a brief hug with Wendy before going in to join her sister at Chloe's bedside. She'd been given another private room after being brought up from post-operative care, and she'd still been very woozy. They'd been told by the surgeon that the operation had gone well, but because of the amount of time the blood supply had been compromised and the extent of the torsion, Chloe had lost both her left ovary and fallopian tube. Zara had gone into the room to be with her as soon as she was brought back up, while Wendy waited outside, relief flooding her body when Alice had turned up to join her sister. She'd thought about going in with Zara, but she didn't want to do anything to make Chloe feel uncomfortable. But Alice's tone was insistent. 'She wants to see the baby, but she says she can only do it if you're in there with her.'

'Me? Is there no one—' Wendy stopped herself before she said any more. She already knew the answer to the question she'd been about to ask. Chloe didn't have anyone else, at least not family. She might have had friends, but Mike had been quite skilled at encouraging Wendy to drop her own friends when they were together, to focus on friendships he could control – the wives and partners of his buddies, those same men, like Tony, who'd help him keep whatever secrets he chose to keep. There was a good chance he'd done the same to Chloe, and that was why there was no one else she could call on right now. Wendy could only imagine the desperation she felt to see her child, and to hold him.

One of the midwives, a woman called Jess, had come along to talk to the next of kin while Chloe was having her operation, which was a mantle Zara had been forced to adopt in her father's absence. Jess had been so kind, and had explained that because Chloe was twenty-six weeks pregnant, the loss of her son was classed as a stillbirth and not a miscarriage. His birth could be registered as a result, and she'd said that could often give bereaved families comfort, knowing their baby's life was recognised in that way. She also told them that there were a team of volunteers, from the Friends of St Piran's, who knitted bonnets and blankets for babies like Chloe's, and that a special memory box would be made with his hand and footprints. Jess had said that Chloe would be told all of this when she'd recovered sufficiently from the operation, and that the decision about whether to see her son would be down to her, but the memory box would be put together either way, because sometimes it was later – after the shock had receded a little bit – that parents desperately wanted those things to hang on to.

It was after the conversation with Jess that Wendy had needed to hide in the toilets, and she cried for a mother who'd never get the chance to see her son grow up, and the little boy who hadn't even got to take his first breath. And if Chloe felt having Wendy there when she saw him would help in any way, then that was what she was going to do.

'Okay.' Wendy stood up and followed her daughter into the room, her heart breaking again as she looked at Chloe lying in the bed. She seemed even younger and more delicate than before, and the grief she was so obviously feeling was etched on her face in a way Wendy wasn't sure could ever be erased. It hit home in a completely different way than it had before that Chloe was just a few years older than Wendy's girls, yet she'd had to face the worst thing imaginable without her partner or her parents. The thought of either of the girls going through something like that alone made Wendy's chest ache, and the rage she felt towards Mike threatened to spill out. Alice and Zara had been forced to witness Chloe's pain, and it was just one more thing Mike should have protected them from but had spectacularly failed to do. Far worse than that was what he'd done to Chloe, by failing to be there for her and their son at a time when nothing else should have mattered. Chloe was already scarred by the hand that life had dealt her, but Mike would probably never comprehend just what his absence had done to Chloe or his daughters, because he simply didn't care.

'Oh darling.' It was all she could say, and instinctively she reached out towards the younger woman, who lurched forward, almost throwing herself into Wendy's arms. Her sobs echoed in the room, just as they had when she'd been told he was gone, and it was all Wendy could do not to give in to tears again too. She had to remember this wasn't her pain, even if it felt like she was far more involved than she was.

'I should've done something, I should've known.' Chloe's words were muffled as she pressed her face into Wendy's shoulder, but it did nothing to dull the torment within them. 'I could have had an operation for the cyst, but I was worried it might put the baby at risk. I didn't know what to do and when I tried to talk to Mike...' She trailed off as sobs wracked her body again. Wendy knew now she *was* capable of murder, with her bare hands if it came to it, and God help Mike when he finally turned up.

'Remember what the doctor said. This was something they or you could never have anticipated. What happened is incredibly rare. The cyst was quite small and they can't say why it suddenly increased so much in size, or even if that was why the placenta stopped working the way it should. I know it's awful, sweetheart, but this isn't your fault. *None of it.*' She emphasised the last part. Mike wouldn't feel guilty. He wasn't capable of it, otherwise he couldn't have lived the life he'd shared with either Wendy or Chloe. But another of his skills was managing to make other people feel like they should shoulder the blame for his behaviour. She didn't even know if Chloe was taking in what she was saying, or whether she understood what Wendy was inferring, but she hoped the words would come back to Chloe when she needed them most.

'I want to see him. To tell him I'm sorry and that I wish he could have stayed, but I don't think I can face it on my own.' Chloe pulled back slightly, her eyes sliding towards Zara and Alice. 'And I don't want the girls to see him until I'm sure he doesn't look...'

It was just one more sentence Chloe couldn't finish, and she didn't need to. She might not get to hold a living, breathing baby in her arms, but she was a mother, and she would have been, even if she'd never been pregnant. She was already a mother to Alice and Zara in all the ways that really mattered, putting them first at the darkest time in her life. And an overwhelming surge of something that felt a lot like affection for Chloe welled up inside of Wendy.

'I'll go and find someone and ask them to bring him to you. The girls can wait in the hospital restaurant until you decide what you think is best.' Wendy nodded as she spoke. This was a decision she was happy to leave entirely in Chloe's hands. She trusted her to do what was best for Alice and Zara, and she'd go along with whatever decision she thought was right. The girls didn't argue either, both of them seeming to understand that it was up to Chloe who got to see her son, and that the choices she made would be because she cared about them so much.

* * *

Wendy's hands were shaking when Jess brought the baby into the room. He was wrapped in a blanket of purest white, his tiny face perfect beneath the knitted bonnet on his head, and his rosebud mouth slightly open, as if he might suddenly take in the breath they all wished he would.

'He's beautiful, Chloe.' Wendy desperately tried to blink back yet more tears, as Jess put the baby in his mother's arms, but she couldn't and, when she looked up, she could see that Jess was crying too. It was only Chloe who had yet to shed a tear at the sight of her little boy. Instead, her face was a picture of awe, as she gently loosened the blanket to get a better look at her son. He couldn't have been more than about eight inches long, like a tiny doll. But he really did look perfect; he'd just needed more time to grow.

'He is beautiful, isn't he?' Chloe looked up at her for a second. 'We were never sure about a name, we couldn't agree on one, but I know what it should be now. I want to call him Beau.'

'That's lovely.' It felt so strange, watching Chloe's instant bond with the baby she'd never get to take home. It was still heartbreaking, but there was a beauty to the moment that Wendy would never have been able to describe to someone who wasn't there. The bond she was witnessing couldn't be broken by death; Beau would always be Chloe's son, even when she couldn't see him, or touch him, any more.

'I think it would be okay for the girls to meet him, if that's alright with you?'

'You don't need to ask my permission. Beau is their brother and you're his mum, so whatever you think is right, is fine by me.' Wendy put a hand on her shoulder and Chloe leant her head against it. There was something unspoken exchanged between them again. And when Wendy looked back on it later, she realised that was the moment they'd somehow become family, in a way that had absolutely nothing to do with Mike, and never would.

* * *

Wendy had always been proud of Alice and Zara, but never more so than on the day they met their little brother. They'd both decided to hold him, something Chloe had encouraged, and Wendy had done what she could by capturing as many photographs as possible. Mike had finally phoned Alice, with some utter rubbish about being in a valley with a no-signal area, but when he'd asked to speak to Chloe she'd shaken her head. Alice had told her father that Chloe wasn't up to talking yet, and had relayed the message that he was on the way. He'd also pre-empted any conversation that might be coming about the discovery of his lie, by saying that Tony had been forced to pull out of the golf trip at the last minute, which was why Wendy hadn't been able to reach him that way; a message that Alice had also passed on. What he didn't know, was that Wendy had never told Chloe she'd tried, or that she'd discovered Mike was using his old friends to cover up his lies yet again. So, what he'd managed to do was to out himself with absolutely no help from his ex-wife. That was something else that Wendy might once have imagined would give her satisfaction, but just like before she'd been wrong about that too.

When Mike crashed through the doors almost ninety minutes after the phone call to Alice, he was panting like a marathon runner, his face a picture of devastation, until he spotted his ex-wife.

'What the hell is she doing here?' It was the first thing he said, before he even moved to comfort his fiancée, or noticed his son lying in the special cuddle cot, which allowed the parents of still-born babies to keep their children with them for longer than they otherwise might.

'Wendy brought me to the hospital, and she's been by my side the whole time.' There was a note of defiance in Chloe's voice, and a strength in the look she gave Mike that Wendy had never seen from her before. 'Thank God I found someone I could rely on, because I couldn't rely on you.'

'I suppose she's been feeding you poison, has she?' Mike snarled, but the only effect it had was for Chloe to pull her shoulders back straight, as she turned towards Alice and Zara.

'Girls, could you go and get me a drink please?'

'We can stay and hear this; we all know what Dad's been up to. It's bloody obvious. And he hasn't even said he's sorry about Beau.' Zara shot her father a look of absolute disgust, but Chloe was right, the girls didn't need to be part of this conversation and Wendy shouldn't be there either.

'Come on, love. Chloe wants a drink, and I'll come down with you. I think she needs to be on her own with your dad for a little while.' She turned to look at Chloe, and silently mouthed the word, 'Okay?' waiting until the other woman had nodded before hurrying the girls out of the door.

'He's doing to her what he did to you, isn't he?' They were barely out of the door before Alice asked the question, and Wendy wasn't going to lie for him any more.

'I think so, but what happens now is for Chloe to decide.' Ushering her daughters along the corridor, she wanted to say so much more, and to tell them she hoped Chloe found the strength to walk away far sooner than she had. What Mike had already done to Chloe was unforgiveable, but the way he reacted in the next half an hour or so would be the true measure of the man, and Wendy had a horrible feeling he'd come up shorter than ever.

* * *

Alice had got another call, this time from Chloe, asking if they could all come back up to the room, and telling her that her father had left.

'I think I might hate Dad.' Zara looked down at the floor and then up at her mother, as they reached the corridor where Chloe's room was. 'How could he just go off and leave Clo after this? Do you think he's even held Beau?'

'I don't know, sweetheart, but maybe Chloe asked him to leave.' The last thing Wendy wanted to do was defend her ex-husband, but she didn't want her daughters to hate him either; for their sake, not his. She didn't need to make any space for Mike in her life any more and, if she could, she'd have arranged it so that she never had to see his face again. But she understood that the girls might want him in their lives, and she wasn't going to stand in their way if they did. Sometimes children were capable of forgiving a parent for unimaginable wrongs, and if there was even a slight chance that her daughters might one day want to try and rebuild their relationship with Mike, she was going to encourage them to leave the door open so that they could. But if it was him that wanted it, and not them, she'd happily help them slam that door in his face when the time came.

'Clo asking him to go doesn't excuse what he's done.' Zara was adamant and, when Alice agreed, all Wendy could do was nod. Zara might not technically be an adult yet, but her daughters were grown women in so many ways. They were far from stupid; they'd seen Mike's behaviour with their own eyes. They knew he hadn't been playing golf, and they'd seen him lash out and try to blame Wendy for Chloe's reaction to his excuses.

Wendy looked at her daughters as they reached the hospital

room. 'All we can do is be there for Chloe; I've got a feeling she's going to need as much support as she can get.'

'I always knew I had the best mum.' Zara planted a kiss on her cheek, giving Wendy a warm glow. It wasn't a sentiment her youngest daughter had ever shared before, and it hadn't been one she'd anticipated either. 'But even I didn't expect you to be this kind to Chloe. I doubt she'll ever forget it, and I know I won't.'

'Me neither.' Alice linked her arm through her mother's on the other side, and Wendy tried and failed to blink back tears for what felt like the hundredth time that day. Whatever bitterness she'd held on to for all the wasted years with Mike, he'd given her the most amazing children.

'Chloe.' Wendy said her name gently as they entered the room. At first glance it looked as if she had fallen asleep, but she was staring down at her son, who she was holding close to her chest, and her head shot up as they came in. Chloe's eyes were bloodshot and the shadows beneath them almost violet. Wendy had an overwhelming urge to wrap her arms around both Chloe and Beau, so instead of second-guessing whether she should act on it, she just did it. When Chloe rested her head on Wendy's shoulder, she knew she'd done the right thing.

'He didn't even want to hold Beau, he barely looked at him.' Chloe gave a shuddering sigh as Wendy finally released them both. 'He just kept saying I needed to put all of this behind us, and that we could try again. Like Beau is replaceable. You understand he's not though, don't you?'

There was so much hope in Chloe's voice. She needed someone to say that they understood, but it wasn't something Wendy needed to pretend to go along with. She completely agreed with Chloe. Another child might fill her empty arms, but it would never replace her son, and she'd always feel his loss and wonder what might have been.

'Of course I do. But maybe Mike is in shock.' She was slipping back into old habits, despite telling herself she wouldn't do it any more, and defending him, not for his own sake but for Chloe's. But Chloe was already shaking her head.

'He wasn't shocked enough not to try to lay the blame at everyone's door but his own. He said you were trying to turn me against him, but he did that all by himself.' Chloe looked towards the girls, but Alice shook her head.

'You don't need to try and protect me and Zara. We've seen it for ourselves.'

Chloe nodded, wiping away a fresh crop of tears with the back of her hand. 'I asked him if he'd ever really loved me, or whether he only proposed because I was pregnant. I didn't need to wait for an answer, I saw it in his eyes.'

'He doesn't deserve you, he never has.' Wendy put an arm around Chloe's shoulders, and she could feel her shaking.

'Maybe not, but I can't help thinking that I'm fundamentally unloveable. It was part of the reason why I wanted a baby so much. Children always love their mums, don't they? Even the mums who aren't any good.' Chloe couldn't stop the tears any more, no matter how hard she tried to wipe them away, and one plopped on to the blanket swaddling Beau.

'You're an amazing mum, not many mothers would have the strength you're showing and you're far from unloveable.' Wendy looked towards her daughters, knowing she'd have their support. 'The girls love you. That's been obvious to me from day one.'

'We do.' Zara's response was emphatic, and Alice was nodding too.

'I wasn't expecting to, when I found out you weren't that much older than me. Dad is many things that aren't all that great, but I can at least say he has impeccable taste in the women he's asked to marry him.'

'Thank you.' Chloe managed a half-smile, but the tears still weren't slowing down. 'I'm just so scared of being on my own again, especially when I have to leave Beau. The last thing I want is to go back to Mike, but I don't know where to go, or where to start trying to find somewhere else to live.'

'You don't have to.' As she said the words, Wendy knew she should probably have run it by Gary before she made the offer she was about to make. But she was even more certain that she needed to make the offer. She also knew that, unlike Mike, Gary was everything a good man should be, and that he'd never turn someone like Chloe away. She needed a safe space to stay until she was strong enough to face the future, and Wendy would do whatever it took to make sure she had one. 'I want you to come and stay with me and Gary. It means the girls can see you whenever they want to.'

'I couldn't ask you to do that.'

'You didn't. You and Beau became a part of my daughters' family when you got pregnant, which means you're a part of my family too. And, right now, you need to be with your family.' Wendy held her gaze. 'I'm not taking no for an answer.'

'Thank you.' Chloe's bottom lip trembled, as a fresh crop of tears began to fall. Wendy couldn't fix Chloe's heartbreak, but she'd do whatever she could to help her find a way through it. After all, no one was better qualified to navigate the devastation that Mike was capable of leaving behind than she was.

17

Danni knew how easy a decision it had been for Esther and Joe to get married at the beautiful St Jude's church in Port Agnes. There were so many factors in its favour, not least of which was that the church in Port Kara was where Esther had planned to marry Lucas. But the vicar at St Jude's, Noah, was a huge draw too. He radiated warmth and kindness, and had made them all laugh at the rehearsal a couple of days before the wedding, when Esther's nerves had been obvious. His wife Issy, one of the midwives who worked out of the Port Agnes midwifery unit, was pregnant herself, and Danni had enjoyed chatting to her about their impending arrivals.

Making new mum friends was something she knew she needed to do once the baby arrived, but she'd been apprehensive about finding people she'd have enough in common with. At the pre-natal classes she'd gone to, she'd been the oldest of the expectant mums, and most of them already seemed to know one another. The Three Ports area could be like that and, although Danni had grown up in another part of Cornwall, she wasn't local and she didn't have the kind of long-established friendships the other women in her group already seemed to have, except with her colleagues at the hospital. Her bond with Esther, which had started well over a decade before in London, was stronger than any friendship she could ever imagine building with anyone else. But Issy was someone she could see herself building a bond with too, and by the time the rehearsal was over the two women had exchanged numbers.

The day of the wedding itself dawned bright, and the view from St Jude's across the clifftop to the sea was almost as breathtaking as the sight of the bride. Danni, who'd agreed to be maid of honour, despite feeling like an ostrich egg on legs, had welled up the moment she saw her best friend when Esther had come down the stairs at her parents' house.

'My brother is officially the luckiest man in the world.'

'You look beautiful.' Esther's father, Patrick, had been even less successful at holding back the emotion than Danni, and her mother didn't even try.

'My darling girl. You deserve the best day and the happiest marriage, and I know you're going to have that with Joe.' Caroline had slipped an arm around her daughter's waist as she spoke, and she'd held out her other hand to Danni. 'What makes it even better is that today you two finally become sisters. Call it in-law if you will, but we know it's a deeper bond than that. We've called you our girls for years, and now it's official.'

It was typical of Esther's family to make Danni feel special and loved, even on their daughter's big day. She wouldn't have her parents standing watching her descend the stairs when she eventually married Charlie, but she had a found family she knew she could rely on. Nicola had accepted the invitation to Esther and Joe's wedding, but both Danni and Joe knew it wasn't a certainty that she'd turn up. Even if she did, there'd be no heartfelt sentiments for her only son. Like Danni, Joe had long since learnt to cultivate other relationships. After his return from Australia, he'd quickly grown close to Charlie, and so it had been no surprise when he'd asked Danni's fiancé to be his best man. Esther's other bridesmaid was Angela, a friend of Joe's from Brisbane, who'd recently moved to the UK to take a job at St Piran's, and whom everyone called Chooky. Aidan and Jase were ushers, and there were so many of the team from A&E on the guest list that the hospital had needed to arrange extra agency cover. It felt all day as though Danni was surrounded by family, and she could tell her brother felt the same way.

Nicola eventually put in an appearance, turning up late and clattering in with her partner Paul to the back of the church, midway through Esther and Joe's vows. Later on, she loudly gave unwanted and unnecessary advice to the captain of the boat that took them along the coast from Port Agnes to the reception venue in Port Kara. Esther and Joe had arranged a vintage double-decker bus to take guests from the church down to the harbour, which was lovely, but the boat trip itself was spectacular, passing the dramatic cliffs at Dagger's Head and showing off the Cornish Atlantic coast at its finest.

The reception was being held at Bocca Felice, an Italian restaurant, with a beautiful terrace overlooking the bay below, which made it look and feel as though they were in Sorrento. There was a marquee pitched in the grounds, where there'd be dancing late into the evening. Every moment of the wedding had been carefully thought out, and Danni couldn't imagine anything that would have made it more perfect. It was everything a wedding should be and more, until shortly after eight o'clock, when the band had begun playing, and Esther and Joe had just had their first dance. That's when something happened to change the atmosphere.

'Doesn't it embarrass you?' Lucas suddenly appeared out of

the shadows, the sneer on his face twisting the features Danni had once thought so handsome.

'What, you turning up uninvited?' She'd been on her way back from the marquee to the terrace, the heat getting to her far more quickly now that she was so far along in her pregnancy.

'Huh!' He grabbed her arm, his fingers digging into the flesh and making her gasp in pain. 'Standing up there pretending to be Esther's best friend when you spent all those years desperately fantasising about what you wanted to do to her fiancé. Every time I so much as looked at you, you were like a bitch on heat.'

This time it was his words that made her gasp; it couldn't have made her reel any harder if he'd slapped her across the face. What made it worse was that she knew there was some truth in his words. The sight of him made her flesh crawl now, but even that didn't compare to her gut-wrenching reaction when she thought about how close she'd come to betraying her best friend for such a repugnant man. But she hadn't, and she knew that was all that mattered to Esther. So she refused to let Lucas see that he still had the power to get to her.

'Take your hands off me, Lucas. Now!' As she tried to yank her arm away from him, he just tightened his grip.

'Maybe I should give you what you wanted all that time. Wouldn't that be a thrill, us finally living out all your fantasies, behind Esther's back, not to mention the father of your baby?'

'I'd rather die, now let me go!' She screamed the words this time, trying to kick out at him as he held on to her, and instinctively wrapping her other arm around her bump.

'You heard her. Let her go. Right now.' Esther was running towards them, barefoot and with the skirt of her dress hiked up to aid her movement.

'What, are you still jealous?' Lucas laughed, finally releasing

Danni's arm, the angry imprints of his fingernails visible even under the muted glow of the festoon lights.

'Just go, Lucas, no one wants you here.' Esther's tone was calm, but there was a flash of defiance in her eyes. She was the kindest person Danni had ever met, but she'd also seen how fearless her friend could be when she was protecting the people she loved.

Suddenly Lucas's expression changed, the laughter dying in his throat as he looked at her. 'There was never any need for you to be jealous, you're still the love of my life. You always will be.'

'It's unfortunate for you that you didn't turn out to be mine.' There was no glee in Esther's tone, just a matter-of-factness that made it all the more convincing.

'And I suppose Joe is?'

'Yes, he is, but so is Danni. You tried for all those years to come between us, and you never managed it. So why don't you do us all a favour, yourself included, and just leave St Piran's and start again?'

'You don't really want me to go, not deep down.' His arrogance was breathtaking and, if Danni hadn't seen it for herself, she wasn't sure she'd have believed it.

'It would be the best wedding gift anyone could give me.' Not waiting for him to reply, Esther took hold of Danni's hand, and turned them both around to head back to the marquee. When they were about twenty feet away, she turned slightly.

'Is he following us?' Danni whispered the words.

'Nope, just standing there watching, like the sad, lonely man he deserves to be.'

'I'm sorry.' Danni bit her lip as they reached the marquee, the sound of laughter and singing filling the air around them.

'Don't you dare, you've got nothing to apologise for. I love you and there's nothing I wouldn't do for you, and I know you feel the same way about me, because you've already proved it. Are you okay?'

'I'm not sure.' Danni was shaking and Esther hugged her so tightly that for a moment it was hard to breathe, but then she stepped back.

'Did he hurt you?' Fire flashed in Esther's eyes and she looked ready to launch herself in Lucas's direction.

'No, but I think he wanted to, and he knew he was scaring me.'

'Bastard.' Esther took hold of her hand. 'I heard you tell him to let you go, but I didn't hear what happened before that.'

'He said...' Danni hesitated for a moment, bile rising in her throat. 'He said he'd give me what I've always wanted. It felt like a threat, and I told him the thought disgusted me, but I'm scared of what he might have tried if you hadn't turned up.'

'Oh Dan, it'll be okay, I promise. I'm never going to let him hurt you.'

Tears stung Danni's eyes as she looked at Esther, she had no idea how she'd got lucky enough to find a friend who was so loyal, but she knew she didn't deserve it. 'I was such an idiot to ever let myself get close to him. I'd give anything to take that back. I'm so sorry.'

As Danni repeated her apology, Esther shook her head, still clutching her hand. 'I'd never allow that idiot to come between us, and this has got to stop. Right now. Lucas has always been a nasty piece of work, but what he's done tonight has crossed a line and we've got to report it.'

'Who to?' Danni was still shaking, part of her wanting to just forget what had happened, but a bigger part of her knowing that Esther was right. Lucas was never going to stop unless someone made him, that much was obvious now.

'I don't know. To the hospital first, the HR department, and then to the police if we have to. But we need to do something.'

'You're right.' Danni nodded, placing a hand on her bump. This wasn't just about her any more, or even Esther. She had a child to think of, and she wouldn't let Lucas Newman spoil that. It was time to close the chapter on the past, once and for all, and if Lucas wasn't prepared to let it go, they'd have to make him.

'We'll do it once I'm back at work.'

'No.' Danni's response was resolute, and the shock on Esther's face was obvious.

'I thought you said—'

Danni cut her off. 'I just meant there's no need to wait. I'll do it on Monday. It's time I stood up to him and took away the last bit of power he thinks he's got over me.'

'He's never had anything over you, you're far too brilliant for that.' Esther planted a kiss on Danni's cheek and hugged her again. Only letting go when her new husband called out.

'Come on you two, you're missing all the fun.' Joe strode over towards them. 'Amy is leading a rendition of Lijah Byrne's latest number one: "That Woman's My World". She stormed the stage when the band started the song, and she grabbed the mic to tell everyone he wrote the song for her when they were still at school. I think she might regret all of this in the morning!'

'She's actually got a great voice.' Charlie arrived behind Joe, moving forward to put his arm around Danni, and all the horror of Lucas's sudden appearance began to fade away.

'She has and an even bigger benefit is that it got our mother off her chair and onto the dancefloor. She actually looks like she's enjoying herself.' Joe smiled, and if it hurt him to think Nicola might be anything but happy at her son's wedding, he didn't show it, but Danni couldn't help asking.

'Does it ever bother you the way she is? It's your wedding after all and your family should be making it special for you.'

'You have.' Joe dropped a kiss on her forehead and the feeling of belonging got even stronger. 'As long as I've got you, I've got all the family that matters. Now let's get back in there before we miss the finale of Amy's performance; the sentiment of the song sits right for today.'

It was Danni's turn to smile as Joe kissed his new wife on the lips. 'That woman really is your world, big brother, and I couldn't be happier for the two of you.'

'And you're mine.' Charlie held her closer still, as they made their way into the marquee, just as Amy attempted to hit the highest note of the song. Danni had found her place in the world and there was no one she'd rather share her life with than the people she was surrounded by. Not even Lucas had been able to spoil that feeling, and she couldn't imagine anything ever could.

Danni had barely seen her mother in hours, except from a distance. She'd spent a lot of the evening after Amy's song on the dance floor with Paul, flailing her arms around and seeming not to care that she'd made herself the centre of attention. Yet when the toastmaster had asked, earlier in the day, when the main speeches were over, whether anyone else had something they wanted to share about the bride and groom, she'd been as quiet as a mouse. And, when Danni had looked over, her mother seemed to sink deeper into her chair, like a school kid desperately trying to avoid eye contact with the teacher. It had been left to Danni to represent their side of the family, and she hadn't been able to stop herself from crying when she'd spoken about just how much Joe and Esther meant to her. Even then her mother had seemed unmoved and, when Danni had looked in her direction again, her face had been masklike. Even a casual observer would probably have reacted more to the speeches than Nicola had, but Danni hadn't really expected anything else. So, when her mother grabbed hold of her elbow and pulled her into a quiet corner of the marquee, to tell her that she and Paul were heading off, the last thing Danni had envisaged was any kind of meaningful goodbye.

'I'm glad you made it; I know it meant a lot to Joe.' Danni gave her mother a perfunctory peck on the cheek. It was the kind of polite parting she might have had with a friend of a friend.

'It was good to see you both.'

'Was it?' Danni hadn't been able to stop herself from asking the question. Her mother hadn't chosen to spend her time at the wedding with her children, but then it would probably have felt more uncomfortable if she had. This was their normal, after all.

'Of course it was. You've both grown up to be people your father would have been very proud of.' Nicola's expression was still blank, like a very bad actor reading from a script she didn't really understand.

'But we don't make you proud, do we?'

Nicola shook her head, although for the first time her mask-like expression slipped, and she frowned. 'I've got no right to claim any pride in you. None of what you've achieved is down to me. Any parental input came from your dad; he was always the nurturer when you were little, and you're both far more like him than you are me. It's only because of him that you got the education you had. He put money aside for it before we were even married. Having kids was one of the first things we talked about, and he was already planning for it.'

'So, you wanted children then?' Danni couldn't keep the surprise out of her voice. She'd often wondered if Joe had come along by mistake, and then her mother had thought she might as well have a second, as much as anything to take the pressure off having to provide companionship for Joe. Or whether they'd both been mistakes. It was hard to believe Nicola had actively planned to become a parent, but she was nodding.

'I wanted children because your father did, and because it was what everyone did back then. Both families assumed we would, and I lost count of how many times I was asked on our wedding day whether we'd be trying for a baby straight away. Even before I met your dad, and realised how desperate he was to be a father, I knew I'd have children at some point, because I didn't think I had a choice. It's not like now. Yes, there were a few people who were career driven and adamant they didn't want kids, but I didn't even have that reason. I just didn't have those maternal feelings you were supposed to have. The few women who were honest about not wanting children were told they'd regret it, or that there must be something wrong with them. So, I went with the flow and hoped the feelings would come once you arrived.'

'And did they?' Danni was willing her mother to give even the slightest hint of a nod, but instead she shook her head, and the space in her chest that her mother's love should have filled felt emptier than ever.

'No.' For a moment Nicola looked down at the floor, and then she met Danni's gaze. 'But I could see how incredibly happy being a father made your dad, and that made me happy in return. He was my world, and you two were his. I didn't feel guilty about not feeling the way I should, because you had all the love you needed from him. And because of that I knew we'd muddle through okay, but then, when he died… I had no idea what to do with you.'

'So, you sent us off to boarding school and tried to forget you even had us?' Danni wrapped her arms around her bump. She couldn't imagine anything happening that would ever make her send her child away. And as much as it hurt to hear her mother admitting how easy it had been for her, Danni wanted to at least try to understand.

'I knew it would be better for you than staying with me. With your dad gone, I couldn't keep up the pretence that I knew what I was doing, or that I was one day going to wake up and be the mother of the year.' Nicola sounded as though she meant every word, and maybe she was right. Maybe the distance between her and her children really had been the best thing for all of them, despite how much they'd longed to go home. But there was something else Danni had to ask.

'Do you regret having children?' Danni had instigated the conversation, so she only had herself to blame for the way it was going, but once she'd started, she couldn't stop. It was like a barely healed over scar that she didn't seem able to resist ripping open.

'Yes and no. I don't regret having you, because you brought your father so much joy, and you've done a lot of good things that make the world a better place.' Her mother's eyes had gone glassy. It was like seeing a mannequin suddenly expressing emotion and Danni had to rub her own eyes to make sure she wasn't imagining it. 'But I regret becoming a mother; I was never up to the job. Mothers are supposed to love their children more than they love anything, or anyone, else. But I could never prioritise you in that way. Your father was always the most important person to me, and now it's Paul. I don't know, maybe there's just something missing in me. Or maybe it's just that there are some people, like me, who aren't meant to be parents because they don't want to be. That would have been fine if I'd followed my gut, but I didn't. I should never have assumed those feelings would suddenly develop out of nowhere. If I was young now, I'd be honest with myself and everyone else, and say I don't want to have children, because I'm not prepared to put them ahead of myself, or my partner. Choosing to become a parent, when I knew that, meant I dealt you and Joe a bad hand in life. I wasn't a proper mother, in any true sense of the word, but I don't regret having you, because raising two such accomplished children is probably the best thing I never did.'

It was a mic-drop moment and, if it had been a movie, the two of them would have hugged and cried, and told each other that this was the start of a whole new era in their relationship. Except Port Kara was a long way from Hollywood, and all Nicola did was give a small nod of her head, before turning her back on Danni and walking away. There were no promises to come and visit the baby, or to use his impending arrival as the chance to try again, and for Nicola to be a far better grandmother than she had been a mother. Yet somehow it was still enough. Knowing that Nicola's parenting hadn't been a reflection on her children, only on herself, turned out to be all Danni had needed to hear. And, even without the Hollywood ending, it was a life-changing moment.

It had been a beautiful wedding, but Wendy still found herself looking at her watch far more than she should have done. It had nothing to do with her being bored, and everything to do with worrying about how long she'd left Chloe on her own. Both of the girls were away in the camper at another music festival, which had been arranged months before, when the idea of Chloe coming to stay with them indefinitely would have felt as unlikely as Wendy being asked to join an astronaut training programme. She'd kept herself shut up in the spare room for the majority of time since leaving the hospital with Stan, Gary's Border Terrier, the only company she seemed able to tolerate. But even though Chloe wasn't interacting with them in a way that offered any reassurance that she was eventually going to be okay, at least Wendy could check on her. She was terrified she might do something stupid, and that included responding to Mike's attempts to contact her. She'd been adamant at first that it was over, convinced that Mike had only ever proposed because she was pregnant. But the hurt and the loneliness made her vulnerable, something Wendy knew Mike was skilled at spotting. If he got through to Chloe at the right moment, there was a chance he could change her mind, and the thought of her going back to him made Wendy's blood run cold.

'Do you want to leave?' Gary asked the question when he caught Wendy looking at her watch for the second time in the space of about two minutes.

'No, don't be silly, you're having a great time.'

'I've already had my great time. I've seen my two wonderful friends get married, eaten a fantastic meal, had a laugh with my mates, and best of all I've danced with the most beautiful woman in the room.' Gary leant forward and kissed her briefly. 'I'm ready to go home and I know you are. You're not going to relax until you know Chloe is okay.'

'I'm sorry, I must be driving you mad.'

'It makes me love you even more. I'm not sure I could be nearly so charitable if Rachel's new husband needed help.' Gary pulled a face.

'Me neither.' Wendy had met him once, at Albert's birthday party, and Rachel had definitely downgraded. He'd spent the whole afternoon talking about how much bonus he was going to earn, and what kind of car he was going to buy as a result. He was a boring arse, and she'd caught Rachel watching Gary a couple of times, the look of regret on her face painfully obvious. But Wendy never once had cause to wonder if Gary felt the same way that day. It was strange, having been cheated on by Mike, that her thoughts hadn't immediately gone there. It was probably because Gary was so good at making her feel secure in his feelings for her, and it was another reason she found it easy to care about Chloe.

Mike's actions would have undermined whatever self-esteem she might once have had – Wendy knew that because she'd been there, and Chloe had no family support to help her build that back up. It had made Wendy realise just how lucky she was. 'It's different with Chloe, though, isn't it? She didn't get involved with Mike until long after we'd separated, and she's been through a lot in life.'

'I know, but she's going to be okay.' Gary squeezed her hand.

'How can you be so sure?' Wendy held her breath, hoping that whatever he said next would be able to convince her of that, because she really wanted it to be true.

'Because she's got you now.' Taking hold of her hand, he stood up, gently pulling Wendy to her feet. 'Let's go home.'

'You've got no idea how much I love you.' She took a step towards him, holding his gaze.

'If it's even half as much as I love you, I'll consider myself far luckier than I deserve to be.' Gary smiled. 'But today has made me realise something.'

'What's that?'

'That I can't wait for us to get married.'

'Me neither.' Wendy didn't have a shred of doubt that it was what she wanted, but she also knew she couldn't even think about it until Chloe was more settled. Luckily, she was engaged to the kindest and most patient man she'd ever met, and she was almost certain he'd understand. But getting Chloe to start taking steps towards a new life was a problem for another day. For now, Gary was right, all she wanted to do was get home and check on the young woman they'd taken into their home, and she was praying that the sense of foreboding that had plagued her all day would come to nothing.

18

Danni's last job before going on maternity leave was to glue together the eyebrow of a boy who'd had a somewhat over-enthusiastic conker fight with his sister. According to their mother, it had started off in a fairly civilised way but when Poppy had accidentally glanced the side of Roman's face with her conker, he'd retaliated, and from that point on, an all-out war had ensued. The truce had only arrived when there was too much blood pouring into Roman's eye for them to continue.

'You'd imagine that at eight and ten I could take my eyes off them for a moment, wouldn't you?' Roman's mother, Maxine, pulled a face. 'I thought the days of me having to watch them like a hawk were over, but oh no, they can still get themselves into all kinds of trouble. You must think I'm a terrible mother.'

'Far from it. You can't watch them every second and, even if you did, accidents still happen.' Danni had learnt not to judge most situations a long time ago. The majority of the time she could put herself in the shoes of the people she was helping. Only the week before she'd had a distraught couple in, new parents of a very colicky baby who barely seemed to sleep. The mum had already been up three times with the baby in the night, so her partner got up the fourth time and had taken the baby into the sitting room. He'd been up at 4 a.m. the morning before, to start his shift as a delivery driver, so it was hardly a surprise that he'd dropped off with the baby in his arms. At some point the baby had slipped from his grip, sliding down his body and on to the floor, waking both of them up with an almighty scream. They'd been terrified at the harm that might have been caused to their little girl, and blaming themselves for something that could so easily happen in a tough situation, when exhaustion made it hard to think straight and the decision to just sit down on the sofa with the baby for a while seemed so obvious.

Danni did everything she could to reassure people in those sorts of situations that what had happened could happen to anyone. There were times when Danni did judge, however, and none more so than when parents deliberately hurt or neglected their children. It had always got to her, partly because without her father there was a chance her mother might have strayed from indifference to neglect. As much as Danni had hated boarding school, she suspected it was what had saved her and Joe from that. But the hardest part about dealing with cases like that was because innocent children had put their trust in someone who had let them down in the worst possible way. She'd wondered whether having a child of her own might heighten those already intense feelings, or if that might affect the way she did her job, but she couldn't know that until it happened.

Thankfully the baby who'd slipped on to the floor had been absolutely fine. Her parents had taken her home after saying thank you about a hundred times, and pledging that they'd never, ever take the risk of falling asleep with her like that again, despite Danni's reassurances that exhaustion was to blame and not them. She wouldn't judge Maxine for her son having sustained an injury when the play fighting with his sister got out of hand either. This was parenting and she was going into it knowing there'd be hard bits and that she would undoubtedly make mistakes, but she still couldn't wait for the biggest adventure of her life to start with Charlie by her side.

'Well one thing I know is that I'll be telling their father he was wrong. The banning of conker fights at school isn't health and safety gone mad, there's a very good reason for it and I'll be banning them at my place from now on too. I don't expect him to follow suit, but he can't say I haven't warned him. And he'll be the one needing a wound glued if he lets the kids get blood on the carpets at his place. His new wife has got it right and puts him in his place when he needs it. She's probably the one I should be speaking to if I want to make sure the kids are looked after properly.' Maxine lowered her voice to almost a whisper, which Roman would have struggled to hear, even if he hadn't been engrossed in playing a game on her phone, with his sister watching his every move. 'I like her better than him anyway.'

Danni couldn't suppress the smile that was tugging at the corners of her mouth. Maxine was clearly one of those people who said what she thought, and it could only be a good thing for the children that she seemed to have a positive relationship with their father's new wife. It made her think of something else she'd wondered from time to time: what her father would have made of Paul, her mother's new partner. He wasn't an awful person, just equally as indifferent to Nicola's children as she was. But then he'd never had any of his own and he was probably just following her lead. Danni and Joe were always treated politely, with the kind of cursory enquiry about their wellbeing that you might make to a casual acquaintance, but that was as far as the relationship went. When Richard had asked Danni if her stepfather would be giving her away at the wedding, she'd been confused for a moment about who he meant.

It wasn't a role Paul held, even in name alone, because he and Nicola had never married, and her mother had made it clear why. When Danni had told her mum that she was engaged, Nicola's response had been 'What on earth for?', and when Danni had said it was because she loved Charlie, she'd been rewarded with a speech about how traditional marriage ceremonies were outdated, and that she should consider a handfasting ceremony instead, which Paul had apparently performed several times for other couples. Her mother had revealed then that she and Paul had been through the ceremony, and that it had been a wonderful day, surrounded by their closest friends. Danni had been angry with herself, that she still allowed her mother's actions to hurt, when nothing Nicola did should surprise her. Her mother did it in such a casual way, like she wasn't even aware of it, but the revelation had still been like a physical blow. Nicola valued the circle of friends she had down in Bristol more than her own children, and Danni couldn't pretend that wasn't painful to discover that she and Joe had been sidelined once again. Although the conversation with her mother at Joe's wedding had helped with those feelings. She knew now why Nicola was the way she was, and it was easier not to take her prioritising other things and other people so personally.

Danni already knew it would be different for her. She adored Joe, and she valued her friends too, some of whom couldn't have meant more to her even if there had been blood ties between them. But the love she had for Charlie, and that they already shared for their unborn son, had a power like nothing she'd ever known before. She would never really understand her mother, but the best thing she could do for her own wellbeing was to accept that nothing she did was ever going to change the way Nicola felt.

'Okay Roman, you're all patched up and ready to go.' Danni smiled as the young boy finally looked up from his phone. 'You need to try not to touch the wound for at least the next twenty-four hours, and avoid getting it wet for five days.'

'Does that mean I don't have to have a wash?' Roman's face lit up and Danni couldn't help laughing.

'Not quite, but I'd suggest a bath rather than a shower, and it might be a good idea to carefully put a shower cap on and pull it down past where the wound is, just in case. Which means you'll probably get away with not having to wash your hair for a few days.' She winked and Roman let out an excited 'woo hoo' in response.

'Thank you so much.' Maxine touched her arm briefly. 'You certainly know how to handle children and your little one is going to be very lucky to have you.'

'That's really lovely of you to say, thank you.' Danni opened the door of the consulting room. 'Enjoy the rest of your day, and maybe stay away from conkers from now on.'

'Oh, they will be, don't you worry!' Maxine ushered the children out of the room and, as Danni closed the door behind them, she took a deep breath. The next time she was on duty, she'd be returning to work after her maternity leave. She just hoped in the meantime she could prove Maxine right, and be the best possible mum she could be to the son she couldn't wait to meet.

* * *

Danni had specified that she didn't want a big send-off. So, when Esther had suggested they go for a coffee and cake at The Cookie Jar café in Port Agnes, as a low-key way to mark her last day at work, it had sounded ideal. Anything more than that and she was worried the emotion of it might get to her. It was silly really, she'd be able to see her friends on a regular basis and she knew they'd all still be there for her, but it wouldn't be the same. These were the people who'd got her through one of the toughest periods in her life, and they'd also been there when she'd found the sort of happiness she'd never really believed she deserved. It would be weird going into this next phase of her life without having them around every step of the way.

'Do you think they'll have any of that pistachio cake?' Danni had thought about the cake she'd had on a recent visit to The Cookie Jar far more often than was probably acceptable. If she closed her eyes and concentrated hard enough, she could almost taste it. But not quite. The idea of getting there and discovering they'd sold out for the day was something she might have to steel herself for. Given that they were going at almost closing time, it was almost certain that the best stuff would be long gone.

'When I called them to ask if they were still doing late closing on a Friday, Sandy did mention they'd be getting a delivery of cakes from Mehenick's tonight, ready for the weekend, so your luck might just be in.' Esther grinned as she pulled into a space two roads away from The Cookie Jar. Mehenick's Bakery on the harbour in Port Agnes was run by Jago and Ruth, who were Ella's parents, one of the local midwives, and the bakery was renowned throughout Cornwall and beyond. Despite Mehenick's having its own small coffee shop, it was Jago who made quite a lot of the items sold in The Cookie Jar, and it would have been no surprise to learn that the pistachio cake was one of his creations. 'By the way, what was the verdict on whether you could consider giving birth at the midwifery unit?'

'Not recommended.' Danni hauled herself out of Esther's car as she spoke. It was getting harder and harder to get out of a low seat without looking a bit like a beetle stuck on its back. 'I'm just too damn old apparently, and because we've had a few incidents of low foetal movement, they think I should err on the side of caution.'

'And don't forget you can get much stronger drugs in the hospital!' Esther laughed. 'If I ever have a baby, I think I'd like to be numbed from the neck down and woken up when it's all over.'

'You'll be amazing, if the time comes. You might not be the tallest person I know, but you are the toughest.' Danni had seen Esther go through things that would break most people. The worst of which was when a former patient who'd developed an obsession with her had abducted her. Danni had been worried that the experience might fundamentally change who her friend was, and she'd have understood if it had. She'd also have understood if Esther hadn't felt able to go back to nursing, even though that would have been an awful loss to the medical profession. To Danni's huge relief, Esther bounced back in a way no one had believed possible, and Danni admired her so much for how she'd dealt with it. She had no doubt Esther could handle everything that motherhood threw at her, she just hadn't dared hope that children might be on the agenda for her best friend any time soon. She was seven years younger than Danni, which meant there was less pressure in some ways, but Joe was almost forty, so it wouldn't have been a surprise if it was something he'd started to think about. Despite promising herself from the moment Esther and Joe got engaged that she wouldn't ask, somehow, on the short walk to the café, she couldn't help herself.

'So, is it something you and Joe have talked about? Starting a family I mean.'

'It would have been a bit crazy of us to get married without talking it through.' Esther grinned. 'And, yes, we both want kids.

But we want to find the right house and have a few adventures together first. There's no rush.'

'Of course not.' It wasn't fair for Danni to feel even a little bit disappointed that she and Esther wouldn't be embarking on motherhood at the same time, but she still wished they would be.

'The upside is, me and Joe will be able to get tonnes of practice with our little nephew, whenever you and Charlie need a bit of time to yourselves. That way, I'll be ready to have my first baby by the time you're having your second.'

'Let's not get ahead of ourselves. I think we should see how I do with number one first!' Danni laughed, but the frisson of fear that she'd been working so hard to push down suddenly fizzed in her stomach again.

'Okay, no pressure; for now at least.' Esther grinned again and hooked an arm through Danni's as they walked the final stretch towards the café. Then Esther let go, moving ahead of her. 'Let me get the door.'

'Surprise!' The chorus went up almost before the door was fully open, and Danni's hand flew to her mouth, half in shock and half to stop herself swearing. All of her closest friends from the hospital were there, and there was a table laden with what looked to be all her favourite foods. Right in the middle was a huge pistachio cake, with her name and the words *'World's Best Doctor'* piped on the top.

'We said no grand gestures!' Danni looked at Esther for a moment, who gave an apologetic shrug.

'You didn't think I was going to let my best friend go without a proper send-off, did you?'

'I guess I should have known.' Danni hugged her. 'Thank you so much.'

'As lovely as this display of affection is,' Aidan called over from the far end of the table, 'there's literally a cake with your name on it waiting to be eaten, and there are at least seven sausage rolls with my name on them too.'

'I think you might have some competition on that front. I've seen how much food the A&E staff can hoover up at the end of a shift.' Gwen raised her eyebrows. 'You can always do what my nephew used to do at all our family parties.'

'And what was that?' Whatever it was, Aidan looked ready to give it a try, if it meant he got his pick of the sausage rolls.

'He used to lick everything he wanted. That way no one else would even try to take them off him. Although he did stop when he was about seven.'

'If you even try to lick the sausage rolls before I get my share, I swear to God I'll put this fork right through the back of your hand, and Danni will have to come off maternity leave straight away to save you.' Amy shot Aidan a look that suggested she meant business.

'Are you going to miss all of this bickering?' Isla smiled as she looked at Danni, and for a moment all she could was nod in response, the emotion she'd been so worried would overwhelm her threatening to do just that. Finally, she found her voice.

'You've got no idea how much I'm going to miss it, but I am coming back.'

'Yes, you bloody well are, even if we have to come and drag you back to work.' Esther put an arm around her waist. 'Now let's get this party started before Aidan and Amy get so hangry they decide to fight to the death over who gets the biggest sausage roll.'

'Good idea.' Danni leant into her friend for a moment, looking around the table at all the people who'd made the effort to come and celebrate with her, many of them at the end of a very long day. If it took a village to raise a child, she already had it in the friendships she'd made, and suddenly it was far easier to push that frisson of fear that had been in danger of coming back up the surface, back down where it belonged.

* * *

Wendy's heart sank as she scraped the food off Chloe's abandoned plate and into the bin. She'd finally agreed to join them for dinner, instead of hiding out in her room, where she'd been holed up for almost twenty-four hours a day since she'd come home from the hospital. Wendy had hoped that joining them for dinner would be a tiny step towards Chloe making some kind of recovery from what had happened. She'd never just 'get over it', no one ever did when they lost a child, but Chloe would have to find a way to learn to live with it and Wendy was willing to do whatever it took to help her. She'd read everything she could about child loss, in the hope it would stop her from accidentally saying the wrong thing, and most of the sites said the pain would eventually lessen, but that it would take a long time and that Chloe would almost certainly need some help to work through her feelings. She'd been referred to a specialist counsellor, but she hadn't made the call to set up the first appointment. She'd also said she didn't feel ready to arrange Beau's funeral yet, even though she'd been told that the hospital's rules meant he couldn't stay in the mortuary for more than twenty-one days, and Wendy had wondered at that point if she should contact Mike. But it wasn't her place, so instead all she could do was to be ready to listen and help in whatever way Chloe needed. That didn't make it any easier for Wendy not to worry herself sick about the desperately sad young woman who'd sat silently at the dinner table, pushing her food around her plate. She'd always been very slim, but she was beginning to look painfully thin. And, knowing her history, that terrified Wendy too.

'What are we going to do? She's not eating anything.' Tears burned at the back of Wendy's eyes as she looked at Gary. It was concerning enough how little Zara ate, and she was still watching her daughter much more closely than she wanted to. Now she had two of them to worry about, and Chloe's disinterest in food seemed far more extreme.

'I don't know, sweetheart, but she looks so pale. I'm really worried.'

'Me too. Do you think we should try and force her to eat? I know it sounds stupid, but maybe if we said she has to eat something if she wants to stay. I don't want to resort to that but—'

'That's the worst thing you could possibly do.' Zara suddenly appeared in the kitchen, her eyes wide as she turned towards her mother. 'It'll just make things worse; she needs help, but that's not it.'

Wendy caught her breath. Zara was still her little girl in some ways, even at seventeen, but at that moment she seemed older and wiser than Wendy had ever felt. 'I know you're right, but we're really worried about her.'

'I am too and it's weird because she was the one who helped me.' Zara swallowed so hard it was audible. 'She noticed I was skipping meals, and telling you and Dad that I'd already eaten, when it was obvious to her that I hadn't. Clo told me that she went through the same as a teenager. I denied it at first, but I started to talk to her about it a lot more a few weeks before Beau died.'

'Oh sweetheart.' Wendy wanted to tell Zara that she'd known too, and that she'd even talked to Chloe about it, but that would just have muddied the waters and this wasn't about her. It must have been huge for Zara to admit this, and it was clear she'd done it out of her own concern for Chloe. So, if Wendy really wanted to help both of them, she had to avoid saying anything that would make Zara shut down again. 'Is there anything you can think of that she said, which might help us to support her?'

'It's not about the food, it's about having something you can control. When I talked to her about it, I realised that was something we had in common. She was struggling at home when she stopped eating as a teenager...' Zara looked at her mother again, and it was as if Wendy had been punched in the gut.

'And you were too?' She was desperate not to cry, or to put her own feelings at the centre of all of this, but the tears welling up in her eyes were completely out of her control. She'd cried more in the last few weeks than she could ever remember doing in her life, even when Mike had left, but her heart felt like it had been broken over and over again just lately.

'I wasn't struggling here, with you and Gary. But with Dad, it was like he'd forgotten I existed most of the time, once he'd left, and I don't think me and Alice would have seen anything of him if it hadn't been for Clo. I couldn't do anything about how he was acting, and it made me feel useless, like I didn't have any control over a huge part of my own life.' The maturity in Zara's words was breathtaking, and Wendy knew that a lot of that must have come from her daughter's conversations with Chloe. They had a shared experience which had allowed Zara to gain more insight than Wendy could ever have given her, but it turned out there was more to come. 'The only thing I could control was what I was eating, but I didn't even realise that's why I was doing it, until Clo told me that she'd done it too. It was because of her that I agreed to go to the support group at the hospital.'

'I had no idea you were going.' A few weeks before, this revelation would almost certainly have angered Wendy; the idea that Chloe would overstep the mark like that and not even tell Wendy what was going on, acting like she was Zara's mother instead. But all Wendy felt now was an overwhelming gratitude towards

Chloe, and another one of those waves of affection for her crashed over Wendy like a tsunami.

'I didn't want to worry you, and I've been making progress.' Zara straightened her shoulders. 'It's not a quick fix, the counsellor told us that and Clo knows it too. Things can trigger an eating disorder and make it come back, and I think that's what's happening to her. So the best way I can think of to help her, is to tell her I need her to come with me to the support group and that I can't face going any more if she doesn't. She offered before, but I wanted to go by myself. I'll just tell her I've changed my mind and that I'm struggling doing it on my own.'

'Do you think she'll go for it?' Wendy held her breath, until her daughter nodded. 'I'm so proud of you, sweetheart, you do know that, don't you?'

'I always have.' Zara suddenly closed the gap between them, wrapping her arms around her mother. 'I'm so lucky I've got you and Gary, but Clo hasn't really got anyone.'

'Yes she has, she's got all of us and we'll do whatever it takes to help her get well again.' Gary's tone was resolute, as he put his arms around the two of them. Chloe might not realise it yet, but she had a family now who weren't going to give up on her. Wendy just hoped that Zara's hunch was right, and that they already held the key to getting her the help she so badly needed, because the alternative was too scary to even think about.

19

Wendy had done her best to back off from trying to fix Chloe's relationship with food, since Zara had made her realise it went way beyond her skill set, and that her eating disorder was so deeply embedded she needed the kind of professional help the support group could offer. But that still didn't make it possible to stop worrying about Chloe almost constantly. She seemed glued to her phone a lot of the time and, when Wendy had gently suggested that a walk on the beach and a break from her phone might be good for her, she'd reluctantly agreed, but only if Wendy went with her. She'd said she couldn't do it alone and that just the thought of being outside by herself made her feel panicky. Wendy had been more than happy to accompany her and, in the research she'd done about how best to support Chloe, panic attacks were listed as a fairly common response to the kind of trauma she'd been through. So the last thing she wanted was to push Chloe too hard. Thankfully being out on the beach had seemed to be doing her some good, but less than ten minutes into the walk she'd started to get twitchy.

'I wish I'd brought my phone.' Chloe had started pulling a

her clothes as she spoke, and moving in the kind of jerky way that suggested she couldn't have kept still even if she'd wanted to, almost like an addict waiting for their next fix. The moment they'd got home, she'd grabbed her phone, frantically scrolling like her life depended on it.

'Are you messaging Mike?' Wendy had tried to keep her tone level, doing her best not to sound like she was making a judgement. It would hardly have been surprising if Chloe was talking to him. There was a funeral to arrange for Beau after all, but whenever Wendy had tried to broach the subject with Chloe, she'd just said she wasn't ready. Wendy understood why she couldn't face saying her final goodbyes to her baby, but Chloe couldn't put it off indefinitely. If she didn't organise a funeral herself, Beau would be cremated without her even being there. Talking to Mike about that might even have helped her feel ready, but what worried Wendy was if Chloe was talking to him for other reasons, especially if that meant she might end up back with him. Chloe deserved so much more than he could offer her, but Mike was excellent at playing on people's deepest fears and insecurities to get what he wanted, all of which could make talking to him a recipe for disaster.

But Chloe's response to Wendy's question had been determined. 'I never want to talk to him again.'

She hadn't doubted for a moment that Chloe meant what she said, relief washing over her that Mike hadn't managed to manipulate the situation. 'I'm spending a lot of time on a forum for women who've suffered a stillbirth or neonatal loss, that's all. It's really helping me to talk to other people who've been through something similar. If I'm honest, it's the only thing getting me through the days right now.'

Chloe's eyes had filled with tears then, and Wendy had wrapped her arms around her, as relief flooded through her again.

At least she was talking to people who understood, and like the eating disorders support group she'd turned to for help, that understanding was what Chloe needed more than anything right now. Wendy had tried not to worry after that about just how much time Chloe spent on her phone, and how disengaged she was from everyone and everything else. But there was still a nagging feeling inside of her that there must be something more *she* could do.

Wendy had been at the latest get-together of the Miss Adventures club for all of about fifteen minutes, before she'd asked the others for advice.

'How do you support the women you care for when they've lost a baby?' She blurted the question out to Frankie, just as the waiter who'd brought over their tray of drinks disappeared from view. They were at a new cocktail bar in Port Tremellien, Merlin's Cauldron, where all the drinks came with some kind of special effect, from glowing, to smoking, and even changing colour. When Caroline had suggested they give it a go, it was the kind of adventure that had been easy for Wendy to get on board with.

'Not the sort of question I was expecting over a smoked Old Fashioned.' Frankie frowned. 'But I've been thinking about Chloe a lot too.'

Wendy's friends knew about what had happened, and the fact that she and Gary had invited Chloe to live with them until she decided what was next for her, but this was the first time Wendy had seen them in person since Beau had died. 'On the outside she probably looks like she's doing really well. The crying finally seems to have stopped and she's getting support from a group of other women online who've been through a similar loss. But she's barely eating, and she won't talk about a funeral for Beau. I don't want to push her so hard that she feels like she wants to get away from us, but she needs to start making some decisions about Beau's funeral soon.'

'That poor girl. It was hard enough letting go of Charlie, when I made the decision for him to be adopted, but I can't even imagine what it's like for Chloe to have to think about saying goodbye to her baby.' Connie shook her head, and Wendy's heart ached for her too. So many women had to go through pain and loss as mothers, and those were things they couldn't ever fully recover from. But Connie had found a way to live her life without Charlie and, even though the circumstances were completely different, there had to be hope for Chloe too.

'It's so difficult to know how to help, but one thing I'd say, and I'm pretty sure that Gwen would too, is don't try to force Chloe to see too far into the future until she's ready, even if you're trying to get her to think positively.' Frankie exchanged a look with Gwen, who nodded. 'You're going to want to try to fix this. That's what women do, especially mums like us. I'm sure you'd never do this, but saying things like "at least you're still young", or "you've got plenty of time to try again" won't help, it'll just make Chloe feel as if the loss of Beau is being minimised.'

'Frankie's right, nothing can make this better.' Gwen shook her head. 'So, you can't try to achieve that; instead you just need to listen when Chloe wants to talk. Saying Beau's name is something else that's important. The woman I've worked with over the years, who've lost a baby, have often told me that one of the things that hurts the most is people acting like their child never existed. Chloe needs to know she's not the only one thinking about him and wishing he was still here. I'm sure Alice and Zara can help a lot with that too.'

'They've been great, especially Zara, because she's home with us all the time, and she's even managed to persuade Chloe to get some support for her issues with food, which seem to have come back since she lost Beau.' Wendy reached out for her glass. It was reassuring to hear they'd taken the right approach so far, but she still had no idea how to get Chloe to think about arranging a funeral. 'Beau's at the hospital, but if Chloe doesn't make some decisions soon, I'm worried they'll go ahead and arrange a cremation without her.'

'Has she spoken to Issy?' Frankie looked at Wendy as she spoke.

'I don't think so, why?' Issy was one of the team from the Port Agnes midwifery unit where Frankie worked. She also spent part of her week as a midwife within the hospital's maternity department. It was a role some of the midwives decided to take on when St Piran's first opened, so that they could care for a wider range of women with differing needs which couldn't all be accommodated at the unit.

'She's the lead midwife for the hospital's maternity bereavement service, and she offers help and advice to patients who've been through a stillbirth. It helps that she's married to Noah, the vicar at St Jude's, if the parents are thinking about a church service.'

'I think it would be really good for her to do that.' Wendy just hoped it was something she could persuade Chloe to consider.

'The only thing that might make it even tougher, is that Issy is quite heavily pregnant herself at the moment.' Caroline bit her lip. 'She was chatting to Danni at Esther's wedding rehearsal, and her bump was obvious to me then. I know Chloe can't avoid seeing other pregnant women, but I'm guessing that would make the conversation even harder for both of them.'

'Good point and I haven't asked Issy how she's handling the role while she's pregnant herself.' Frankie sighed. 'It might be that she isn't doing the face-to-face sessions at the moment, but I can certainly check if you want me to? And Issy will be able to recommend someone else if not.'

'That would be great, thank you.' Wendy took a sip of the cocktail she'd ordered, which was a marbled combination of purple, green and blue that gave the drink its name of Mermaid's Tail. It would be good to put Chloe in touch with a professional who could talk to her about Beau's funeral arrangements, so that Wendy could follow her friends' advice and just be there to listen when Chloe was ready to talk. She couldn't fix this, no matter how instinctive it was for her to want to make things right for Chloe. All she could do was continue providing the safety net that she and Gary had willingly offered, and which would be there for Chloe for as long as she needed it.

* * *

Wendy had asked her friends whether they thought she should go ahead with hosting the bonfire night get-together that she and Gary had planned in lieu of throwing an engagement party. Their response had been a resounding yes, and she'd been ready to explain that she'd understand if Chloe didn't feel up to being sociable. As it was, Chloe had seemed excited about the idea and had admitted to Wendy and Zara that she'd never been taken to a bonfire night celebration as a child, at least not after her mother had died. When Zara had talked about the idea of making a Guy for the bonfire, Chloe had put down her phone and asked if she could join in. Wendy hadn't been able to suppress a smile when she'd seen the finished results, and Gary had picked up on the reason for her amusement straight away.

'Is it just me, or does that Guy bear more than a passing resemblance to Mike?' He'd laughed as Chloe and Zara had trundled past, with their creation in a wheelbarrow, heading towards the unlit bonfire.

'It's not just you.' She'd laughed too, and she'd begun to allow herself to feel much more hopeful about how Chloe was doing. Two hours later the party was in full swing, and the weather had been kind to them. It was a clear, crisp night, but the now raging bonfire made it possible for the guests to spend the evening in the garden, and the baked potatoes, sausages, and spiced rum punch were all helping to keep everyone warm too.

'Well, if this is what you guys do for a bonfire night party, I cannot wait to see the wedding.' Danni smiled as Wendy came to join the group from A&E, which Gary was already in the middle of. 'Although I appear to be taking the eating for two to extreme levels tonight. I was weighing up whether a third jacket potato was one too many, but seeing as I already look like one, I thought what the hell!'

'You look beautiful.' Wendy wasn't just saying it. Danni could genuinely have been described as glowing, and it wasn't just because they were standing in the reflected light from the flickering flames. 'How are you feeling?'

'Really good. It's been nice to have a bit of time to sort things out after finishing work, and I finally feel ready for when the baby arrives. Although Esther has told me under no circumstances am I to give birth before she gets back from her honeymoon.'

'When is that?'

'On Tuesday, thank God.' Aidan pulled a face.

'Are you missing her at work?' Wendy couldn't help laughing at Aidan's expression.

'Too much, with her and Danni off, I'm stuck with your fiancé and the woman the press are calling Lijah Byrne's muse.' Aidan laughed and then poked his tongue out at Amy and Gary. 'I gave her a lift home from work the other day, and there was actually a photographer in the bushes by my car. I need some warning if I'm going to be papped!'

'So that's all still going on?' It had been the talk of the hospital, when two weeks before, one of Amy's old school friends had sold a story to a national newspaper. She'd told them that Amy had been Lijah Byrne's girlfriend from the age of fourteen to eighteen, and that there was no doubt in her mind that Amy was the inspiration for most of the songs on his new album. She'd also supplied the papers with photos of Amy and Lijah from back then.

'Thankfully most of them lost interest as soon as I told them I'm not in contact with him any more.' Amy affected an air of nonchalance, but there was a hint of something in her eyes that Wendy couldn't quite read, and when she'd had a bit too much champagne at Esther and Joe's wedding, she'd seemed quite keen to lay claim to being Lijah's muse. 'There are one or two desperados hanging on and trying to make a story out of nothing, but I suspect they're from the *Three Ports News*, rather than the tabloids.'

'I still think there'd be no harm you getting back in touch with him. You never know where it might lead.' Isla's suggestion was met with a snort of derision from her friend.

'Just because you and Reuben are madly in love, it doesn't mean we're all destined for a happy ever after. And I still haven't forgiven Reuben for persuading my best friend to go travelling for months on end, and leaving me behind at the hospital.' Amy winked, and it was clear there was no malice in her words. After what Isla had been through following a diagnosis of chronic myeloid leukaemia the year before, everyone was happy that she was making such exciting plans, but no one more so than Amy.

'You'd just better be back by the time Aidan goes on paternity leave, or I really am going to sulk that I've been deserted by everyone.'

'Oh, and what am I, chopped liver?' Gary pretended to look offended, but he couldn't quite pull it off, especially once Amy had thrown her arms around him.

'Sorry Gaz, you know I love you to bits, but if I'm planning what to text to the latest guy I'm talking to online, I don't think you've quite got what Aidan and Isla can offer me in the way of advice.'

'Fair point.' Gary shrugged. 'Although you can always go to Gwen.'

'Hmm, last time I did that, she told me to be upfront and just ask the guy what it was he was looking for.' Amy was already laughing.

'Dare I ask what he was looking for?' Gary raised his eyebrows.

'Someone to call mummy.' Aidan was laughing so much as he interjected, that Wendy wasn't sure she'd heard him right.

'Please tell me you're joking.'

'I wish he was.' Amy shook her head. 'What makes it worse is that he was nearly ten years older than me, and somehow he still saw me as a mother figure. I need to get rid of this hairstyle, because it's clearly making me look old before my time. Although I'm beginning to think I should give up on dating altogether and just get more dogs.'

'More dogs are never a bad thing.' Isla put an arm around her friend's waist. 'But if you decide you want to find someone, you will, and they'll be incredibly lucky that they get to be in your life. Just look at Lijah, he's still pining for you after all these years.'

'Is that what you want?' Wendy looked at Amy as she waited

for her to respond. When she'd first split from Mike, some of her friends had assumed that all she wanted to do was replace her ex with another man, someone to become the new permanent fixture in her life, and that would somehow make everything okay. It was as if being in a relationship was the only goal in life, but back then tying herself to another man who might well turn out to be just like her husband had been unthinkable. Her decision to date had been more of a knee-jerk reaction to the way Mike had made her feel, rather than a desperate need to find a partner and she hadn't expected to ever want to live with another man, let alone marry one. Meeting Gary again, and discovering that she felt just as strongly about him as she had in her teens, had been an unexpected surprise. But, as much as she loved him and as grateful as she was to him for the part he'd played in rebuilding her self-esteem, her relationship with Gary still didn't define Wendy, and she'd never go back to allowing her self-worth to be measured by the man she was with. It was why her job, her family, and her friends were all so important to her. And she didn't want Amy to feel like being with someone was the only thing that mattered either.

'I guess so, but I'm telling myself if it's meant to happen it will.' Amy grinned again. 'I thought I might be in with a shot of being yours and Gary's daughter-in-law one day, when he introduced me to his son. But it looks like Drew's hitting it off with Chloe.'

Wendy looked towards where Chloe and Drew were chatting animatedly. She was laughing at something he'd said, and she looked happier than she had since before she'd lost Beau. Wendy didn't think for a moment that anything would come of it; Drew was a lovely lad and the whole family had gone above and beyond to make Chloe feel welcome. But whatever it was that was making her smile, Wendy was just glad to see it. Mike had been responsible for so much pain over the years, and Chloe deserved to find true happiness, whether that was with someone else, or because she realised it was every bit as possible to love being single. Either way, Wendy just hoped that Chloe knew she had a family now, and that she didn't need to settle for anything less than the best, if she did eventually embark upon another relationship.

20

During one of Danni's antenatal classes, the discussion had got around to how many of the women were planning to have their mother in the delivery room, as well as their partner. There was a mixture of responses, with around half saying they would have their mother there, and one woman who was intending to have both her parents with her. It had been another moment when Danni's heart had contracted, and that familiar emptiness had threatened to swallow her from the inside out. But then Charlie had reached for her hand, squeezing it tightly, as if to remind her that he was there and that she didn't really need anyone else. She might not *need* anyone else, but the conversation with the other expectant parents had made her realise she wanted them.

On the way home, she'd asked Charlie if he minded Esther being at the birth. Maybe she should have felt odd about her best friend seeing parts of her that even the closest of friends didn't usually get to see, but they were both medically trained and there wasn't much that fazed them. Charlie had said he was happy as long as she was, and she'd asked Esther if she wanted to be there. It still made her smile when she thought about her friend's reaction: she'd run around whooping like she'd won the lottery. And it clearly meant every bit as much to her to be there, as it did to Danni. The only thing that worried her after that was that no one in the room, other than possibly her midwife, would actually know what it was like to give birth. So when she'd discovered that she could have a third person, at the discretion of her midwife, Danni had known she wanted to fill that gap.

She'd considered asking Caroline, who'd been so much like a mother to her. But she hadn't wanted to take that moment away from Esther, who would no doubt want her mother with her when the time came for her and Joe to have a baby. Someone else had immediately sprung to mind, though. Who better to have with her, than a friend who not only had children of her own, but who also had almost five decades' experience as a midwife, not to mention the fact that she was a mother figure to almost all the staff at the hospital. Having Gwen there also allowed Danni to avoid having to choose between her two mothers-in-law. Charlie was so lucky to have two loving mums, but it would have hurt Connie or Gilly if one of them had been left out, and Danni wasn't entirely sure she'd have felt comfortable with either of them being there. At least this way all four parents on Charlie's side could start their lives as grandparents on an equal footing. They'd all be in the baby's life from day one, and it would be like a fresh start for Connie and Richard.

When the labour pains first started, Danni had grimaced telling a concerned Charlie that it was probably just Braxton Hicks, the practice contractions she'd been having for almost four weeks. Maggie had known before she did that something more serious was happening. As she'd rested her head on Danni's lap as was her habit, and looked up at her with the big soulful eyes that said more than words ever could, Danni had been forced to acknowledge that this pain was different. It suddenly felt as though it was gripping her insides in a vice, and she knew these weren't practice contractions any more.

'Charlie,' Danni had called out to him, concentrating on keeping her voice as level as she could, even as the wave of pain continued to build, 'I think the baby's coming.'

She'd never doubted that Charlie would rise to the occasion, and his actions had been urgent and calm all at the same time. He'd got her into the car, making sure that her carefully packed bags weren't left behind, and he'd proceeded to call everyone they'd promised to let know, while they were en route to the hospital. Esther and Gwen had both said they'd head straight to St Piran's, and Connie and Richard would come over to collect Maggie and Brenda. Thankfully the baby had decided to hold off until a week after his aunt and uncle had returned from their honeymoon. He was going to be a little bit early, but not drastically so, and there was no reason why he wouldn't be leaving hospital with his mum a few hours after delivery, as long as everything went according to plan.

'Can you believe this is it?' Charlie had gripped her hand when they arrived at the hospital and she'd nodded.

'It feels like the moment I've always been waiting for.' She'd kissed him then, before drawing in the longest breath and readying herself to start the next phase of her life, as a mother. Now here they were, in the labour room – six hours, and what felt like half a lifetime, later – and it finally looked as though that moment was about to come.

'You're doing so well, Danni, you just need to carry on with what you've been doing and listen to your body when you get that next contraction. Just a few more and you'll get to meet your little boy.' Jess was such a reassuring presence as a midwife, and Danni had been so grateful that she'd gone into labour while she was near the start of her shift. Danni hadn't felt the need for an epidural, and although she'd tried the gas and air it had made her feel spaced out and horribly sick. Jess had said there were other painkilling options she could try, but she'd decided to hold off until she got to a point when the pain was too much. She was almost certain she'd have reached that stage already if it hadn't been for Jess encouraging her about how well things were progressing, and making her believe she could do it. Charlie, Esther and Gwen were all still there too. The plan had been that Gwen would leave when Danni got this close to delivery, but it had turned out to be a very busy day in the maternity unit, and Jess seemed grateful for the additional support that her former colleague and old friend could offer. Danni had wanted her to stay too, knowing that there were no better hands she could have been in. Gwen had done everything Danni could have wished for if she really had been her mother, from whispering words of encouragement, to tracking down iced water from somewhere when Danni got so hot it had felt as if she might pass out.

'Oh Dan, you're so brilliant, I can't believe you're about to become a mum.' Esther was already crying, and the baby hadn't even put in an appearance yet.

'Are you sure this is not going to put you off for life? Some people have said it's worse watching it than going through it.' Danni was getting close to exhaustion, but she still managed to raise a smile at the expression that crossed Gwen's face.

'Oh yes and I bet they were all men.' Gwen gave Charlie a pointed look, as if it was his fault that his fellow men had dared make that kind of comment. 'Let them try passing a golf ball, or an avocado, down their urethra, and then they can say what's worse.'

'To be fair, that probably would be quite traumatising to watch!' Esther laughed. 'But this has been nothing but magical to be a part of, and I'm so honoured you've allowed me to be here.'

'I think she was worried I wouldn't cope on my own.' Charlie dropped a kiss on to Danni's forehead as he spoke. 'I've always known you are the stronger of the two of us, Dan, but watching you today has taken my breath away.'

'Thousands of women do it every day and I'm just—' She couldn't finish the sentence, gritting her teeth as another contraction took hold, and dropping her chin to her chest to focus all her energy on pushing, as Charlie held her hand.

'That's it, Danni, the baby's head is crowning, keeping going like that.' Jess's words tapped into a source of energy Danni didn't even know she had, and a sound filled the room that she would have sworn hadn't come from her, even though it must have done.

'Oh Dan, his head is out, he's here.' Charlie's eyes were shining as he looked at her, and a wave of exhaustion washed over her, but she had to keep going.

'There's another contraction coming.' Danni clenched her jaw, ready to get this baby out, but Jess put a hand on her leg.

'Okay sweetheart, I want you to try not to push. Blow out through your mouth in short breaths when the pain comes, and let your body do the rest.' Jess's tone was calm and she made it all sound so easy.

'That's it, you're doing great.' Gwen was her cheerleader on the opposite side of the bed to Charlie. 'Taking this bit nice and slowly is best for your body; it allows the muscles to stretch. Just keep breathing exactly the way you are.'

'I love you so much.' Charlie said the words aloud, but Danni could already feel so much love in the room and there wasn't a single thing she would have changed about the people she was surrounded by, when the biggest moment of her life finally arrived.

'That's it, he's here and he's just beautiful.' Jess lifted the baby straight up on to Danni's chest and, when he immediately cried, it was the sweetest sound she'd ever heard. Although he had plenty of competition, because everybody else seemed to be crying too.

'Hello my darling.' Danni's biggest fear had been that she wouldn't experience a rush of love for her son. She knew that a lot of women didn't get that, especially after difficult deliveries, but she was terrified that not getting that initial rush of love meant it would never come for her at all, and that she was exactly like her mother. Thankfully, as she looked down at her newborn son, it was as if love was rising up inside her with a strength so over-whelming she knew, without a doubt, that she'd die for the little boy who was lying on her chest.

'He's so perfect, he looks just like you. The two loves of my life are like peas in a pod.' Charlie was laughing and crying, and kissing Danni again.

'Oh my God, you've got a baby and I defy anyone to say he's not the best baby they've ever seen.' Esther couldn't seem to drag her eyes away from him. 'I'm your auntie Esther and I promise to spoil you and take you on adventures, and to look after you when-ever your mummy and daddy need a break.'

'He's going to have the best auntie, and so many wonderful people around him.' Danni looked towards the end of the bed, where Jess had her arm around Gwen, both of them looking as if the emotion of the moment had got to them too, even after all the deliveries they must have witnessed. 'Thank you both so much for giving me the best birth experience possible.'

'It's been an absolute pleasure. I am going to have to borrow your beautiful boy in a moment to check him over, and that's got nothing to do with me wanting to get a cuddle in... Well maybe a bit!' Jess laughed. 'But we've delayed the cord cutting for long enough to help baby adjust to being out in the world. So is Charlie going to do the honours?'

'Absolutely.' Charlie's hands shook as he followed Jess's

instructions, and then there was a flurry of activity as another midwife finally arrived apologising profusely for not making it in time for the delivery. Danni was given a shot of vitamin K, while Jess checked the baby over, and they ensured the placenta was delivered safely too.

'Right, I've borrowed this little man for long enough.' Jess smiled as she brought the baby back to Danni and Charlie. 'We're doing kangaroo care, aren't we?'

'Yes, and I want Charlie to have him for a couple of minutes first.' Danni's voice was already thick with emotion, and her breath caught in her throat as Charlie put the baby against his bare chest. Kangaroo care was something that had been covered in their antenatal classes, and the suggested benefits for both the parents and the baby had been huge. During her pregnancy, she'd researched every method of bonding with a child, because she'd been so fearful that it wouldn't come by itself. But when she looked at her two boys, she knew she'd never experienced love like she had in that moment and it was more powerful than she'd ever dared dream of. Her life as a mother had got off to the perfect start, and she couldn't imagine anything that would ever make her wish she'd done things differently.

21

Chloe was jiggling around in her seat like a child who needed a wee, but had left it far too late to get there. She couldn't seem to keep still as they waited for the consultant to call them in. It was hardly surprising, because Chloe was waiting to hear how her fertility might have been affected as a result of the ovarian torsion. Wendy hadn't spoken to her about the prospect of trying again, because all the reading she'd done had told her that would be a mistake. Beau was irreplaceable, but what Chloe needed now more than anything was hope for the future. Wendy was scared of what it might do to her if the doctors said there was a reduced chance of a falling pregnant again and it felt as though there were butterflies fluttering inside Wendy's chest too. Chloe desperately needed some good news, even if another baby was the last thing on her mind right now.

'Chloe Adlington please.' The consultant who'd called Chloe's name was a kindly looking woman, who appeared to be in her sixties, and had the sort of warm demeanour that immediately made Wendy feel a bit more relaxed. She couldn't say the same for Chloe, whose legs were still frantically jigging up and down even as they sat opposite the consultant's desk. Wendy had looked up the doctor's details on the system before the appointment, and Miss Cohen had decades of experience as a consultant gynaecologist and surgeon, which had reassured Wendy that Chloe would be getting the best possible advice.

'I'm so sorry about what you've been through.' Miss Cohen's gentle tone finally seemed to make Chloe's legs stop moving.

'Thank you.' Her response was barely audible, and Wendy instinctively reached out and took her hand.

'I can't imagine how difficult this has been for you emotionally, but it's obvious you've got a lot of support and hopefully you're drawing on what the hospital can offer you in that respect too?' As Miss Cohen waited for a response, Chloe gave an almost imperceptible nod and Wendy had to stop herself from saying that she wasn't sure Chloe was taking full advantage of professional help. 'That's good and I'm here to support you with the physical side of things.'

'Can I still have a baby?' It was as if someone had suddenly turned the volume dial up, and Chloe's question sounded almost like a shout.

'Yes.' As Miss Cohen spoke, all the tension seemed to be released from Chloe's body, like air being let out of a balloon, and she slumped slightly in her chair. 'Your left fallopian tube and ovary had to be removed as a result of the torsion, but the good news is you're in the optimal age range to fall pregnant without this affecting you too much. Up until around the age of twenty-eight, as long as your right ovary and tube are healthy and functioning normally, you'll have an 85 per cent chance of falling pregnant within two years.'

'That's great news.' It was Wendy who spoke, and when she turned to look at Chloe the young woman had an unreadable expression on her face.

'I'll be twenty-five soon and I'm single now.' Chloe touched the place on her finger where her engagement ring had sat for such a short period of time that there wasn't even a hint of an indent or tan line left behind.

'Try not to worry about that for now. The important thing is to make sure you're maintaining good physical health, and I am slightly concerned about how underweight you are.' As Miss Cohen spoke, Wendy continued to watch Chloe, and she could see her shutting down. She wasn't listening to anything the doctor had to say, and Wendy had no idea whether that was because she didn't want to hear it, or because Chloe was fixating on the fact that – in her mind – she now only had three years to have a successful pregnancy. All Wendy could do was hope that it didn't weaken Chloe's resolve to stay away from Mike, because at that moment she couldn't imagine a worse outcome than the two of them getting back together.

* * *

'How are you feeling?' Wendy handed Chloe one of the lattes she'd ordered and sat down opposite her. She'd needed to deal with a work issue straight after the appointment with Miss Cohen, authorising the purchase of some supplies that an inventory had shown were urgently needed, but it had taken less than ten minutes to sort out. Wendy had been determined to take Chloe out for a quiet coffee afterwards, so they could talk properly about what the consultant had said, without the risk of Zara over-hearing anything that Chloe might not want her to know. 'I thought the appointment went well and the scan results suggest that everything looks good on the right-hand side too.'

'Umm.' Chloe sounded unconvinced, as she wrapped her hands around the cup Wendy had just passed to her. 'It's just that it suddenly feels like there's a big clock counting down inside me. Three years is such a short time, especially if it could take up to two years to fall pregnant even within that window. I'd have to start trying pretty much straight away.'

'Miss Cohen didn't say you couldn't fall pregnant after that, just that it might be a little bit easier if you're under twenty-eight.' Wendy was still trying to keep her tone light, but if Mike's name came up, she wasn't sure she'd be able to stay anywhere near as calm.

'It doesn't give me long to meet someone.' It was as if Chloe hadn't heard what Wendy had just said, and she couldn't stop herself from responding in the way she'd been trying so hard to avoid.

'Please tell me you're not thinking of going back to Mike, because that would be a disaster.'

'God, no!' The force of Chloe's response was like a weight lifting off Wendy's shoulders. 'There are other options. I don't know, maybe sperm donation, or if I can't fall pregnant... There are lots of other ways I can still have a family, aren't there?'

'There are loads of options, but I really don't think it will come to that.' Wendy put a hand over Chloe's. 'And whatever happens, I want you to remember you already have a family. Beau has bonded you to Alice and Zara forever, and nothing is going to change that.'

'I hope not, and I'm so grateful to you and Gary too.' Suddenly Chloe flung her arms around Wendy, hugging her so tightly that for a moment it was hard to breathe, and then she let go. 'I'm going to get myself sorted out, I promise.'

'I know you will.' Wendy smiled, and resisted the urge to ask Chloe whether she'd made any decisions about the funeral, because time really was close to running out. She was still wary of pushing her too hard about anything else, and asking her whether she'd given any thought to whether she might go back to work at the college could wait too. For now it was just so wonderful to hear Chloe sounding as if she could imagine a future where she would be happy again. That was more than enough for one day.

'Is it something we need to be concerned about?' Charlie furrowed his bow, as Dr Kowalski shook his head.

'A haemorrhage always sounds terrifying, but as Danni will know it's a broad term.' He smiled as he turned from Charlie to Danni. 'A secondary post-partum haemorrhage is most likely caused by an infection, but there's a small chance there may be some retained tissue. We'll get you straight onto antibiotics to clear any infection, and uterotonics to help reduce the bleeding. Have you got any known allergy to penicillin?'

'I haven't got any allergies that I'm aware of.' Danni held her as-yet unnamed son close to her chest. He'd taken to feeding like a dream, and he was happily snoozing, completely oblivious to the conversation going on around him.

'Great, in that case we'll start you on a combination of ampicillin and metronidazole. Hopefully that will resolve things, but we'll also give you a scan to see whether you need surgery to remove any retained tissue. I'm confident it won't come to that, but we'll be keeping you in until we're certain all is as it should be. I'll see you soon, Danni, but for now you need to get as much rest as possible.'

'Thank you, Pieter.' Danni leant back against the pillows behind her, as Dr Kowalski left the room.

'Are you okay?' As Charlie spoke, he gently swept the hair away from her forehead.

'Yes, just a bit tired and feeling guilty that this is going to delay your parents and Joe from meeting the baby.'

'The meeting will be all the sweeter when it comes, and all any of them want is for you to get well. So, even if they have to wait a week, they'll all understand.'

'God, I hope I'm not stuck in here for that long.' Danni pulled a face. 'I love St Piran's, but right now all I want is to go home and be with my boys.'

'That's all I want too.' Charlie reached out and stroked the baby's cheek. 'I can still hardly believe he's ours, and that I got lucky enough to find the most wonderful woman in the world to do this with.'

'Hang on to that feeling, because I think it's going to be a very long time before you get lucky in any other sense of the word!' Danni started to laugh, but even that hurt.

'No one deserves more luck than I've had already.' Charlie kissed her gently before pulling away again.

'We really have hit the jackpot with this little guy, haven't we? Although we probably do need to decide on a name.' Danni breathed out slowly and Charlie nodded.

'I think all of that will be easier when we're back home and we get settled in to our new life as family. I've got a feeling the name will just come to us then.'

'I think you're right and I'm sure from what Pieter said that we'll be home by tomorrow at the latest.' Danni looked down at her little boy again, already picturing the three of them curled up on the sofa together, with Brenda and Maggie at their feet. It might sound incredibly simple to some people, but it was all she'd ever wanted.

22

Ever since the appointment with Miss Cohen, Chloe had seemed much more like her old self. She was still spending a lot of time online, but she seemed more animated and hopeful than she had before. Even when a friend of hers from work had made the questionable decision to send her a screenshot of Mike's photograph on an online dating app, she hadn't seemed fazed.

'I couldn't care less what he does now.' Chloe had genuinely sounded like she meant it. 'I know what I want my future to look like and Mike isn't a part of that. I've got a plan and, as soon as I feel strong enough, I'm going to start taking steps towards making it happen.'

'Would it help to talk about what you want to do?' Wendy had continued to tread carefully, not wanting to shatter the fragile progress Chloe seemed to be making.

'I know I need to work out how to say goodbye to Beau and find a way to move forward without him, that's my priority. After that, I want to have the chance to be a mum, whatever that might look like, and I'm not scared of doing it on my own. After all, nothing could be worse than losing Beau, could it? If I've survived that, I can survive anything. One thing this has taught me is that I'm stronger than I'd ever have believed.'

'You really are.' It had been an easy statement for Wendy to agree with. If she'd been asked when she first met Chloe whether she thought she'd have the strength to turn her back on Mike, Wendy would never have believed it, especially as it had taken her decades to do the same thing. It was getting easier and easier to believe that Chloe would be okay, and so she didn't panic when it got to 10 a.m. and there'd been no sign of her, or even the slightest sound coming from the guest bedroom. She was probably just catching up on the rest she so badly needed. Ever since she'd lost Beau, Chloe had insisted on having Stan, Gary's Border Terrier, up in her room with her at night. The little dog was undemanding company, and she seemed to get comfort from having him close by. But she must have recognised the need for a good night's sleep, because when she'd gone up to bed the previous evening she'd shut Stan in the kitchen for the first time.

'Chloe, love, are you okay?' When there was still no sign of her at eleven, Wendy tentatively knocked on the door. Zara had told her that they were both due to go to an eating disorders support group meeting in the early afternoon, and she wanted to make sure Chloe had enough time to get ready. When there was no answer, she knocked a little bit harder. 'Chloe, you need to get up now, or you'll miss your meeting with Zara.'

Met with only silence, Wendy slowly pushed the door open expecting to see Chloe still sleeping; instead, the bed was neatly made.

'What's up?' Gary looked at Wendy as she came into the kitchen, after running down the stairs. But that wasn't the only reason her heart was thudding as fast as it was, a horrible feeling of dread had settled in her chest and it was even worse than it had been before. She knew she was overreacting, but she couldn't stop her mind going to the worst-case scenario: that something awful had happened to Chloe.

'She's not in her room and it looks so tidy, almost like she was never there.'

'She's probably just gone for a walk.' Gary held out a hand towards her. 'I love how much you worry about everyone, but you really don't need to. I expect she's just tidied up because she feels a tiny bit better, and she doesn't want to be surrounded by clutter.'

'Maybe.' Wendy really wished she could believe him, but the feeling of dread seemed to be getting stronger all the time, and Gary could obviously see it on her face.

'If you're really worried, why don't you give her a call?'

'I don't want her to think I'm checking up on her, or that I don't trust her to remember that she's due to go to the meeting with Zara.'

'Just ask her what she wants for dinner tonight.'

'Okay.' Even a simple question like that had to be handled carefully, so it didn't sound like Wendy was being the food police, but she'd got used to treading on those particular eggshells with Zara, and that was definitely something she could handle. As soon as she connected the call, she heard the sound of a phone ringing in the distance.

'I think her mobile must be in her room.' Wendy followed the sound, taking the stairs two at a time, reaching the bedroom just as the call went through to voicemail. Disconnecting the call, she was about to ring again, so she could locate the phone, but then she saw it, on the bedside table. As she moved closer, the sense of foreboding threatened to overwhelm her altogether, as she spotted an envelope with her name written on the front. Ripping it open, her hands were shaking, even before she began to read the words.

Dear Wendy,

I can never thank you enough for what you've done for me, but I can't stay any longer. I thought I could say goodbye to Beau, but when I tried to call the hospital yesterday, I just couldn't go through with it. I don't think I'll ever be able to make the decision to let him go, until I'm holding another baby in my arms. I've been trying so hard not to think about it, but after I put the phone down it was all I could see. Beau lying there, all alone, waiting to be laid to rest. I feel terrible that I've left him on his own for so long, and I need to do whatever I can to make sure I'm ready to let him go as soon as possible. I can't wait around to make it happen, and not even you can help me with that.

Hopefully I'll be able to get in touch when I'm settled, and let you know how you can contact me. But I can't risk anyone being able to find me before I'm ready, so I've left my phone behind too. If I can't find a way to say goodbye to Beau, then I'd rather just go with him. That might be the best solution anyway, but I owe it to him to try and make a different kind of life for myself first.

I'm so sorry I couldn't say goodbye to you, Gary, and the girls; you're the kindest people I've ever known.

With love and eternal gratitude.

Chloe xx

'Oh my God.' Wendy's hand flew to her mouth and Gary had to steady her, as he came into the room.

'Is that from Chloe? What does it say?'

'That she can't let Beau go until she's got another baby in her arms and that, if she can't have that, the best solution would be for her to be with him instead.' Wendy's eyes widened in fear as she looked at Gary. 'You don't think she'd do anything stupid, do you?'

'No, but I think we need to find her.'

'What if we can't?' Nausea was rising up inside Wendy now. 'I wouldn't even know where to start.'

'I think we should try the hospital first. It's where Beau is, and she might want to try and see him again.' Gary put his arms around her. 'It'll be okay, we'll find her, I promise.'

'Thank you.' Leaning against him for just a moment, Wendy took a deep breath, desperate to believe he was right and the worst thing she could do was lose hope. 'Okay, let's go.'

Grabbing Chloe's phone, she hurried out of the door, praying that Gary's hunch about her heading to the hospital would prove to be right. If it wasn't, she'd have absolutely no idea where to look instead and it already felt as if grains of sand were passing all too quickly through a timer. The countdown to bringing Chloe home safely and before she did anything stupid, was well and truly on.

* * *

By the time Danni was ready to be taken down for a scan to check that the medication Pieter had prescribed was working, she was every bit as confident as he'd been that it was. So, when Charlie had asked if she wanted him to come with her, she'd said no and left him cradling their son in his arms. She'd been gone less than half an hour, but the longing she had to be reunited with her son was already a physical ache. And when she got back to the room, she was disappointed to see that he wasn't still with Charlie, because it meant he was asleep in the crib by her bed, and it would be hard to justify waking him up just so that she could have the cuddle she was desperate for.

'How did it go?' Charlie stood up as she came into the room, a note of anxiety in his voice. She'd been taken down for her scan in a wheelchair, by one of the midwifery assistants, Sam, but she was beginning to feel a bit of a fraud. Especially as she'd had Geeta, a senior midwife, with her too, so that she could review the results and explain things to Danni. Thankfully, as it was, there was nothing much to explain, but both Geeta and Sam had accompanied her back to the room.

'Everything's fine and the best news is that we can go home as soon as the baby wakes up.' Danni smiled and gestured towards the crib, as Sam wheeled her to the bed.

'Oh, he's not asleep; one of the midwives took him for his day-one blood test a few minutes ago.' Charlie had returned her smile, but a shiver went up Danni's spine. She'd read everything she could get her hands on about newborn babies, in an attempt to feel more prepared, and she hadn't come across anything about a day-one blood test. If they'd taken the baby away, it had to be because they suspected something was wrong with him, and the story about a blood test was just an attempt to stop them panicking. All her fears about something awful happening came rushing to the surface, and when she saw the expression on Geeta's face, her blood ran cold.

'Are you sure they said a blood test?'

'Definitely. She said it's the test all babies have in the first thirty-six hours. She said it would take ten minutes at most, so they should be back any minute.'

'Did she tell you her name?' The urgency in Geeta's tone made Danni's spine go rigid and, even though she'd opened her mouth, no words would come out. A few seconds earlier she hadn't been able to imagine a worse scenario than something being wrong with the baby, but suddenly she could, and she was frozen with fear.

'She said her name was Millie. Why, is there a problem?' Charlie was suddenly looking panicked too, and Danni felt as if she'd forgotten how to breathe.

'We need to raise the alarm. *Right now*. Call security and let them know we'll have more details as soon as we've got them.' Sam shot out of the room almost before Geeta had finished speaking. Danni's lips were moving now, but there was still nothing coming out. It was as if she'd been plunged into freezing cold water and even catching her breath was impossible.

'Oh my God, are you telling me she isn't a midwife?' Charlie's eyes shot open, his face a mask of the same terror that seemed to have paralysed Danni.

'There's no one on the team called Millie, and there are no routine blood tests we give babies until they're five days old. Can you remember anything about this woman?'

'She must have been a midwife, because I recognised her.' All of the colour had drained out of him now. Danni's stomach was churning so hard she was almost sure she was going to be sick, and she'd clamped her mouth shut. This couldn't be real and if she pinched herself hard enough, she'd prove it was all just a nightmare she was going to wake up from. But it didn't matter how hard she squeezed her fingers, or how much pain it caused her, Charlie was still talking and it was all still horribly real. 'I've definitely seen her before, I was sure it was here, but maybe...'

'For Christ's sake, Charlie, you let her take our baby, what the hell did she look like?' The words had suddenly spilled out of Danni's mouth like venom, but she didn't feel any guilt, even when Charlie reacted as if he'd been struck. She couldn't worry about his feelings right now. Getting their baby back was the only thing she cared about.

'She was very slim, about five feet three I guess, fair-skinned and blonde. She was wearing glasses, but I didn't look at her that closely...' There was so much pain in Charlie's eyes as he reached out to her, but she couldn't comfort him. 'Dan, I'm so sorry. I was convinced I knew her, that I'd seen her here, she looked so famil iar, and she sounded so plausible. She knew my name and yours. I just—'

'This isn't your fault.' It was left to Geeta to try and comfort Charlie. 'The security team will put the hospital in lockdown, and with any luck we'll stop her before she even leaves.'

'And if you don't?' Danni was shaking so much as she asked the question, that her whole body seemed to vibrate. And, when Geeta didn't answer, an unearthly scream suddenly filled the air around them. It wasn't until Charlie took hold of her, wrapping his arms around her too tightly for her to be able to scream again, that Danni realised the sound was coming from her.

23

The feeling of dread that had been building up inside Wendy reached new heights when she got an alert on her phone to say that there'd been a major incident at the hospital, just as they were about to leave for St Piran's.

'Someone posing as a midwife has taken a baby from the maternity ward.' Even as she said the words, Wendy didn't want to believe they were true. But, for a second time, it was only Gary reaching out to put a steadying arm around her waist that stopped her legs from collapsing under her. 'Chloe couldn't have done that, she knows what it's like to lose a baby. She just wouldn't.'

'Trauma can twist things so much. If she's done it, she won't be thinking straight. She'll barely be thinking at all, except about how to get what she wants the most: her baby.'

'But it's not her baby.' Wendy still couldn't picture the gentle, kind, young woman who she'd come to care for more deeply than she'd ever have believed, doing something like that.

'In her mind it might be. What she said about empty arms...' Gary sighed. 'All she can think about is having them full again; logic won't come into it in a situation like this and she won't be thinking about how likely it is that she'll get caught. The desperation will override all of that.'

'We've got to get there, but they might not let us in, unless we take our passes and say we're working?' Wendy looked at Gary, and he nodded. There was a chance they could both be putting their jobs at risk with a lie like that, but she had to get to the hospital as quickly as she could, and keep praying that Chloe would still be there somewhere.

'I'll grab my pass.' Gary released her, and Wendy turned away, almost running to the drawer in the kitchen where she kept her own hospital ID.

'Oh God, no.' Her scalp prickled as she flung the drawer open, desperately rummaging in case the pass was somehow hiding in plain sight, despite it being obvious it was gone. 'Gary, she's taken my pass!'

'Bloody hell.' He skidded to a halt next to Wendy, as another terrible thought occurred to her.

'When we were in the hospital for her appointment with Miss Cohen, I had to pop to the laundry to speak to Frank about a housekeeping issue and I was too worried about her to leave her on her own. She could easily have got her hands on a uniform, or she'd know where to go to get one, and there's a chance she might have watched me key in the access code. I never thought—'

Wendy couldn't finish the sentence, because there was no excuse for what she'd done, even if Gary seemed to think otherwise. 'Oh darling, this isn't your fault.'

'Try telling that to the woman whose baby she's taken.' Wendy put a hand to her mouth, as the nausea threatened to overwhelm her again. She had to do whatever it took to put this right and reunite the baby with its parents, even if it cost her more than just her job.

* * *

Danni wasn't even sure what medication she'd been given, but she
didn't care. She'd been so desperate to get any kind of relief from
the terror gripping her body that she'd have agreed to anything.
Whatever it was had worked in a way, because she'd stopped
crying and she felt completely numb, as if she wasn't really in her
body at all, just watching herself from a distance, somehow
unable to connect with all the things she knew she should be feeling. It might not just have been the medication, shock had probably set in too, as her body fought to find its own way to cope with
what had happened. If it hadn't, she didn't think she could have
carried on breathing in and out, because there'd be no point in
doing that if her son was really gone.

'We've reviewed the CCTV footage.' The police officer, whose
name Danni couldn't have recalled if her life depended on it, even
though she'd introduced herself less than fifteen minutes after the
alarm had first been raised, furrowed her brow. 'It seems the
woman was let into the maternity department by some visitors
who'd just been buzzed in. She came up behind them, and she
was wearing a nurse's uniform and pushing a laundry trolley. It
looks like she'd got a hospital pass too, so the visitors probably
thought nothing of holding the door open for what looked like a
member of staff.'

'I need to see what she looks like.'

'She did quite a good job of shielding her face from the
camera, but my colleagues are already working on enhancing the
images so we can circulate them. Do you think there's a chance
you might recognise her?'

'I don't know, but I need to see the face of the woman who's got
my son.' A stab of pain pierced through the numbness, making
Danni double over. She needed to know what this woman looked

like, and whether there was anything in her appearance that could reassure Danni that she wouldn't hurt the baby.

'As soon as we've got a clear image, I'll—'

'Boss, there's been an update.' Another police officer came into the room. 'We've had a tip-off about who the woman might be.'

'Who is it?' Charlie's question took the words out of Danni's mouth, and she wanted to reach out for his hand, but she had no idea if he'd push her away. The things she'd said to him were etched on her brain in a way that even the medication hadn't been able to erase. She'd blamed the only person who could really understand how devastated she was, for something that wasn't his fault, and she knew he'd never have done the same to her. Nothing could be worse than losing her son, but losing Charlie too...

'I'm so sorry, we can't tell you that at this stage.' The female officer shot her colleague a look that would have frozen water. 'But I promise I'll update you as soon as I can.'

'Just bring him back. *Please*.' The numbness seemed to be wearing off by the second, and the all-consuming fear that they'd lost him forever was lodging itself back in her throat, making the task of breathing suddenly feel impossible again.

'They will. We're not going to lose him.' Charlie had reached for her hand, and just the touch of it in hers made her steady her breathing. She trusted him more than anyone she'd ever met, and she desperately wanted him to be right.

'We've got the best team possible working on this, and we won't rest until we find out where he is.' The female officer gave a small nod, before hurrying after her colleague.

'He hasn't got a name yet, we didn't even get to keep him for long enough to give him that.' Danni's throat ached from screaming and despite the effects of the medication, which were now quickly fading, it hadn't been able to alleviate the aching emptiness inside her, which she knew could never be filled unless she got her son back. She'd had a terrible sense of dread for so much of her pregnancy, and she'd tried to convince herself it was all tied to her feelings about her mum, and the loss of her dad, but now it all felt like a horrific premonition.

'Oh darling, don't say that. We'll get to name him, and hold him, and love him for the rest of our lives.' Charlie took hold of her hands. 'He's coming back to us, I know it.'

'Do you really believe that?' Even in her determination to hang on to his words, Danni couldn't help searching Charlie's face, looking for the tiniest hint that he might not mean what he'd just said, but it wasn't there.

'I know we will, and the woman who has him...' Charlie shook his head again. 'I don't know, she was gentle, and warm, the way she looked at the baby. I'm sure she wouldn't do anything to hurt him. I just wish to God I hadn't trusted her, I should have realised.'

'How could you have done? I'm so sorry, Charlie, what I said was unforgiveable.' No medication on earth could have held back the tears that were now streaming down Danni's face. 'None of this is your fault, I was just so scared.'

'I know, me too, but like the police officer said, they've got the best team working on this and they'll find him.' As Charlie pulled her closer, she saw her phone on the unit by the bed light up, as a call from Esther came in. She was the first person Danni had messaged about the baby's disappearance, but she hadn't been able to speak to her. She couldn't face saying the words out loud. Except now she needed to hear that Esther believed the same as Charlie, that they would get the baby back. Breaking free from Charlie's embrace, she snatched up the phone.

'Hello.'

'Oh, thank God, I've been frantic since I got your message.' Esther was breathless, her words coming out in a rush.

'I'm sorry, I—'

'Don't be, I can't even imagine, but I'm calling because we might know who it is. When I messaged the others to let them know what had happened, Gary called me straight back. Chloe has gone missing and she's stolen Wendy's hospital pass.'

'Chloe?' As Danni repeated the name, she tried to process what it might mean. She knew about Chloe losing her own son, and it suddenly made sense why she'd looked so familiar to Charlie, because he'd met her briefly at Wendy and Gary's bonfire night party. Although she must have tried to disguise her appearance, because she hadn't been blonde then.

'Wendy and Gary are trying everything they can to find her, and they've let the police know too. I just wanted to make sure you knew what was happening. They'll bring him back, Danni, I know they will.'

'Thank you.' In the end she hadn't needed to ask Esther the question, and a sliver of hope pushed out a tiny bit of the fear. It wasn't just because Esther had said what she'd so desperately needed to hear, it was because the baby was almost certainly with Chloe. Somehow, the fact that it wasn't a complete stranger made it a little bit easier to believe it would all be okay and hope was the only currency they had right now.

24

Wendy had never been as scared as she was in the hours after discovering that Chloe had gone missing and that in all likelihood she had Danni and Charlie's baby boy with her. Part of her hadn't wanted the girls to know what was going on, but she needed their help to find Chloe. There'd have been no way to keep it from them even if they'd tried, because it was already over social media after the police appeal for information went out, and CCTV images of Chloe wearing a blonde wig and pushing a laundry trolley out of the hospital were released. The trolley must have been how she'd got the baby all the way out without being questioned. The police said they were trying to track the woman's movements using other CCTV in the area, but they'd also asked the public to be alert and call with any information that might be useful. Everyone would be looking for Chloe, and Wendy was terrified of what that might drive her to do. She couldn't imagine any scenario in which she'd hurt Danni and Charlie's baby, but it was all too easy to picture a situation in which she might hurt herself.

Zara had come straight home from college after Wendy had

messaged her, and she'd been able to access Chloe's phone, because she knew the passcode. By the time Alice had made the drive back from university, almost three hours had passed since the baby's disappearance, and Wendy and Zara had gone through as many messages and as much of the search history in Chloe's phone as they could. Gary had been out driving around looking for her. He'd even gone back to the house she'd shared with Mike, who'd predictably been no use at all.

'"I told everyone she was a psycho." Can you believe that's what he actually said?' Gary was incredulous when he got back to the house. 'A woman he claimed to have loved, and who has just lost his child, is missing. And all he wants to do is use that to try and prove he's not the arsehole.'

'There's far too much evidence that says he is.' Alice dropped her bag on to the table as she came into the kitchen.

'I'm sorry, love, I never meant for you to hear that, I shouldn't have said it.' Gary shot her an apologetic look.

'Yes, you should, because it's true.' As she turned towards Wendy, it was obvious she'd been crying. 'You don't think she'll hurt herself, do you?'

'I really hope not.' Wendy held her arms out towards her older daughter, hugging her close, just as she'd done with Zara. She didn't want to lie to the girls and pretend there were any guarantees, because they'd been lied to by their father far too many times already. They also needed to understand just how urgent it was to find Chloe, and not just for the baby's sake. 'When was the last time you spoke to her?'

'I called her last night and she seemed so much more upbeat.' Alice pulled back from Wendy as Zara came into the room and immediately moved towards Gary, who put an arm around her. The girls had the kind of built-in safety net Chloe had never had, and Wendy's heart ached to think that she'd have no one to reach out to, even if she realised she'd made a terrible mistake.

'What did she say?'

'That she was working out how to get back to her happy place again, and that it was only a matter of time before she got there.'

Zara's mouth suddenly dropped open. 'Oh my God, I think I know where she might be. She posted a picture on Instagram a little while ago. I'll show you.'

Zara scrolled on her phone as the four of them gathered close, finding the post she'd been talking about. There was a caption underneath the photograph of a woman and a little girl, both grinning broadly at the camera, with afternoon tea spread out in front of them.

Throwback Thursday! Me and my mama in my happy place, at the last birthday celebration I ever had with her. High standards, even at seven! #BirthdayTea #Love #Family @TheSistersofAgnesIslandHotel

'When Chloe and Dad got engaged, the first thing she said was that she wanted to get married there, because it was the place her mum always took her to when they were celebrating special occasions.' Zara looked at Wendy. 'I really think it might be where she's gone.'

'That doesn't make any sense if she wants to get away with the baby.' Even as Wendy said the words a sudden realisation hit her. 'But maybe getting away was never the point, maybe she just wanted to share something with her baby that she hadn't had since she lost her own mum. That might be all she wants to do.'

'But he's not her baby.' Gary's tone was gentle, but firm. 'And as sad as we all feel for Chloe and everything she's been through,

Danni and Charlie are going through hell every second their little boy is missing.'

'I know, I just hope to God that Chloe is there.' Wendy dropped a kiss on Zara's forehead. 'Well done, sweetheart, you did brilliantly remembering the photograph. But you need to wait here with Alice, while Gary and I go and see if she's there.'

'I'm not staying here.' Alice had folded her arms across her chest, even before her younger sister responded.

'Neither am I. They're going to arrest Chloe, aren't they?' Tears filled Zara's eyes again as Wendy nodded. 'I need to see her first, to tell her that whatever has happened I still love her and that she's not going to be on her own.'

'Me too, because I'm really scared about what might happen if she thinks she's lost us too.' Alice was every bit as resolute as Zara, their maturity and empathy taking Wendy's breath away yet again. Mike might well have wreaked havoc and made one hell of a mess of so many people's lives, but his daughters had grown up to be extraordinary young women despite everything he'd done.

'Right then, if we're all going, we'd better do it.' Gary grabbed his car keys off the kitchen counter. 'I just hope we can make it before high tide cuts off the access road.'

As Wendy and the girls followed him towards the front door, it wasn't just a low tide she was praying for.

* * *

Danni jumped every time she heard a footstep in the corridor outside her room. The police had suggested they leave the maternity department, but she couldn't bear to walk out of the room where she'd last seen her son. Every noise around them seemed heightened, and the sound of talking and even laughing from other families felt so alien. It was impossible to believe that the world could still be turning when her baby was missing. When the police had established that the kidnapper was no longer within the hospital, the lockdown had been partially lifted, although increased security meant only essential access was permitted. But women were still giving birth, and they needed their loved ones with them at the most important moment of their lives. She couldn't begrudge them that, but the distant sound of a baby crying had hit her like a truck, physically and emotionally. Her body had responded all by itself to the cry, making her breasts heavy, despite the fact that she couldn't feed her son and that she didn't know if she'd ever be able to do it again. Her emotional reaction to the sound was every bit as visceral, and it made her feel as if she was drowning on the inside.

'I want my baby, I just want him back.' The effects of the medication had long since worn off completely and she was sobbing so hard her breath was coming in gasps, as Charlie pulled her towards him.

'I know, darling, I know, and I'm so sorry, but we'll get him back. You've got to keep believing that.'

'I can't stand it any more. I can't just hang around, waiting for them to tell us if there's any news. I've got to go and look for him.' There was an almost overpowering feeling of fight or flight building up inside of Danni. The unwillingness to leave the room where she'd last seen her baby was suddenly replaced by an over whelming desire to just run and run, until she found her little boy but Charlie was still holding her tightly.

'I want to do that too, but we'll just get in the way, and you're not well enough. The baby's going to need you here, and for you to be okay, when he comes back.'

'I just feel so helpless.'

'So do I.' He still didn't let her go, the shaking of his shoulder making it obvious that he was crying too. Charlie was the only person who understood the depth of her pain, and deep down she knew he was right about them being in the way if they tried to find Chloe. She just hoped Charlie was right about the police being able to bring their baby back to them too, because she couldn't imagine wanting her life to go on if they didn't.

* * *

Wendy could have cried with relief when they got to the slip road and the tide was still low enough to drive to the Sisters of Agnes Island. They'd discussed calling the police on the journey over, to alert them to their suspicions, but they'd decided against it, reasoning that Chloe was most likely to remain calm if they spoke to her first.

'What are we going to say when we get inside? It's going to look odd, four of us turning up and asking if they've got a woman and a baby staying with them. Although I'm guessing she'll probably have kept the baby hidden away somehow, knowing the police will be looking for him.' Gary turned to Wendy, as he brought the car to a stop in the hotel car park. She'd been running through scenarios in her head all the way over.

'If she's trying to relive the experiences she shared with her mum, I'll think she'll have checked in using her mother's name.' Wendy turned to look at her daughters in the back of the car. 'It was Josephine, wasn't it?'

'Yes.' Alice nodded. 'And Chloe already has her mother's maiden name as her surname. She changed it when she was eighteen and things got even worse with her dad.'

'Okay, I'm going to go in there and say I've come to see Josephine Adlington.'

'They won't just tell you her room number.' Zara pulled a face. 'We'll have to be more inventive than that.'

'How about if I come with you, show my ID card, and we ask them to call her because she said she was staying at the hotel, but discharged herself after coming into A&E. I'll tell them that her test results have shown up something she needs urgent treatment for and it could have catastrophic consequences if we don't persuade her to come back with us.' Gary frowned. 'I know it sounds like something off the TV, but maybe when they call and she doesn't answer, which I'm guessing she won't, they'll be worried enough to give us access to her room.'

'That might work.' Alice leant forward in the chair. 'And if it doesn't, we'll just have to tell them the truth and they can call the police.'

'But then we won't get to speak to her first.' Zara sounded distraught and Alice put her arm around her.

'I know and I want that as much as you do, but the most important thing is to get the baby back to his mum and dad.'

'Alice is right and maybe we should just call the police.' Wendy glanced up at the windows of the old convent and shuddered, trying to work out if they'd open wide enough for someone to try getting out that way. It was the level of desperation Chloe might feel, if she was backed into a corner, that Wendy was most scared of now.

'Let's give it one go like this and, if it doesn't work, we'll tell them everything. I still think this is our best shot of keeping Chloe as calm as possible.' Gary seemed to have read her mind and Wendy nodded. It was time to go.

Some small element of fate must have been on their side, because the receptionist on duty seemed to accept Gary's story without questioning any of it, as soon as he confirmed they had a Josephine Adlington staying with them. Just as Gary had predicted, she didn't respond to the phone call the receptionist put through to the room. His age meant he was probably quite new to the role and the drama of Gary's story might have appealed to him too. Either way he got another colleague to cover the desk for him, and took them straight up to Chloe's room. Gary had explained on the way that it might be best if he didn't tell 'Josephine' why they were there, as she might have the same reaction she'd had in the hospital and that it was probably best if he and Wendy, who was posing as another nurse, spoke to 'Josephine' alone once she'd let them in.

Rapping on the door, the receptionist announced his arrival loudly enough for guests in the neighbouring rooms to have heard too. 'Miss Adlington, if you're there can you come to the door? It's Oliver from the hotel reception.'

'Is there any chance she could have collapsed?' Oliver looked horrified at the idea, and Wendy watched as Gary nodded.

'I'm afraid it is possible.'

'I think I should just let you in then.' Swiping a pass key over the sensor, Oliver tentatively opened the door. 'Miss Adlington, I'm coming in. We've got a concern for your welfare and I just want to check that you're—'

'Don't come in!' Chloe called out, but it was too late, Oliver had already pushed open the door. When Chloe spotted Wendy and Gary, she clapped a hand over her mouth as if she was trying to stop herself from screaming.

'It's okay, Josephine, it's Gary from the hospital, remember we met earlier when you came in?' He was speaking really slowly, as if he was explaining something to a very young child, and Chloe eventually nodded, seeming to cotton on to the fact that Oliver had no idea who she was, or what she'd done. 'I need to speak to you about the results of some of the tests we ran for you.'

'Okay.' Chloe's eyes darted towards a large black holdall on the sofa under the window, which had two of the bathroom towels draped on top. She turned towards Oliver, her voice shaking as she spoke. 'Thank you so much for bringing them up. I had a migraine, which is why I didn't answer.'

'No problem at all, Miss Adlington.' Oliver looked almost disappointed that there wasn't more drama, and that she hadn't been found sprawled out on the floor, unconscious. 'Can I do anything else for you?'

'No, thank you.' Chloe all but shoved the young man out of the room, and the second she closed the door behind him, she sank to the floor, covering her mouth with both hands for a second time, and swaying backwards and forwards as silent sobs wracked her body.

'Where's the baby? Chloe, where the hell is he?' Wendy hadn't been certain of what she'd say if they managed to get to Chloe before the police did, but her only priority was making sure the baby was okay.

'In the bag.' Wendy almost threw herself in the direction where Chloe had gestured, her heart thudding so hard it felt as if it was coming out of her chest. If something had happened to that little boy, if he was dead... Her legs were shaking as she reached the sofa, and she wasn't sure they'd hold her up, but then she saw a little foot poking out beneath one of the towels and it was moving.

'Oh, thank God.' Snatching the baby up, she cradled him against her chest, sinking down on the sofa and gently rocking him to and fro, and repeating the same words over and over. 'He's okay, he's okay, he's okay.'

'I didn't mean to do it. I only wanted... I'm sorry, I'm so, so sorry.' Chloe moved as if to stand, but then she slid straight back down again.

'It's okay.' Gary stepped towards her, pulling her into a standing position and she collapsed against him as Wendy got to her feet too, with the baby still in her arms.

'No, it isn't, I've done something terrible and nothing is going to be okay ever again.'

'You haven't done anything that can't be undone, and we're going to be there with you every step of the way.' Wendy crossed the room towards her. Now that she knew the baby was unharmed, she could focus on Chloe again.

'I don't deserve that. I've already lost Beau and the girls are going to hate me too.' Chloe's eyes were so bloodshot, they looked almost completely red, and the blotchiness of her cheeks could have been sunburn. It didn't seem as if taking Danni's baby had brought Chloe a single moment of joy. She looked broken and hopeless, and the fear at what she might do was building inside Wendy again, even before Chloe broke away from Gary and grabbed something from the dressing table. And as Wendy turned to look at her, she realised Chloe was holding a pair of scissors millimetres away from her neck. 'I just want it to be over, I want to be with Mum and Beau.'

'You can't do that.' Wendy fought to keep her voice steady, even though she felt as though the floor was moving beneath her feet.

'Why not? The world would be a better place without me and no one would care.' Chloe sounded so certain she was right, nothing she was saying was for the sake of being dramatic.

Gently handing the baby to Gary, Wendy inhaled slowly. She had to make Chloe believe what she said next, and not just because it was true. 'Plenty of people would care very much, including me. I told you before, you've got family now. At this very moment, Alice and Zara are downstairs desperately waiting to hear that you're okay.'

'They're here?' Chloe's tone was incredulous.

'We didn't want to let them come, but they insisted. They love you, and they want you to know that. So, if you think no one would care if you weren't around, and that they'd be better off without you, then you're very much mistaken. It would hurt the girls, and it would hurt me and Gary too. I'd also bet everything I own that it would even cause pain to the people you think you've hurt the most. Danni and Charlie wouldn't want you to do something like that; all they want is to have their son home where he belongs.'

'I don't know why I did it.' Chloe was crying again, which made it was almost impossible to make out what she was saying, and Wendy took the chance to inch closer to her. 'I just thought if I could have another baby, even for a little while, it would be easier to let Beau go. But as soon as I was outside the hospital, I wanted to take the baby back, and to undo what I'd done. But then I heard the sirens and I couldn't do it.'

'You've been through so much, and people will understand that you never wanted to hurt anyone.' Wendy could almost reach out and touch Chloe now, and suddenly the younger woman seemed to notice how close she was.

'Don't come any nearer.' Her eyes widened and she frantically waved the scissors in the air.

'You're not going to hurt me either, are you?' Wendy took another step forward, reaching out to try and take the scissors, but Chloe raised them higher and out of her grasp.

'Wendy, don't!' Gary called out her name, making Chloe jump and then shoot forward, the scissors glancing Wendy's arms as she did so. The pain made Wendy gasp and she felt the blood trickling down towards her elbow before she saw it.

'No!' Chloe dropped the scissors and screamed, as Wendy looked down at her arm. The pain seemed to have passed, but there was more blood than she'd ever seen in her life. For a second the room seemed to swim around her, and she was only vaguely aware of Gary running towards her before she passed out.

* * *

'Don't ever scare me like that again.' When Gary came back into focus, he was leaning over Wendy, holding her arm in an elevated position, with a blood-streaked white towel pressed against it.

'What happened?' She blinked again, but everything still looked and felt fuzzy, like she was under water.

'The scissors slashed an artery in your arm, and you fainted.'

'Where's the baby?' Wendy tried to get up, as she spoke.

'Don't try and move, sweetheart. Alice has got him; Chloe ran down to get the girls as soon as it happened.'

'Where is she now?'

'Waiting for the police with the girls.'

'She didn't do it on purpose. I don't want them to know about this.' She tried to get up again, and Gary gently put a hand on the shoulder of her good arm.

'I know it was an accident, but I've got a feeling she'll tell them everything.'

'How long did I faint for?' It didn't make any sense that all of that had happened, when it felt as if she'd only just dropped to the ground.

'Ten seconds or so at the most, but you weren't making a lot of sense at first and you kept closing your eyes, almost like you were going in and out of consciousness. I was focusing on controlling the bleeding when Chloe ran out and I didn't know if she'd come back. I didn't try to stop her, I was too worried about you. Alice was up here within about two minutes, and she said Chloe had asked Oliver to call for an ambulance and the police.'

'I need to be there when they speak to her.'

'Alice said she'll go with her, but now you need to rest. The blood seems to be clotting and I don't think you'll need surgery, but I'm not taking any chances.' Gary fixed her with a look that dared her to argue. 'I knew you were special before today, but I had no idea just how amazing you were. And I am not going to lose you for a second time. Alice will look after Chloe, but me and all four of our kids need you to look after yourself. You're the glue that holds this family together.'

For a moment Wendy's eyes felt so heavy she wasn't sure she could respond at all, but then she opened them and focused on Gary's face.

'Has anyone spoken to Danni and Charlie?' She couldn't even begin to imagine what they'd been through. The terror she'd felt when she'd thought the baby might be dead inside the bag was something she'd never forget, but it had only been a couple of seconds before she'd been able to see that he was okay. They'd been waiting on news and no doubt fearing the worst, for hours.

'I gave Alice my phone and told her to call them, so they'll know by now that he's okay.'

'I wish I could have stopped this.' Wendy's arm was throbbing now, but it wasn't the pain that was making the tears slide out of her eyes again, straight into her hair.

'Me too, but Chloe needs more help than we can give her and at least now she's going to get it.'

'If she ends up in prison, it's going to kill her.' The thought of that was like a knife twisting in her gut. After what Chloe had put Danni and Charlie through, some people might argue that she deserved to rot in a cell somewhere, but that wouldn't undo what she'd done and she needed help, not incarceration.

'I hope it doesn't come to that, but if it does, all we can do is be there for her. And you can't do that if you don't take the time to get better. So, for now, you're going to focus on yourself, whether you like it or not.'

'I never knew you could be this forceful.' For the first time since she'd got Chloe's letter, Wendy managed to smile, and Gary leant forward again to gently kiss her. He'd never lied to Wendy, or misled her, which made it easy to choose to believe what he was saying now too. Closing her eyes for a few seconds, she breathed out. The baby would be back with his parents soon, and Chloe hadn't done the one thing that Wendy had feared the most and decided to join Beau. There was a road back for her, and they'd all be cheerleading her journey to recovery when the time came. But Gary was right again, she couldn't do that unless she got over her own injury first. She had someone she could completely rely on, for the first time in decades, and she was going to lean on Gary until she was strong enough for Chloe to lean on her. That was what love was after all. The last few weeks had taught her there was enough of it to go around, and that it could flourish in the most unexpected of places, but she had no idea just how unexpected the power of love could still turn out to be.

25

When the police had tried to suggest that Danni and Charlie wait at the hospital for the return of their son, she'd told them in no uncertain terms what she thought of that idea. There wasn't a force on earth that could have stopped her getting to him. The message must have got through, because the detective inspector who'd been leading the hunt for the kidnapper had agreed that they would be taken to the hotel by the police. The tide was too high for the island to be accessible by road, and a police vessel had been dispatched to the harbour to meet them there. But Danni would have swum across to the island if she'd had to.

'You don't think there's any chance they've made a mistake, do you?' Her teeth were chattering, as Charlie took her hand to help her off the boat.

'None and he's going to be back in your arms in the next few minutes. Let's go and get him.' As soon as they were both on land, they started to run, hand-in-hand, towards the hotel. The police officers with them didn't even try to tell them to slow down, and they were running too, all of them desperate to know that the reports about the baby being unharmed were true.

'Danni!' Wendy's daughter called her name, as they charged through the doors of the hotel. She was holding the baby in her arms and he was sleeping, blissfully unaware of all the drama of the last few hours.

'Oh darling.' Taking the baby from Alice, Danni drank in every millimetre of her little boy, with even more wonder than she had in the first moments after he was born, as Charlie put his arms around them both. But she had to say the words out loud to really believe they were true. 'He's fine, he's absolutely fine.'

'He is and he's never going to be taken away from us again.'

'I'm sorry, I'm so sorry.' The voice of the woman in front of her made Danni's head shoot up. A police officer was holding on to the woman's arm, keeping her back from Danni and Charlie, and another officer had stepped between them, probably out of fear that one of the newly reunited parents might launch themselves at Chloe. In the time the baby had been missing, when Danni couldn't be certain whether he was dead or alive, she'd known without doubt that she was capable of murder if he had come to any harm. But standing there, with him safely in her arms, looking at the broken-hearted woman in front of her who'd never get to take her own son home, all she felt was pity.

'Don't make the situation any worse, Chloe.' The police officer who already had a tight grip on her arm, pulled her further away from Danni and Charlie.

'She's not making it worse.' The force of Danni's words surprised her. She couldn't tell Chloe it was okay, because what she'd put them through had been the most traumatic thing she could ever have imagined. She couldn't even say for sure yet whether she forgave her, but she needed Chloe to know that she didn't want her to suffer any more than she already had, so she turned to face her. 'I know you've been through hell too and I really hope you get the help you need.'

'Thank you.' Some of the tension seemed to leave Chloe's face, and she dropped her gaze as the officers led her away.

'I'm never going to ask for anything again; you and Caleb are all I'll ever want.' Danni looked up at Charlie, as he raised his eyebrows.

'Caleb?' It was a name Charlie had suggested a few months before, and Danni hadn't been sure. But she'd looked up the meaning at the time, and now she couldn't think of anything more fitting.

'It means the whole of my heart, and that's what the two of you have got. I love you both so much.' Danni leant into Charlie, the utter joy she felt to have her son back tinged by only one thing. 'I wish I could take back the things I said when we realised Chloe had taken him.'

'I love you too, and none of that matters. All I care about is that we've got him back and I'll never stop being grateful.' Charlie kissed her and, even though they were far from alone in the hotel foyer, she didn't care. She had her boys, the life she was terrified she might have lost for good was hers for the taking, and she was just as determined as Charlie never to take it for granted again.

Caleb was always going to be incredibly loved. His four adoring grandparents thought his every gurgle and murmur was the most momentous thing ever to happen, all of which had been heightened by his terrifying start in life. His Uncle Joe and Aunt Esther were equally besotted with him, and even Danni's mother had begun texting a bit more often, asking after him. She still wasn't a doting grandmother, but it was far more than Danni had expected from her. Caleb was also adored by Danni's friends and colleagues at the hospital.

Aidan and Jase had been particularly regular visitors, and they'd been getting in lots of practice as the weeks ticked down to the birth of their own baby. They'd offered to babysit, as had everyone else, but Danni and Charlie were nowhere near ready to take anyone up on the offer yet. They couldn't bear the thought of Caleb being with anyone but them, and she knew it was something they needed to work on. They'd started counselling and, in the New Year, they'd be having more sessions to make sure they got to a place where their anxiety about being separated from Caleb didn't end up damaging him. In the meantime, they were focusing on enjoying their first family Christmas, and the mountain of presents under the tree was yet another indication of just how loved their little boy was.

'What time did you tell Connie we'd be there?' As much as Danni loved all of her in-laws, she was in no hurry to dash over to Trengothern Farm. They'd be sharing the day with the people they cared about most, and would even be taking Maggie and Brenda with them. Connie and Richard had insisted on organising everything, so that Danni and Charlie wouldn't have to lift a finger. She was incredibly grateful, and she was really looking forward to it, but right now, sitting on the sofa with Charlie, both of them still in their Christmas pyjamas, and with Caleb snuggled against her chest in his Santa Claus onesie, there was nowhere she'd rather be.

'Not until 1 p.m., so we've got plenty of time.' Charlie stroked the side of Caleb's face as he spoke.

'I think Maggie wants us to get a move on; she's after a walk.' Danni laughed as the Labrador nudged at her leg. 'Although Brenda will probably happily give up her walk, if it means she's at the farm in time to get a look in when the turkey is carved.'

The Basset Hound opened her eyes at the mention of her name, lumbering over from her position by the fire, and promptly lying down again on top of Danni's feet.

'Sitting in the kitchen during meal prep is always Brenda's favourite place to be, so that would definitely be her perfect Christmas. Especially as Connie's such a soft touch.' Charlie grinned. 'But I'm already having my perfect Christmas.'

'Me too.' As Danni looked down at her son, her breath caught in her throat, and her thoughts drifted to Chloe again, as they had so many times before. In quiet moments, Danni often found herself wondering how she was doing, and whether she was getting the right help. Those feelings had intensified in the run-up to Christmas, as Danni and Charlie prepared to spend their first one as a family. Chloe should have been looking forward to the birth of her son, and to her first year of motherhood. Now she'd never get to watch Beau grow up. Instead, she was spending Christmas in a mental health facility, and her future was still unclear. In the days after being reunited with Caleb, Danni and Charlie had made the decision to write to the CPS to say they didn't feel a criminal prosecution for Chloe would be in anyone's best interests. It was clear that she'd been out of her mind with grief at the time she'd abducted Caleb, which they both believed had impaired her judgement to such an extreme that she hadn't been able to grasp the consequences of her actions until it was too late. But there'd been no confirmation yet that Chloe wouldn't be prosecuted. There were times when it felt like the wait for a decision was a dark cloud hanging over Danni's head, so she had no idea how it must feel for Chloe.

'Wendy and Gary are going in to see Chloe today.' Charlie put his hand on top of hers.

'How did you know I was thinking about her?'

'Because I've seen that same look on your face so many times, and because I've been thinking about her too.'

'I wish there was something else we could do for her. When it first happened, I wasn't sure I could ever really forgive her, but I think I have now.' Danni looked down at Caleb, his eyelids fluttering as he dreamt whatever it was that babies dreamt about. Despite the anxiety that they would need ongoing counselling to deal with, in the end it had been easy to forgive Chloe. What she'd put them through had made Danni realise once and for all that her fears about not loving her son enough were ridiculous. Whatever part of Nicola it was that made it easy for her to turn her back on her children wasn't hereditary, because Danni loved Caleb with a fierceness that had left her speechless with fear, the moment she'd realised he might be in danger. Without Chloe doing what she'd done, Danni might never have fully realised just how powerful that love was, and the lengths she'd be prepared to go to in order to keep her son safe. She couldn't say she was grateful for what had happened, but it had changed her forever in ways that weren't all negative. And she was holding on to the hope that something positive might come out of it for Chloe too, but it was hard to imagine what that could possibly be.

'Maybe you could tell her that? I think if I was in her position, that might help me.' Charlie tucked a strand of hair behind Danni's ear. 'Just when I think there's nothing you can do or say to make me love you even more, you find a way to surprise me.'

'I've got something else that might surprise you.' Danni reached under the cushion where she'd hidden an envelope and passed it to Charlie.

'What's this? We've already done presents.'

'It's something for me as much as you, and for Caleb too.' Another smile tugged at the corners of Danni's mouth, as she watched Charlie read the card in the envelope.

'You've re-booked the wedding at the registry office in Truro? I'd marry you in a car park and it would still make me the happiest man alive, but I thought you wanted to wait until the summer and do it all like we planned?'

'All of that stuff we were going to do doesn't matter any more. I just want it to be you, me, Caleb and all of our favourite people. And to be honest I've already spent some of the money we were going to use for the wedding on something else.'

'Should I be worried about what?' Charlie was so lovely and she knew, even if she'd spent it on something ridiculous, like a rare coin collection or a flashy car, that he wouldn't be upset, as long as she was happy. But she really hoped her investment would make him happy too.

'Look at the picture on the back of the card.'

'It's a camper van!' Charlie's smile as he looked at her said it all. When she'd first fallen pregnant, it was something they'd talked about buying, especially after Gary had told them all about the one he was renovating. They'd even planned some of the adventures they'd eventually be able to take their son on, with Maggie and Brenda along for the ride. Except with a wedding to pay for, it had definitely been a case of 'one day' rather than something they'd do straight away. But after what had happened with Caleb, the idea of putting off happiness of any kind had seemed crazy. When she'd seen the perfect camper van for sale, she'd found herself making an offer before she'd had the time to change her mind, let alone talk to Charlie. It was only when she realised how much of the wedding budget it had used up, that she'd started to worry whether or not it was the right decision. Looking at his face again now, there was absolutely no question, but she had to ask anyway.

'Did I do the right thing?'

'You always do the right thing for us, Dan. Every single time.' As Charlie kissed her, his words seemed to echo in the air around them and she made another decision she'd been weighing up for a while. It was time to try and do the right thing for someone else too, and there was no time like the present.

* * *

Wendy, Gary and the girls were due to join Beth and her family for Christmas Day. Gary's son, Drew, would be there too, and they were all looking forward to seeing how excited Albert was now that the big day had finally come. But there was somewhere they all wanted to go first.

'Oh my God, I can't believe you're here!' The look of pure joy on Chloe's face when she came into the visitors' room and saw them made Wendy smile too. It might not be the ideal location to spend Christmas morning, but seeing her looking so well was the best Christmas present they could ever have asked for.

'How are you doing, sweetheart?' Wendy hugged her close, and Chloe nodded.

'Better. I've had a message from the hospital and they've got permission for another extension to keep Beau with them. So, I'm hoping he'll be able to stay there until my doctors say I'm well enough to go to his funeral.' Chloe's relief was obvious. Wendy had discovered that the hospital could seek special permission to override the usual twenty-one-day rule in extenuating circumstances and, after Chloe was arrested, she'd personally gone to speak to senior staff in the hospital mortuary to beg for their help. Thankfully, they'd been incredibly kind and it sounded as if they were doing everything possible to make sure Chloe could be there to say a final goodbye to her son.

'That's great news.' Wendy hugged her again, releasing her so that Zara could hand over the gifts bags they'd brought in.

'We bought you some presents.'

'I haven't been able to get you anything.' Chloe's face fell slightly, and Wendy reached out and touched her arm.

'All any of us wanted was to see you today.'

'Zara and I definitely don't need anything, Dad's been trying to bribe us, and he dropped off loads of presents, so the house looks like an explosion in John Lewis.' Alice wrinkled her nose.

'Yeah, it won't change anything, but I might as well let him furnish the flat I'm going to get when I go to uni.' Zara laughed and to Wendy's surprise and relief, Chloe did too.

'I made you one of my famous chocolate logs too.' Gary handed over the tin and it was no exaggeration to say the contents were famous. There was more chocolate than sponge involved and it was the best cake Wendy had ever tasted, although she could only manage a small slice at a time, even though she considered herself a semi-professional connoisseur of cake. She was convinced it could turn the worst Christmas around too. She just hoped Chloe wouldn't need anything to turn her Christmas around, once she'd handed over the letter that felt as though it was about to burst into flames in her pocket. She might as well get it over with.

'I've got something else for you.' She took a deep breath, holding the letter out to Chloe. 'Danni and Charlie dropped it off, just before we left. She wanted you to have it today.'

'What does it say?' Chloe had gone deathly pale, and she didn't reach for the letter, her hands still clamped to her sides.

'I don't know, sweetheart, I haven't read it.'

'Will you read it to me now? I don't think I can do it.' Chloe bit her lip and, as she held Wendy's gaze, it was easy to see just how scared she was of what it might say.

'In front of everyone?'

'Yes.' Chloe nodded, and Wendy peeled open the envelope and took out the letter, all the time willing it not to say anything that would hurt Chloe, but knowing there was a chance that even people as kind as Danni and Charlie might find it impossible not to lay some kind of blame at her door.

'Okay, here goes.' She blew out her cheeks, before starting to read. 'Dear Chloe. We wanted to write to you today as Christmas is a time of year when anything is supposed to be possible. I've got to admit that, when we first got Caleb home, I wasn't sure I would ever be able to forgive you for what we went through. But in the last couple of weeks, it's got easier and easier to do that. What happened has made us realise just how lucky we are, and that's something we won't ever be able to forget or take for granted again, the way most people do. It's changed the way we do things, but I really believe those changes are for the better. I've already written to the CPS saying I won't support a prosecution, and I'm going to write again in the New Year. The only thing I hope for, is that you find a better way of living, and a new perspective because of all of this too. Good things can come from the most difficult of situations, and it turns out that at Christmas anything really is possible. Yours, with hopes that the year to come brings you brighter days. Danni, Charlie and Caleb.'

Wendy didn't know how she managed to get the whole letter out, especially as the words were already blurred by her tears when she reached the second line. And by the time she looked up, everyone around her was emotional too.

'I can't believe they've forgiven me.' Chloe finally reached out and took the letter from Wendy, scanning over the words again, until she was crying and laughing at the same time. 'They've really forgiven me, haven't they?'

'They have.' Wendy held out her arms, and Chloe rushed into them. 'It's going to be okay now, and if Danni writes to the CPS again in the New Year, I can't see them wanting to bring a case against you.'

Suddenly Chloe stepped back. 'I got a call from the police yesterday, telling me they weren't going ahead with a prosecution and that they wanted me to know in time for Christmas. They said they'd be writing to Danni and Charlie to let them know. And when you told me Danni had sent me a letter, I thought it was because she was so angry about the police dropping the prosecution.'

'They might only get notified in writing, and you'll probably get a follow-up letter too.' Wendy tilted her head as she looked at Chloe again. 'You don't look as happy about the news from the police as I thought you would.'

'I'm not.' Chloe shook her head, a slow smile spreading across her face. 'At least I wasn't until I got Danni's letter. I couldn't understand why I wasn't going to be punished, because I felt like I deserved to be.'

'No, you don't. You've been through more than enough.' Wendy squeezed her hand. When Danni had turned up with the letter earlier, they were the exact words she'd said. Chloe had been through so much, and no punishment the courts could hand out would be any worse than losing Beau. 'You can start looking forward to the future now, and when you can come home.'

'*Home.*' For the second time, Chloe went deathly pale, as if the idea of leaving the facility was suddenly horrifying. 'I can't say I like it here, but the thought of being on my own is even worse.'

'You're not going to be on your own, you'll be coming home. To our house.' It was something they'd already discussed and agreed upon as a family, and Gary was as on board with the idea as everyone else. So, when Wendy fixed Chloe with a look, she was ready to argue for as long as it took to persuade her that moving in, until she was really ready to be on her own again, was the best solution for all of them. Except there was no argument from Chloe, just another broad smile as she flung her arms around Wendy.

'The girls are so lucky to have a mum like you, and I feel even luckier to have you as a friend.'

'I'm so glad you feel that way and I don't even mind you seeing me as a mother figure, as long as you don't actually call me mum. That would be a bit too weird!' Wendy pulled a face, as everyone else laughed.

'Okay, I promise not to call you mum, but I will find a way to thank you for what you've done for me. I've got no idea what, because I can't think of anything that would ever be enough.'

'Just be happy, that's all I want.' As Wendy wrapped her arms around Chloe again she realised it was true. All she wanted for any of the people she loved was for them to be happy, and there was no question now that she included Chloe in that number. Everything they'd been through had taught her that love really could be found in the most unexpected of places. There was no such thing as loving too many people, or being loved by too many people in return. For years, Wendy had thought she was unlovable, but all she'd needed was to open her heart to let that love in. Just like Danni, it had changed the way she lived her life for the better, and she'd never forget the lessons she'd learnt along the way.

ACKNOWLEDGEMENTS

I can hardly believe this is the fourth book in *The Cornish Country Hospital* series already. Although it feels very much like home to me now, especially with some of the characters from previous books putting in an appearance, and some even taking up permanent residence at St Piran's!

As always, I want to start with a huge thank you for all the support I get from my wonderful readers. I'm so grateful to you for choosing my books and I will never take that for granted. The messages and comments I receive are incredibly kind, and they are what keep me going when it feels like the next deadline is impossible to reach.

I really hope you've enjoyed this fourth instalment in the series. The caveat I give for each new book is that I'm not a medical professional, but I've done my best to ensure that the details are as accurate as possible. If you're one of the UK's wonderful medical professionals, I hope you'll forgive any details which draw on poetic licence to fit the plot. I've been very lucky to be able to call on the advice of a good friend, Steve Dunn, who was a paramedic for twenty-five years and to whom I can go to for advice on medical matters when I need to. I've drawn on the expertise of another friend, Kate, a hospital consultant, and, as ever, I continue to seek support and advice in relation to maternity services from my brilliant friend, Beverley Hills. There's quite a bit of midwifery in this book, so if you're missing the Port Agnes midwives, I hope this was a welcome return to labour and delivery!

This book is about both motherhood, stepmotherhood, the challenges and joys that can come from being part of a blended family, and the surprising sisterhood that can arise in the most difficult of circumstances. I think nearly all mums and stepmums spend a lot of time wondering if we're getting it right or wrong, I know I do, and it was this thought that gave me the idea for Wendy's story. The novel is dedicated to my cousins, Tammy and Maria, two amazing mothers who have faced challenges others would find insurmountable, and I could fill another entire book telling you about all the things they've got so incredibly right.

Part of the plot features eating disorders, which is something I have personal experience of. Facing this kind of issue is different for everyone and what I have written here is not intended in any way to represent how such a situation should be handled. If this part of the story has affected you in any way, a great source of information and advice can be found here: https://www.beatea ingdisorders.org.uk.

This is the point where I begin to thank all the other people who have helped get this book to publication. At the end of *A Found Family at the Cornish Country Hospital*, I wrote a long list of book reviewers and social media superheroes, who have played such a big part in bringing this new series to readers and spreading the word to others, including by regularly commenting on and sharing my posts. I wanted to take this chance to thank as many people as possible again and, as such, my thanks go to Rachel Gilbey, Meena Kumari, Wendy Neels, Grace Power, Avri McCauley, Kay Love, Trish Ashe, Jean Norris, Bex Hiley, Shreena Morjaria, Pamela Spearing, Lorraine Joad, Joanne Edwards, Karen Callis, Tea Books, Jo Bowman, Jane Ward, Elizabeth Marhsall, Laura McKay, Michelle Marriott, Katerine Jane, Barbara Myers

Dawn Warren, Ann Vernon, Ann Stewart, Nicola Thorp, Karen Jean Wright, Claire Proudler, Kath White, Allissa Oldenberg, Mary Morphy, Beryl Colman, Helen Rachel, Imtiaz Riyad, Amanda Broad, Pamela Spearing, Joanne Edwards, Karen Callis, Charlotte Schwab, Sharon Martin, Julie Shynn, Michelle Hallowes, May Miller, Helen McEntee, Lesley Brett, Adrienne Allan, Sarah Lizziebeth, Margaret Hardman, Vikki Thompson, Mary Brock, Suzanne Cowen, Debbie Marie Sleigh, Melissa Khajehgeer, Sarah Steel, Laura Snaith, Sally Starley, Lizzie Philpot, Kerry Coltham, May Miller, Gillian Ives, Carrie Cox, Elspeth Pyper, Tracey Joyce, Lauren Hewitt, Julie Foster, Sharon Booth, Ros Carling, Deirdre Palmer, Maureen Bell, Caroline Day, Karen Miller, Tanya Godsell, Kate O'Neill, Janet Wolstenholme, Lin West, Audrey Galloway, Helen Phifer, Johanne Thompson, Beverley Hopper, Tegan Martyn, Anne Williams, Karen from My Reading Corner, Jane Hunt, Karen Hollis, @thishannahreads, Isabella Tartaruga, @Ginger_bookgeek, Scott aka Book Convos, @teaandbooks90, @carlalovetoread Pamela from @bookslifeandeverything, Mandy Eatwell, Jo from @jaffareadstoo, Elaine from Splashes into Books, Connie Hill, @karen_loves_reading, @wendyreadsbooks, @bookishlaurenh, Jenn from @thecomfychair2, @jen_loves_reading, Ian Wilfred, @Annarella, @Bookish-Jottings, @Jo_bee, Kirsty Oughton, @kelmason, @TheWollyGeek, Barbara Wilkie, @bookslifethings, @Tiziana_L, @mum_and_me_reads, Just Katherine, @bookworm86, Sarah Miles aka Beauty Addict, Captured on Film, Leanne Bookstagram, @subtlebookish, Laura Marie Prince, @RayoReads, @sarah.k.reads, @twoladiesandabook, Vegan Book Blogger, @readwithjackalope, and @staceywh_17. Huge apologies if I've left anyone off the list, but I'm so thankful to everyone who takes the time to review or share my books and I promise to continue adding names to the list as the series progresses.

My thanks as ever go to the team at Boldwood Books, especially my amazing editor, Emily Ruston, my brilliant copy editor, Candida Bradford, and fabulous proofreader, Rachel Sargeant, all of whom shape my messy early drafts into something I can be proud of. I'm also hugely grateful to the rest of the team at Boldwood Books, who are now too numerous to list, but special mention must go to my marketing lead, Marcela Torres, and the Director of Sales and Marketing, Nia Beynon, as well as to the inimitable Amanda Ridout, for having the foresight to create such an amazing company to be published by.

As ever, I can't sign off without thanking my writing tribe, The Write Romantics, including my fellow Boldies Helen Rolfe, Jessica Redland, and Alex Weston, and to all the other authors I am lucky enough to call friends, especially Gemma Rogers, who is another fellow Boldie. I owe another of my best friends, Jennie Dunn, a big thank you for her support with the final read through.

Finally, as it forever will, my most heartfelt thank you goes to my husband, children and grandchildren. Everything I do is for you and you teach me lessons in love every single day.

ABOUT THE AUTHOR

Jo Bartlett is the bestselling author of over nineteen women's fiction titles. She fits her writing in between her two day jobs as an educational consultant and university lecturer and lives with her family and three dogs on the Kent coast.

Sign up to Jo Bartlett's mailing list for a free short story

Follow Jo on social media here:

 facebook.com/JoBartlettAuthor
x.com/J_B_Writer
instagram.com/jo_bartlett123

ALSO BY JO BARTLETT

The Cornish Midwife Series

The Cornish Midwife

A Summer Wedding For The Cornish Midwife

A Winter's Wish For The Cornish Midwife

A Spring Surprise For The Cornish Midwife

A Leap of Faith For The Cornish Midwife

Mistletoe and Magic for the Cornish Midwife

A Change of Heart for the Cornish Midwife

Happy Ever After for the Cornish Midwife

Seabreeze Farm

Welcome to Seabreeze Farm

Finding Family at Seabreeze Farm

One Last Summer at Seabreeze Farm

Cornish Country Hospital Series

Welcome to the Cornish Country Hospital

Finding Friends at the Cornish Country Hospital

A Found Family at the Cornish Country Hospital

Lessons in Love at the Cornish Country Hospital

Standalone

Second Changes at Cherry Tree Cottage

A Cornish Summer's Kiss

Meet Me in Central Park

LOVE IN EVERY CHAPTER

WHERE ALL YOUR ROMANCE
DREAMS COME TRUE!

THE HOME OF BESTSELLING
ROMANCE AND WOMEN'S
FICTION

 WARNING:
MAY CONTAIN SPICE

SIGN UP TO OUR
NEWSLETTER

https://bit.ly/Lovenotesnews

Boldwood

Boldwood Books is an award-winning fiction publishing company seeking out the best stories from around the world.

Find out more at www.boldwoodbooks.com

Join our reader community for brilliant books, competitions and offers!

Follow us

@BoldwoodBooks

@TheBoldBookClub

Sign up to our weekly deals newsletter

https://bit.ly/BoldwoodBNewsletter

Printed in Great Britain
by Amazon

48215377R00155